Once Upon a
Caveman

Cassandra Gannon

Published by Star Turtle Publishing
www.starturtlepublishing.com

Visit Cassandra Gannon at starturtlepublishing.com or on the
Star Turtle Publishing Facebook page for news on upcoming
books and promotions!

Email Star Turtle Publishing directly:
starturtlepublishing@gmail.com

We'd love to hear from you!

Also by Cassandra Gannon

The Elemental Phases Series
Warrior from the Shadowland
Guardian of the Earth House
Exile in the Water Kingdom
Treasure of the Fire Kingdom
Queen of the Magnetland
Magic of the Wood House
Coming Soon: *Destiny of the Time House*

A Kinda Fairytale Series
Wicked Ugly Bad
Beast in Shining Armor
The Kingpin of Camelot
Coming Soon: *Happily Ever Witch*

Other Books
Love in the Time of Zombies
Not Another Vampire Book
Vampire Charming
Cowboy from the Future
Once Upon a Caveman
Ghost Walk

You may also enjoy books by Cassandra's sister, Elizabeth Gannon.

The Consortium of Chaos series
Yesterday's Heroes
The Son of Sun and Sand
The Guy Your Friends Warned You About
Electrical Hazard
The Only Fish in the Sea
Coming Soon: *Not Currently Evil*

The Mad Scientist's Guide to Dating

For Lulu,
Who lounges on windowsills, surrounded by toys and treats and love,
and smugly dreams of those glorious days when her sabretooth ancestors hunted mine.

Prologue

Her hair is a beautiful, amazing mass of midnight black.

Rhawn lifts his hand to touch the fire lit curls, amazed that she allows it. Amazed at how soft it feels. The incredible, miraculous strands fall around both of them, as she leans forward. No one has a hair color like hers. It's like something from a story of the gods. She is so perfect that he cannot breathe. All his life he has dreamed of her, in bits and pieces, but this time it's like she's really in his arms.

Like she's real.

She isn't, of course.

This woman doesn't actually exist. She can't. No woman would ever be with him. Especially not a woman like this. But inside this dream, he can pretend she's actually in his arms, welcoming him. She's straddling his body as he reclines on the pelts, the warm perfection of her curves sliding against him. Rhawn has no clue what he's done to lure her here, but – stupid as he is– he's not stupid enough to question it.

Once a cycle he has a dream of her, always on this day. It is the highlight of his life. And the dream this cycle is better than he'd ever imagined.

Her eyes are brilliant green, filled with mischief. His lungs cannot get enough air when she looks at him and smiles. No one ever looks at him like that.

Why is she never repulsed?

His hands are calloused on her skin. They're too big and too rough to touch someone so delicate, but he can't gentle his hold. Rhawn is the largest man in the Clan. Tempering his strength is difficult and this woman is driving him past all control. She always has. The shine of her hair and the light of her smile. This is the clearest he's ever seen her and he is overwhelmed with emotions. The woman means everything to him.

Imaginary or not, she is his mate.

He's trying to remove the foreign clothing that his mind has created for her. Obviously, they're a sign of his masochistic leanings, because he never has an idea how to get her out of the damn things. This covering is made of some waterfall of scarlet fabric that's so much finer than anything the Clan could create. The material is nearly as soft as her skin and reveals more than it covers. It's making him crazy.

She's making him crazy.

"You're always in a hurry when we get this far." She says with a laugh. "Luckily I always am, too."

Rhawn shifts himself into a sitting position. His fingers catch hold of her left hand, shackling it behind her back. Her wrist is small enough that he could break it between his fingers, but she doesn't seem to be afraid. She never has been. Instead she gives a teasing smile as he tugs her onto his lap, enjoying his growl of frustration.

She truly is sent by the gods to torment him.

Whatever the flimsy red garment is made of, the thin straps rip easily enough under his free hand. He tears it from her body, his breath shuddering out at the sight of her naked flesh. All she's wearing now is some nearly transparent scrap covering the junction of her thighs. The acres of pale skin contrast with the dark color of her hair and it pushes his arousal to new heights.

Finally.

Rhawn's head dips to run his tongue over the dusky pink tips of her perfect breast. Finally, he can touch all of her. It's been so long since he could have her in his arms.

"Oh God… you're sooooooo good at this, caveman."

He appreciates the praise. Keeping her still, he switches to her other breast and repeats the whole process with new techniques. He's always been a man who strives for perfection in his work. He'll do something once and then do it even better the next time and the next, until he's satisfied it's right. And it's never fully right. There are always new variables to test. When Rhawn gets an idea, he wants to experiment.

The Clan views his repetition of the same tasks as evidence of his stupidity. To them, he is nothing but a big, dumb oaf who never learns from mistakes.

The woman doesn't seem to agree.

Her head goes back with a moan as his teeth graze the underside of her breast, offering him more. Her fingers curl into his golden hair, holding his head in place. She doesn't need to worry. He isn't trying to escape. He wants to taste all of her. Rhawn tugs her closer, his hand still holding her wrist, determined to memorize every inch of her, so he can relive this moment in the long cycle ahead. Her nipples tighten into hard points, even as the rest of her softens.

He gives a low growl of desire and she grins at him.

"You really are a caveman, aren't ya?"

Rhawn understands her strange language. He's dreamed in the tongue since he was a boy. He has no idea what all her words mean exactly, but he knows that when she calls him "caveman" she is teasing him. No one else ever dares such a thing. Just her. It always melts his heart. His mouth curves and he nips her shoulder in small punishment.

She laughs again. "Alright. Alright. Hey, what is the politically correct term for your living arrangements, anyway?" She arches a playful brow and glances around. Her cheeks are rosy from passion and the frigid air. "How about, 'modernity challenged'? For real, you never heard of houses with doors and windows and maybe central heat?"

No, he hasn't.

He's never even heard of a "house," although he works hard to understand her language. The woman fascinates him. Baffles him. He tries to learn all he can, because he wants to know her. He wants her to know him. It's a difficult task. Usually, the dreams are fragments. The scent of her hair. The feel of her touch. The sound of her voice.

One year, he was very sick from a boga bite when she arrived. He'd dreamed of her lying beside him, humming quiet songs and begging him not to leave her all alone in the world. He fought through the poison, because she asked him to. Because he could not stand to disappoint her.

Because, even if she is just an image in his head, she is the only thing he has ever loved.

There is not even a word for "love" in the Clan's tongue, but Rhawn knows the feeling straight down to his soul.

Her lips suddenly find his and it startles him. Rhawn's whole body jerks at the unknown feel of her mouth against him. His head pulls back in surprise. "What are you doing?"

"Kissing you. I keep wanting to do that, but we never seem to have time."

"Kiss-sing?

Her head tilts. "You don't know how to kiss?"

"No." *But he suddenly wants it. Rhawn's biggest weakness has always been his curiosity. Even when he knows it will lead to his downfall, he questions and seeks. He wants to experience everything for himself.* "Show me."

She obediently leans forward with a smile. "Don't worry. It won't hurt a bit."

Her mouth is close to his, their breath mingling. Rhawn's mind goes blank with helpless lust. He doesn't understand what this "kissing" is meant to do, but he wants more of it. Her lips brush against his again. Soft. Warm. Moist.

Oh gods...

The "kiss" rushes through his system like an inferno and he cannot think.

He doesn't want to close his eyes. It's so rare that someone holds his gaze without recoiling and he doesn't want to look away from her, but he can't help it. His lashes flutter down and he surrenders to the unknown. She sucks gently on his lower lip, seeking entrance and he's hypnotized. This cannot have anything to do with mating. The necessary parts are not involved.

Except they are.

The jolt of the "kiss" slams into his blood and Rhawn has to bite back a hiss. Something untamed rises within him. A wild desperation. She is everything he's ever searched for. Rhawn has always questioned when he should obey. Looking for something not even he can fully explain. This moment makes the frustration and derision and setbacks he's faced completely *worth* the struggle. Her mouth opens against his and he knows he's discovered magic.

She tastes like all the pure, clean things in the world. Her tongue touches his and his skull nearly blows apart with need. Rhawn still can't breathe for wanting her. Acting on instinct, he massages her tongue with his own and she gives a moan. He wants more. He will never get enough. She is the only good part of him.

"You catch on fast." She teases, coming up for air. "You like kissing, huh?"

"Again." Rhawn gets out and drags her mouth back to his.

The "kiss" turns hotter. More insistent. Rhawn knows that none of this is real and he doesn't care. He can't lose her.

His hand comes up to caress her breast and her nipple beads tight, enjoying his touch. She smiles and his heart turns over in his chest. No one smiles at him. No one but her.

"I missed you." She says. "I never know when you're going to show up and I start to think you're gone for good. Then you're finally here again and I'm so happy you're back."

"You always appear on the same day." He is surprised she hasn't noticed that. The woman is usually so bright and observant he worries that he will bore her with his stupidity.

"Nope, sometimes I dream of you in September, sometimes in February, and sometimes in May."

Rhawn has no idea what she was talking about. "On Fangard, I always dream of you." He insists. The holy day always ushers her into his mind. It is why he continues to believe in the gods, even when he questions everything else. This woman's presence is proof of their divinity.

"I have no fucking clue what Fangard means." She says as if he's the one talking in riddles. "But, whatever."

Then, she's "kissing" him again and he forgets everything except the feel of her. She'll be gone any second. Given his luck, it's inevitable. He might believe in them, but the gods have never listened to his prayers before, so there's no reason to think they'll begin now. While he has this small window of opportunity, he has to make the most of it.

Determined now, Rhawn flips her around, so he can pin her beneath him. Black curls cascade over the thick pelts. They fall against his hands, as he plants his palms on either side of her head. He wants to drown in that perfect hair. It is so beautiful. She *is* so beautiful. His instincts are screaming at him. To take her, now. Hard and fast. His hands catch hold of her wrists, pinning them above her head.

The men of the Clan have never cared for wooing women. They just Choose the one they want and she submits. Why should it be different now that he's found a female of his own? And she is *his*. He knows that. Desperate thoughts fill his head. He will somehow convince her to stay with him and fight any other man who seeks to steal her away. Except, when he traps her delicate body, her gaze flies to his in surprise.

...And he hesitates.

The beginnings of caution stir in her eyes. For the first time, she's paying attention to the differences in their sizes. She has a strong spirit. He's always known that and he admires it. Nothing scares her. The woman's sudden awareness of her vulnerability doesn't make Rhawn feel powerful. It makes him feel... wrong.

Like he is on the edge of betrayal. Like he should stop.

But, why is she upset in the first place? She is not unwilling. Far from it.

His mind races for some explanation, trying to reason it out. She is his mate. He is big, but he will use his strength to defend *her*, not hurt her. Doesn't she see that? Injuring this girl is the last thing he wants.

"Vando." He says quietly.

The woman doesn't understand. She tugs against his hands, wanting her wrists freed. Rhawn's grip tightens for a beat, trying to figure out how to proceed. She is not going to follow the rules of mating and meekly acquiesce to his demands. It is astonishing. As far as he knows, nothing like this has ever happened before. He flounders for an explanation.

What is he supposed to do?

"Stop." *She says, twisting her hands to get free.* "Please."

Rhawn blinks. ...And releases her wrists. He knows her worries are groundless. He should keep going and show her that their mating is nothing to fear. It's the logical solution. Certainly, no other man in the Clan would be stupid enough to let this woman escape.

So, why is he easing back from her, making soft sounds to calm her? Why is he petting her hair and coaxing her to relax again? Why is he stopping just because she asks him to? He really is an idiot. Five seconds more and he can have everything he wants.

...No, not everything *he wants. He wants so much more than just surrender.*

He wants her to want him back.

Imaginary or not, she is what Rhawn treasures most. If he frightens her, she will never smile at him again. He won't risk such a thing happening, no matter how hard desperation is beating at him. Her acceptance is what he values. It doesn't matter that her fears are perplexing, they are real to her. Therefore, he has to soothe them. It is his duty as her mate.

So, Rhawn does what no man in the Clan has ever done with his female: He relinquishes control. He is still confused by her resistance to their mating, but it doesn't matter. All that matters is regaining her trust.

"I'm sorry." *He soothes, adjusting the pelts around her so she feels more secure.* "I went too fast." *After dreaming of this girl for so many nights, Rhawn doesn't think it seems "fast" at all, but her opinion is all that matters.* "Are you alright?"

She swallows, gazing up at him. "Yes, I'm fine. Sorry. I just got a little scared. I know it's a dream and that cavemen probably have way different social mores and all. I know that you would never hurt me. You were just suddenly so... intense."

He stifles a wince. "You do not ever need to fear me. I will do nothing you do not wish. You have my word."

The wariness fades, as she realizes that he will not force compliance. She begins to look embarrassed. "I don't do this a lot. I mean, except with you in these dreams, but most of them are less... real. Kinda fuzzier and more like bits and pieces."

"Yes." She's right. The dream this cycle seems very different somehow.

"So, can we just start again and go a little slower?"

He nods, dizzy with relief, because she doesn't wish to stop all together. He tries to touch her as she likes –carefully and with patience– but he's still too desperate for much finesse. Despite his best intentions, Rhawn's hands are still rough with need. Goddamn it, why does he have to be so big?

She gives a breathless laugh that sounds like music, not concerned about his lack of tenderness. Her confidence is back. Her faith in him restored. It is a miracle. "In a hurry, huh, caveman?"

"Rhawn." Telling her his name suddenly seems more urgent than even his raging need for her. He's afraid of marking her skin, just from touching her. She is so delicate. He is all but shuddering with his lust, but still he whispers: "I am Rhawn." He's always wanted her to know him.

"Hi, Rhawn." She says gravely, as if she isn't pinned under his naked body.

Again.

Damn it, how has that happened again? He promised her he would go slowly. No wonder she is terrified of him, if he cannot even do as she asks. Perhaps his failure is to be expected. He tries to live a life of worth, but the gods send dreams to plague his mind and have marked his eyes with their disfavor. His fate is dark. And now he cannot even be considerate of the mate that he isn't supposed to have. He should stop this and let her go.

Ashamed, he tries to look away.

She moves her head to follow his, not letting him break eye-contact. He doesn't like to meet her gaze and have her see his deformity, but she never seems disgusted by it. "Nice to finally meet you." She lifts her palm to rest it against his cheek, in case he tries to drop his eyes, again. "I'm Lucy."

Rhawn's mouth curves at one corner, giving up any notion of letting her go. It was a hopeless thought. He cannot find the strength. Without her, he would be completely alone. "Nice to meet you, Lou-ceee." He echoes, softly.

She grins and leans up to "kiss" him, again.

The woman is perfect.

Rhawn runs his hand down the curve of her hip, nudging her legs apart and pressing closer. It's not enough. He wants to slam inside of her and lose himself in her heat. Holding back is so damn hard, but his restraint is worth the effort. She doesn't try to pull away from him. Instead, she arches against his body, her breasts pillowed between them. Her thighs willingly part, her knees tighten on his hips and Rhawn groans.

"Rhawn." She breathes, her lush body opening to his and her mouth curving in bliss. "Wow... I wish I could dream of you every night."

He loves that she says his name in that breathless tone.

Her eager response lights a fire in his already overheated blood. His methodical process of discovering what makes her happy has earned her desire. In return for his efforts, she's giving him back more than he ever imagined. Her body welcomes him... Her clear eyes are heavy with passion and excitement... She smiles in anticipation at his touch...

Rhawn's hand grips the small triangle of fabric shielding her black curls, trying to rip it off her. He's still tempering his strength, but it should be enough force to shred the thin covering. Instead, the edges of the fabric unexpectedly stretch in his grasp. Rhawn frowns in confusion, trying to get her free of it. Somehow, he ends up flipping her over so she's on her stomach. That position will work fine for him.

"Hang on. It's elastic." She pants. "Here." She takes over, moving beneath him. She slides the material down her legs, her back towards him. Rhawn instinctively shifts to give her room.

...And that's when he sees the marking.

His jaw drops open in shock.

Rhawn's hand clamps down on her thigh, stopping her

from moving. He gapes at the patch of skin just above the thin, top band of the fabric. Her skin is branded with a very familiar image.

He doesn't want to believe the ramifications.

"What is this?" He whispers, although he already knows. He's seen it before. Knows what it means and what it is.

Knows what she is.

Rationally, there's no other explanation. According to the Clan, rationality has always eluded him before and he wishes he could switch it off, again. Because the truth is going to kill him.

"The tattoo?" She asks blankly and cranes her neck around to look down at the mark. "It's supposed to be Times Square. Yeah, I know. It sucks, right? I got it a couple months back. There was a bachelorette party and lot of tequila involved. Trust me."

Rhawn swallows hard and slowly raises his eyes to meet hers. "Who are you?" The words leave aching holes inside of him and he already has too many pieces missing. At this moment, he can feel himself shattering into nothing.

"What?" She seems confused.

Rhawn forces himself to let go of her. To move off the unbelievable softness of her body and into the isolated cold. He crouches on the pelts and struggles not to give into mindless despair. "This is... a lie." He brings the heels of his hands up to press against his temples. "You are a lie."

"You don't want me, all of a sudden?" She has the audacity to look hurt. "After all this time, all the nights I needed you, you're just stopping? Because I have a tattoo?"

"No!" Rhawn roars. "I can't have you because of what you are!"

"What I am?" She echoes blankly. "Well, I mean, I don't have the greatest job in the world, but a lot of people who are over-educated in useless fields have to work in bookstores, so..."

He cuts her off. "Why did you pick me? Because you

know that I'm stupid?"

"You're not stupid! That's idiotic." The woman —who isn't just a woman— winces at the phrasing, but keeps going. "Seriously, why would you think that?"

"Stop lying!" Rhawn stands up, pulling her to her feet along with him. "I know *your* marking! I have seen it before, in more dreams than you can imagine." He half carries her to the wall of the cave. It's covered in his artwork, even in this fantasy world. Countless pictures stain the stone in every direction, one on top of another. "Look!" He gestures towards the rough depictions of his dreamscapes. "Look at it! And tell me this isn't your homeland."

She stares at the drawings, her head tilting.

The impossible images fill Rhawn's head when he sleeps. He remembers all of them, so he doesn't even have to look at the wall to know what she sees. Every time he closes his eyes, he pictures that world in vivid, incredible detail. When he awakens, he tries to recreate it, but it's so hard to capture all the colors and shapes. Structures that tower over the ground. Lights that shine in the night. Boxes that move along smooth trails that stretch off into infinity.

That place —that fantastic, beautiful place— is what he dreams of when he doesn't dream of Lucy.

"New York?" Her fingers moved to brush the painted image of a stoic woman in flowing robes holding a torch above her head. "Yeah." Her expression is baffled. "Of course, I live there. Well, I live in Jersey, but I commute."

"Newyork?" Was that where Earth, the home of the gods, was located? It had to be.

She shakes her head. "This dream is some kind of symbolic thing, because of the reunion, right? Fifteen years out of high school and —okay fine— I'm not the most successful graduate that Woodward High's ever seen. I didn't live up to my potential and do something special. I never changed the world. But, I'm certainly not ready to curl up in a cave and die just because..."

He cuts her off. "Tell me." It's hard to get the words out. Even now, Rhawn knows he's a fool for asking. For *needing her to verify what any child would already know. But, how could it be true? How could she possibly be evil?* "Are you... the Destroyer?"

Her face crinkles into a baffled squint. "The what...?"

The world begins shaking around them, cutting her off. Under their feet, the small pebbles slide back and forth on the stone floor. He can feel the vibrations running up from the ground, through his entire body, and causing the island to sink another foot into the Infinite Sea.

What other answer does he need, besides that?

Lucy glances at him in surprise, pretending not to understand. "Is it an earthquake?" *She reaches over to steady herself on his arm, as the floor moves beneath them.*

"It's the *Ardin.*" *He corrects, softly.* "The sinking."

She, of all beings, knows that.

"The what?"

"The end of the world."

"The WHAT?"

Voices shout outside.

Rhawn's head turns to look at the entrance of the cave, although he already knows that he won't see anyone else inside this dream. He never does, when she's here. It's always just the two of them. The yelling comes from the waking world. They're already coming for him.

He's about to wake up. They can both feel it.

"Wait! Don't go. Not yet." *Her fingernails dig into his arm. For some reason, she's tinted them a red so dark they're nearly black. It's probably a mark of evil, but that does nothing to lessen how pretty he finds them.*

Or how much he wants her.

Even knowing that she's manipulated him for cycle upon cycle with dreams and that she's the Destroyer of All, destined to sink the world... Everything inside of Rhawn still wants this woman. Still loves her. Still knows that she is his.

He really is an idiot.

"Tell me what's going on?" *She gazes up at him in bewildered worry.* "Will you be alright?"

"No." Rhawn intones. He will be blamed for the shaking and possibly executed. The Clan is too on edge for reason.

...But, if he's going to die either way, he'll die with the taste of her seared into his memory. Rhawn yanks her forward, his mouth slamming over hers, again. The woman's lips part beneath his, welcoming and sweet. "Kissing" her is worth anything. Her naked body presses against his, her arms going around his neck. And, honestly, he doesn't care if this damns him. Not a bit.

"Rhawn!"

His eyes snapped open at the shout. The world was still quaking underneath of him, but the dark comfort of the dream had faded. The cave felt twenty degrees colder without the warmth of the woman beside him. He turned to look towards the paintings on the cave wall as if she might somehow still be standing there looking at them. An echoing hollowness filled him when he saw that Lucy was gone.

But then, she'd never really been there, at all.

It had all been a dream, hinting of what was to come.

The legends of the Clan had long predicted the *Ardin*, a battle between the gods. A heroic man and an evil woman would return to the island in its final days and determine the fate of the world. The Savior would pluck the worthy from the sinking island and lead them to a glorious new home. The Destroyer would try and stop him, wanting to doom them forever.

No one knew which deity would emerge from the fight victorious. The last chronicle would be written by the gods and their respective followers, during the *Ardin*.

The final days.

These days.

Rhawn stumbled to his feet and made his way to the mouth of his cave. He'd deliberately picked a spot away from the others. For obvious reasons, Rhawn didn't do well with neighbors. His visions ensured that they did not welcome him in their midst.

No one welcomed him.

His home sat on the southern end of the island, with an unobstructed view of the ocean and the volcano. Every day the waves below got closer. When he was a boy, he remembered the vast width of the beach and the variety of animals that had lived on the island. Each passing cycle saw the land growing smaller and the creatures growing rarer. The water was swallowing them so quickly. He wasn't sure if the entire island would sink before the Clan ran out of food or if they would starve before the final plunge occurred.

One way or another, they would all be dead very soon. It was inevitable.

Rhawn reached the entrance and blew out a long breath at the sight of the unforgiving sea. It was so close, now.

"Rhawn!" Notan, the Clan's leader climbed up the twisting pathway to Rhawn's cave. In his youth, he had been the Clan's greatest hunter, but then a mammoth stepped on Notan's leg and left him with a permanent limp. The old man's hair was gray now and he supported himself on a walking stick, but righteous anger kept him moving at a quick pace. "What have you brought upon us?"

Damn it, why did things like this always happen to Rhawn?

He was deemed responsible whenever anything went wrong. His dreams. The color of his eyes. His massive size and lack of intelligence. It all worked to ensure that Rhawn was the scapegoat for every unsuccessful hunt and bad omen that came the island's way. He was forever hated by the other members of the Clan, no matter how hard he tried to be worthy.

Of course, they'd blame him for the *Ardin*. He'd been marked by the gods. He had dreams of their lands. The Destroyer had sought him out. For better or worse, his destiny was tied to the darkness.

It was Rhawn's own fault they distrusted him. As a child, he'd told Notan about his dreams of "Newyork." The old man was understandably alarmed by the possible ramifications of Rhawn's curse. After that, he did his best to keep Rhawn away from the others in case of contamination. Rhawn couldn't even blame him for it.

"Of course Rhawn is to blame." Skoll, next in line to be the Clan's leader, sneered in derision. "We all know he is in league with the Destroyer."

Skoll stood behind Notan, offering protection in case Rhawn went crazy. They were continually prepared for him to do something dishonorable or deranged. Skoll would undoubtedly be pleased if Notan died and he could assume control of the Clan, but he also had designs on Anniah, Notan's daughter. He needed to at least put in a pretense of caring about the old man.

"Rhawn, the Accursed, tell us all you saw or suffer the consequences." Notan thundered. None of them found Rhawn worthy, but they always wanted him to reassure them about his dreams. Everyone knew they often happened in conjunction with the shakings. "The day of the *Ardin* grows closer. Have you at last seen the Destroyer's unholy form?"

The familiar question struck him as darkly hilarious. Rhawn roared with laughter, while the land shook, and their island sunk ever deeper into the bottomless sea, and the end of the world loomed on the horizon.

Notan and Skoll stopped their approach and watched him warily. He could tell they were thinking he was just as stupid and sinful as they'd always believed.

Maybe they were right.

"Yes." Rhawn got out. "I finally saw her."

Every inch of that dark-haired, green-eyed, soft, treacherous, deity from the magical land of Newyork was burned into his mind forever. The Destroyer might've been the embodiment of strategic genius and all-powerful evil...

...But she was also his mate.

Chapter One

There's a caveman staring at her. A really big, really handsome one.

Lucy's eyebrows soar. Her prom night has been such a total loss that she's fallen asleep in her stupid dress, but suddenly things are looking up. She's having a sex dream about a really big, really handsome caveman! Cool! Usually, she just gets random crap about singing Boston Terriers or being late for an AP English exam. She'd much rather dream about a half-naked hottie.

"Hi!" She says eagerly.

The caveman tilts his head to one side, like he is amazed at what he's seeing. Amazed by her. For two seconds, he just stares. Then he shakes his head as if to clear it and starts purposefully towards her. His expression is intent, his eyes scanning up and down her body. He seriously looks like he's ready to ravish her or something.

Lucy smiles. Oh yeah. This dream is going to be awesome!

Rhawn and Lucy's First Dream- Fifteen Years Ago

"Tony the Cruise Director hates you." Marnie-from-third-period-bio stage-whispered. "Like *a lot*."

Lucianne Meadowcroft sighed and took a sip from her watery margarita. "Yeah, I noticed. Thanks."

"It's because you didn't show up for the official class reunion picture this morning or the mixer last night or the..."

Lucy cut the list short, getting right to the bottom line. She was a bottom line kinda girl. "It's because he's married to Taffi and Taffi still hasn't forgiven me for wearing the same dress as her to prom."

Tony and Taffi were the reason Woodward High School's fifteenth reunion was being held on a four day Caribbean excursion out of New York harbor. Tony's job on the small—correction: "boutique" – cruise ship had gotten everyone a really great discount. But, if Tiffany "Taffi" Dawson could've found a way to loose Lucy's invitation for the trip she totally would have.

The biggest mean girl at Woodward High, Taffi would *never* get over that stupid poufy ball gown. To hear Taffi tell it, Lucy should have known when she touched the hanger at Macy's that Taffi had *already* selected an identical bouffant vision of blue and lace. Taffi insisted that Lucy should've somehow psychically intuited Taffi's prior claim. Sadly, Lucy's nonexistent ESP hadn't picked up any prom-y signals that day. By buying the same dress, she had singlehandedly ruined Taffi's "MOST IMPORTANT NIGHT *EVER!!!*"

God, just remembering the screaming and tears in the ladies room of the gym gave her a headache. Fifteen years and it was still a recurring nightmare. She hadn't even *liked* that damn dress.

Lucy finished off her watery drink and gestured to the bartender to get her another. What the hell was she doing on this cruise? Bad enough to be in high school. Worse to get suckered into a reunion once you escaped. But, to be stuck on a boat with the same people she'd desperately hoped *never* to see again after graduation was just fucking stupid.

It was all the Alumni Committee's fault. They'd plastered the event all over the email inboxes of every former student, promising a long weekend of unimaginable fun. It had all sounded like one of those travel commercials with the colorful sunsets and pretty people playing volleyball. In a rush of nostalgia, Lucy recalled her teenage life in Clovis, New York like a misty water-colored filmstrip of football games and slumber parties. For the half-an-hour it took her to buy her nonrefundable ticket, the trip had seemed like a great idea.

Now that sanity had returned, she was suddenly remembering that the slumber party thing was actually a scene from *Grease* and that Woodward High's football team sucked.

Lucy had hated high school. Granted, *everyone* hated high school. But, girls with snarky personalities, twenty extra pounds, and a low tolerance for other people's stupidity *really* hated it. Lucy had been the kid whose report cards always read, "academically brilliant, but has a bad attitude" or "talks back and refuses to join in with other kids." Well, she *liked* having a bad attitude and she *didn't* like the other kids. High school had been a nightmare. No way was she pretending otherwise.

So, what the hell had she been thinking signing up for this boat trip to relive it all? Temporary insanity was the only explanation. Still, Lucy wasn't about to walk away from so much cash. She'd *paid* for this miserable trip, which meant she was damn well taking it.

Even if she didn't want to.

Thanks to her brief moment of amnesia and stubborn refusal to write off a week's salary, Lucy was stranded on the high seas with a lot of annoying people screaming "Go Woodpeckers!" every ten minutes. She wasn't exactly sure who most of them were. Her brain must have blanked out half the class in an effort to shield her from remembering the horror.

No wonder she'd never bothered to buy a senior yearbook.

Marnie-from-third-period-bio leaned in closer. She probably had a last name, but Lucy didn't know it. Maybe it started with an "A"? She'd definitely been in Mr. Sonovich's biology class, though. Lucy distinctly recalled throwing a frog at her.

"You were always the special one, Lucy. I think Taffi was maybe a little jealous of you."

Lucy rolled her eyes. "Yeah, that *must* be it."

She would never understand why everyone in Clovis insisted she was special. Sure Lucy had a perfect SAT score, but so did a lot of other people. It was hardly the stuff of legend. For as long as she could remember, though, they'd all been poised for her to do something great. Something *important*, so that the dying town could finally have a citizen to be proud of.

Well, if they were pinning their hopes on her, they were in for a long damn wait.

"Hey, what are you wearing to formal night?" Marnie asked with dramatic concern. "It's not red, is it? Because Taffi's dress is red. If you wear the same dress as her again..."

She trailed off, letting Lucy's imagination fill in the rest.

Lucy paused with her drink halfway to her mouth. "*Shit.*" She looked over at Marnie. "Her dress is red, too?"

Marnie bobbed her head, going pale. "Oh God." She was a bubbly blonde whose greatest achievement in life would always be her status as an alternate on the cheer squad. At age thirty-three, there was still a yellow and blue ribbon in her hair. "What are you going to do?" She gasped in genuine horror. A tragedy of this magnitude froze her round face into an overly mascaraed jack-o-lantern. Wide eyes and a gaping mouth, with nothing but the faintest flicker of light illuminating the empty interior of her skull.

Airhead or not, Lucy didn't blame Marnie for the look of fear, though. Taffi's reaction to Lucy's red dress would make the *Lusitania* seem like a Disney cruise. The tantrum would ruin a trip that was already teetering on the edge of "maybe I should swim for shore" rotten.

Wonderful.

Typically, Lucy wasn't a big drinker. When she drank, she did stupid things, like get tattoos. But, alcohol really was the best option here. She belted back her third margarita and slammed the glass back down on the bar top. "I have to go find another dress. The ship has a gift shop, right?"

"On level three. You'd better hurry. Dinner's in an hour."

God, this whole weekend had been *such* a mistake.

Lucy headed for the elevator, brooding. She hated high school reunions even more than she'd hated high school. Maybe it would've been different if she'd become the kind of super success everyone had imagined. She'd been valedictorian of the class. The smartest kid in school. She was supposed to go out and change the world.

Obviously, the world had made other plans.

If she'd had a super-terrific job or even a husband and some cute pictures of their 2.3 kids to pass around, maybe she wouldn't feel so miserable. But, in the end, Lucy hadn't been nearly so special as everyone assumed. All she'd accomplished was getting a master's degree that couldn't land her a job beyond checkout clerk at Barnes and Noble and having a social calendar so empty little tumbleweeds sometimes blew across the blank squares.

Hell, the closest she'd gotten to a man in years were her dreams.

Actually, the dream last night had been the best part of the trip, so far. Soundly beating highpoint number two: free Mardi Gras beads with every drink. (There were only so many strands a girl could wear and still look respectable.) Last night, though, she'd fallen asleep on her small balcony, rather than go to the tedious class mixer. The antisocial tendencies thing, again. Mrs. What's-Her-Name the guidance counselor would've been so disappointed.

In her nostalgia-and-travel-commercial fugue state, Lucy had sprung for the upgraded room. Rather than eat dry chicken with morons, she'd figured she might as well enjoy the sea view that VISA would be charging her twenty percent interest for until the turn of the next millennium. It had been a warm evening. She'd been wearing her favorite silk nightgown, staring up at the stars and feeling lonely.

Lucy always felt lonely.

Maybe she really should just buy a cute little dog. She was always talking about it. Dogs seemed easier than people. No matter how much she disliked joining in, she'd always wanted somewhere to belong. Somewhere she'd feel welcome. She'd just never found it.

When Lucy nodded off, she'd been seduced by her caveman.

Since high school, she'd been dreaming of the same guy. Bits and pieces of him, anyway. Just enough to make her feel depressed and achy to wake up by herself. About once a year, give or take a couple months, he showed up and it was always like Christmas morning to see him, again.

Looking at the caveman, everything seemed to make sense. It seemed like he was the place she'd been searching for. The spot where she belonged.

...But in the morning she was always alone. It was like

the caveman was taunting her, showing her all the things she could never have. Hell, she'd gotten a paleontology degree, because she'd been so caught up in the fantasy of being closer to him.

Sometimes it seemed like the caveman was the realest part of her life.

Usually, Lucy just had fragments of him, but this dream had been so clear. So *real*. She'd been able to see him better than ever before. Her caveman was... perfect. No one else could compare to his long tawny hair and big calloused hands. He was handsome and tender. And *huge*, with a chest straight out of an action movie and the most beautiful eyes she'd ever seen.

Last night was better than any real sex she'd ever had and they hadn't even gotten to finish. He'd wanted her so badly he was shaking. For a second, he seemed to get overwhelmed by his desire, but then he got himself under control and started touching her like she was delicate. Like he was afraid he might hurt her. Despite the fact he could probably bench press a car, he'd been careful with her. She always felt safe with the caveman. Cherished.

...And incredibly turned on.

God, all she had to do was think about him and her pulse kicked into overdrive. This time it had seemed like she might get to finish *in* the dream. That would've been a first. And she'd been so *close*. But, right as things were about to get interesting, it got all earthquake-y and symbolic. Typical. Lucy had jerked awake with her body weeping for him and her heart pounding.

Also, the straps of her nightgown had been torn. That had been weird.

The elevator door bing-ed open and Lucy shook her head. She started for the small store, still thinking about the dream man. His name was Rhawn. She'd always wondered about that.

Since he only existed in her mind, she supposed she could've just made up a name for him years ago. It had never occurred to her to do that, though. Crazy as it seemed, she'd always known he'd tell her when he got the chance. Just *giving* him a fake name wouldn't have meant nearly so much as him sharing his real one. Which was completely crazy, but...

"Moose-y!"

She froze at the dreaded nickname, horror filling her. Faith came easily in times of disaster and she began to pray for a miracle. "Don't let it be Warren. Don't let it be Warren."

Warren Ples appeared, conclusively proving that God hated her. "Well, I don't know what all those rumors are talking about. You haven't packed on *too* much more weight since graduation." He gave her a thumbs up. "Good for you."

The hate. The *hate*.

It swept over her again, the clearest memory of her high school experience. Warren was Satan in a letterman's jacket. Every day for four years, she'd detested breathing the same air as Woodward High's "star" quarterback and now she was right back in the pit with the bastard.

Lucy slowly turned to face him. "Warren, didn't we have a pact never to speak unless one of us was on fire and needed a heads-up? Even then, I think we had a hand signal worked out."

"Yeah, but that was because you were such a snotty bitch." He told her easily. "We're past that now, ya know?"

Warren had the irritating habit of turning every statement into a question by adding "ya know?" to the end. It was one of the ten-thousand things she detested about the man.

Physically, he looked pretty much the same as he always did. Not quite as attractive as he pretended to be, with the bulky build of a football player who hadn't made the cut for a scholarship offer. His final game at Woodward High had been such a catastrophe that they were *still* shaking their heads about it around Clovis. No college would put him on the field after the Homecoming fiasco, even though he'd been an above average player up until then.

One bad day ruined it all for Warren and nobody was even surprised when it happened.

Warren was a guy who *juuuust* missed the mark in everything he did. Everyone knew it, so they didn't even *expect* him to hold things together. His whole life was an "almost." Bad choices, bad luck, bad timing... He was just doomed to failure. These days, he had two of the meanest ex-wives ever spawned and sold Saturns on his dad's car lot.

And probably *still* made more per hour than Lucy did. Ass hat.

"I'll *always* be a snotty bitch to you, Warren." Lucy assured him and headed off to find a non-red dress. Given the state of her day, it was no surprise that pretty much all the gift shop offered in the way of clothing options were bathing suits, sarongs and terrycloth bathrobes. Why couldn't this be one of the luxury cruises with the onboard malls?

Warren followed her around the small store, not taking the hint. His dark hair seemed to have been affixed to his head with Crisco to hide his developing bald spot. "Seriously, you had —like— some kind of Goth-girl-from-*The-Breakfast-Club* thing going on in high school." He informed her, crossing his arms over his chest. He was wearing his Woodward High football jersey, which was all kinds of sad. "All you did was read books in the library and dress in man-hating flannel and whine about how the ballplayers didn't take the same tests as the rest of the class, ya know?"

"Because, your tests were easier."

"Because, we needed good grades to stay on the team! You fucked up all my weekends with your complaining. I had to stay home and *study*." He frowned at her. "Fifteen years and you still can't admit that you were wrong about that?"

"Fifteen years and you still don't see that I was *right* about that?" Lucy snapped back. But, it annoyed her that Warren was a little bit right, too. Not about the tests, obviously. And she'd never been a full on Goth kid, nor had she hated men. She just hated *Warren*. She'd definitely been a loner, though. It was her nature to stand back and roll her eyes rather than join in.

"Taffi broke-up with me, because I couldn't take her

out on Saturdays." Warren insisted. "Otherwise, we'd probably be married now and this would be *my* boat, ya know?"

Jesus, it was like the Mobius strip of tenth grade debate all over again. "Taffi's husband works for the cruise line, first of all. They don't own this boat. Secondly, *Taffi's husband works for the cruise line*. If she'd married *you*, we wouldn't even *know* about this boat, because we're only here due to the fact she married *him*." She paused. "Also, you broke up because she screwed Craig Turkana at her birthday party."

Warren's eyes narrowed. "You're not going to apologize, are you?"

"That's it. We're reinstating the rule." Lucy decided. "No talking to each other, unless one of us spontaneously combusts." She turned back to the racks of clothes, picking up a t-shirt without much hope. "It's the only way you're getting off this ship with all of your limbs attached."

"The least you could do is..."

"Where is she?" Taffi slammed into the gift shop, interrupting his complaint. Her expression was wild and her eyes narrowed in a way sure to cause premature wrinkles. Her plastic surgeon would have palpitations if he saw. "You *bitch!* You think you're stealing my dress, *again?*"

Damn Marnie-from-third-period-bio. That pumpkin-headed twit always did have a big mouth. She must have rushed off to tell Taffi all about the impending maritime disaster.

"I'm buying a new outfit, Taffi. Just calm down..."

"Damn right you are!" The artful layers of Taffi's hair flew in all directions as she advanced on Lucy. She looked like she was wearing a scaled down version of the infamous blue dress, complete with corsage. Where the hell had she found a freaking *corsage* at sea? The woman just wasn't sane on the subject of proms. "You won't spoil *this* for me, too, Lucy!"

"Hey, Taffi." Warren gave her a leer, somehow managing to telegraph to everyone in the cute little boutique that they'd once had lots and lots of sex. "How you doin', babe?"

"Fuck off, Warren." Taffi didn't even glance his way. Instead, she glared at the shirt in Lucy's hand. "You think you're wearing *that* to Formal Night? Do you *want* to ruin the beautiful dinner that the Alumni Committee has planned? Is that it?" She shook her head. "*This* is why we've been enemies since kindergarten, you freak."

Lucy decided to wear the damn shirt just to piss Taffi off. It was neon orange, with the silhouette of the cruise ship on the front and its name written in gold glitter: *The Arden*. It would serve Taffi right to...

From out of nowhere, Lucy remembered the dream, again.

Rhawn's stark face as he whispered, *"It's the* Ardin. *The sinking."*

A strange premonition swept over Lucy. The same feeling she got the day her grandfather had died a hundred miles away or when she switched seats on a bus just before the driver had sideswiped a telephone pole. A deep, inexplicable *knowing*.

Oh God.

Lucy's eyes widened in panic. Not bothering to put the t-shirt down, she headed out of the shop. "We have to get up on deck! *Now*."

"What?" Warren followed her, but he didn't look happy about it. "Why?" He pulled out his folded shipboard itinerary to double-check the schedule. "All we're missing are shuffleboard lessons, ya know?"

"Lucy, you didn't pay for that shirt." Taffi protested hotly, trailing after them like the eternal hall monitor. "My husband is a vital member of this crew and I'm not going to let you just steal from his ship."

Lucy ignored them. All she could process was the pounding of her own heart as she ran up the stairs. Goddamn it, what level were the lifeboats on? Why hadn't she paid closer attention to that stupid TV safety message they'd played yesterday afternoon?

Craig Turkana, Woodward High's "most likely to get the electric chair," watched her race by. He wasn't some handsome rebel in the Fonzie, James Dean, Luke Perry tradition of high school bad boys. He was just the kind of low-rent scumbag who dealt drugs behind the cafeteria and sold pictures of his sister in the shower.

Lucy had no idea why Craig had even bothered to come to the reunion. Maybe he'd just needed a way to flee the state.

"Where you goin' in such a hurry, Meadowcroft?" He called, a cigarette dangling from his mouth and an ancient shirt that read "Fuck the World" covering his chest. "Brainiac marathon?" He chuckled at his own barely coherent wit. Lucy obviously wasn't the only one taking advantage of the cruise's open bar. "For real, I'm glad you're here, though. There's some stuff I've waited fifteen years to say to..."

Lucy cut him off. "Get up on deck!" She ordered, although she probably should've just spared Craig's future victims the heartache and let him drown. "This boat is going to sink."

"Huh?" Warren said with a typical show of razor-sharp intelligence.

"That's crazy." Taffi sputtered. "This ship can't sink. We have it rented until Monday."

Craig was a bit quicker on the uptake. He might have been a career criminal, but he'd never been stupid. Even half-drunk, he quickly assessed the situation and saw that Lucy was serious.

Perhaps remembering the twelfth grade library fire she'd shown up to douse seconds after he'd started it... Craig believed her. For whatever reason, he'd always insisted that she'd had some kind of psychic flash that day and he held it against her. It was another example of people ascribing Lucy with a specialness she just didn't have. Really, she'd just smelled the kerosene.

"Do we have time to get the life vests from the rooms?" Craig sounded nearly sober.

"I don't think so. I think we just have to get to the..."

She was cut off when the *Arden* suddenly listed to the

left. *Port,* she mentally corrected herself, because nautical precision was important when you were caught in *The Poseidon Adventure*. They were listing to *port*.

Lucy held on as the entire ship rolled to a sickening new angle. All around her, she heard people shouting in panic and objects falling. Metal creaked. Glass broke. Sirens started going off. She thought she smelled smoke.

Oh yeah. Taffi was *definitely* going to be giving her a refund for this "vacation."

Using the decorative bannister of the staircase as a ladder, Lucy pulled herself upward. She had to get to the deck or she'd be caught inside when the ship went down.

Warren and Taffi changed their minds about her mental state and frantically climbed after her, as the ship twisted further onto its side. Behind them, there was a reverberating crash. Lucy turned to see half the steps she'd just climbed fall away. Taffi and Warren barely made it to the jagged piece of landing that remained. If she hadn't left the store when she did, they all would've been stranded down there.

It's the Ardin. *The sinking.*

Rhawn's warning had saved her life.

So far.

"Go!" She shouted at Craig.

He didn't need the prompting. He sprinted for the exterior door at the top of the stairs. It had swung open when the ship made its ominous roll. Outside, Lucy saw lightening flash. It hadn't been raining before, but now a storm raged like something out of a George Clooney film.

Lucy hesitated, suddenly more afraid of what lay behind the door than what she'd face inside. Wait. How could the weather have deteriorated into a typhoon in a matter of minutes? What was going on?

"Move!" Warren shrieked. "Move! *Move!*" He shoved past her, pushing Lucy through the door in the process.

She stumbled out onto the sharply-angled deck, forgetting about the mysterious hurricane. All that mattered was getting to the lifeboats. On the wall, she spotted an emergency sign pointing towards the stern and she automatically headed that way. Just a few more moments and she'd be safe. All she needed was a few more…

The *Arden* plunged further into the water, the whole ship turning onto its side.

Shit.

Lucy had time to lock eyes with Craig. She heard Taffi screech in panic and Warren bellow for help. She tried to find a handhold, but the exterior railing gave way. It was the end. Damn it, she'd *known* she'd never get out of high school alive.

The very last thought in her head was of Rhawn.

Then, Lucy was freefalling through the air and into the bottomless blue of a swirling abyss.

Chapter Two

The caveman comes up behind her, pulling her against his chest.

Lucy tilts her head to stare at him, breathing hard. She's never dreamed of the same person twice before. It seems like that must mean something. Lucy tries to think of what, but her mind is buzzing. She can't process anything except wanting him. He's the handsomest guy she's ever seen. And the biggest. And the gentlest.

He clearly wasn't expecting to see her again, either. His face is dazed and excited as he stares down at her. One of his hands comes up to touch her cheek in something like reverence. He says something in a strange language. Whatever it means, she's guessing it's good, because he sure seems happy to see her again.

Lucy grins, hoping she doesn't wake up for a really long time. "Hi, caveman. Wanna make out?"

Lucy and Rhawn's Dream- Fourteen Years Ago

When Lucy opened her eyes, she realized she wasn't dead. For a second, she wasn't sure whether to be happy about that or not.

She was lying on her stomach, generally feeling like hell. Powdery white sand clung to every bit of her body, from her eyelashes to her shoelaces. Pushing herself up onto her elbows, she swiped grit from her face and tried to swallow down the taste of seawater in her mouth. Her lower half was still partway in the *very cold* water. It took her a second to find the energy to pull herself fully onto the shore, although that wasn't so toasty warm, either.

As far as Lucy could tell, she was on a beach.

Some kind of bizarre genetic mishmash of evergreens and palm trees swayed overhead, growing right up to the edge of the icy grey ocean. Growing *in* the ocean, in fact. As if the dark water was swallowing them, inch by inch. Wherever the hell she was, it sure didn't look like tropical blue waves of the Caribbean. These seemed like the kind of dark and dangerous seas Vikings had sailed on, carving dragons on their ships to protect them from the monsters beneath the murky surface. This ocean was menacing.

...But not as menacing as the volcano.

The damn thing loomed up from a jagged line of mountains, spewing smoke into the overcast sky. Lucy had never seen a volcano before. Well, she'd seen that movie with Pierce Brosnan and the mom from *Terminator*, but she'd never seen an *actual* volcano. It was —she was absolutely positive— *not* part of the cruise's scheduled sightseeing tour.

Where *was* the cruise?

The last thing Lucy remembered was the final deadly roll of the hull and plunging overboard. She'd hit the water like it was a brick wall. Everything after that was a blank. Lucy didn't even know what day it was. How had she gotten here? Did she swim? Float? Did someone bring her to shore? If so, where were they? Shouldn't she be at a hospital or something? She was just in a damn boat crash! Where were the doctors?

Lucy looked around. No ship. No people. No helicopters searching for survivors. No houses or buildings. No news trucks. No ambulance waiting to take victims to the hospital. No lawyers shoving business cards at her and promising to sue the cruise line for every last oar.

No... anything.

The chill that went through her had nothing to do with the weather.

"Hello?! *Hello?* Is anyone there?" A male voice called out.

It was a sad commentary on how scared Lucy felt that she actually breathed a huge sigh of relief at the sound of Warren's panicked cries.

"I'm here!" She struggled to her feet and instantly doubled over in a coughing fit.

It felt like she'd swallowed half the ocean. Lucy braced her hands on the knees of her wet jeans. There was still a strand of green Mardi Gras beads around her neck and they swung forward. She batted them aside. Aside from aching all over and the burning in her lungs, though, she seemed physically okay. Nothing broken or bleeding. Apparently, she'd live long enough to be interviewed on a very special episode of *Dateline*.

Class Reunion Castaway: The Lucy Meadowcroft Story.

"Moose-y! You're alive!" Warren came racing towards her. He was waterlogged and sandy, but otherwise unharmed. Even his slicked down hair had survived the sinking. Science class had been right: Oil and water really didn't mix. "What happened?" He demanded, his blue eyes huge in his pale face.

"We went overboard." She straightened, still wiping at the grit covering her. "Have you seen anyone else?"

He shook his head. "Just you. Where are we?"

"I don't know."

"What do you *mean* you don't know? You're supposed to have a million point IQ! How can you not know, ya know?"

"Because I'm not a fucking cartographer, that's how." Snapping at Warren made her feel better, but it wasn't really helping. Lucy needed to figure out what to do.

"Well, what are we going to do?" Warren demanded on cue.

Oh good. They were a "we," now.

Lucy rolled her eyes and didn't bother to argue the point. He'd just follow her if she didn't let him come along. "We start walking." She decided and headed off down the beach. Since they had no flare gun, phone or taxi available, it was really the only choice.

Trudging through the sand was just exactly as fun as she'd imagined it would be. All the pointlessness of P.E. combined with a growing certainty that she was in deep, *deep* trouble. Plus, Warren was there to add his stimulating observations to their ongoing disaster.

"Is that mountain supposed to be smoking like that?" He asked, pointing at the volcano. "It seems like kind of a bad sign, ya know?"

"I don't think our signs can get much worse, actually." Lucy was keeping track of the sun's position in the sky. They'd been walking for a long time, but it seemed like they were going in a circle. Only she was sticking right by the shoreline, which meant that this was indeed an island and they were headed right back to where they'd started.

"If it comes down to it Warren, I'm going to have to kill and eat you. Nothing personal."

"I have a green belt in karate." He informed her seriously. "I can totally take you in a..." His boast trailed off in a panicked scream as the ground started shaking.

The earthquake felt just like it had in her dream about Rhawn. Sort of a low-grade rumble. It didn't knock them off their feet, but it was enough to send trees swaying and sand shifting. Above them, the volcano's cloud of smoke grew darker in response.

Angrier.

"Oh shit." Lucy whispered. Anyone who'd ever seen a documentary on Mount St. Helens knew this was bad.

"What's going on?" Warren demanded. Apparently, he didn't watch PBS.

"That volcano is going to erupt soon."

"Oh *shit*." Warren agreed in an octave so high that even bats would have cringed. "We have to get out of here!" He started for the ocean, close to hysteria. "I'll take my chances with water over goddamn lava, ya know?"

"We need to think for a minute before we start freaking out."

"You think all you want. I'm dogpaddling outta here."

"That water has to be close to freezing. You're going to get hypothermic." Neither of them was dressed for the frigid climate of this island. The sun was still out and Lucy could already feel the cold biting through her shirt. God only knew what kind of temperatures night would bring. "We need to dry out, not get even wetter."

He didn't slow his desperate flight into the icy sea.

"Warren..." Lucy sighed in annoyance as he floundered out into the waves. A big part of her wanted to leave him, but she couldn't quite bring herself to walk away. Still, he clearly wouldn't listen to logic. Maybe she needed to persuade him with something even more frightening than freezing to death or erupting volcanoes. She thought for a beat. "There are probably sharks out there, you know."

He came splashing back out of the ocean even faster than he'd waded in. "Jesus, what is *with* this place?" Dashing up the sand, he stood by the line of trees, breathing hard and eyeing the shoreline. Apparently, he was waiting for a Great White to evolve legs and creep up onto the beach after him. "This is your fault!" He jabbed a finger at her. "*You're* the one who insisted we leave the gift shop."

"Because the ship was sinking!"

"You don't know that. You don't even know for sure the *Arden* went down, at all. Maybe it's fine. Maybe it's just floating on its side, ya know? Maybe everyone's headed back to New York by now, except us. All we know for sure is that we're stuck here in *Lord of the Flies*, all thanks to *you*."

Back in high school, Lucy had been smitten with Teddy O'Connell, president of the senior class and co-founder of the computer club. She'd always had a weakness for smart guys. Teddy, the kind-of-nerdy hunk, had gone on to make billions with some internet whatsit. Of course, *he* couldn't be stuck on this island with her. Oh, no. It had to be *this* asshole.

"Warren, if you keep it up, I will personally hold you under the water and you can see for yourself if the ship is down at the bottom of..." Lucy stopped short.

A sabretooth tiger was staring at them.

For real.

It was a *sabretooth fucking tiger.*

Lucy's master's degree in paleontology couldn't land her any job beyond retail book sales, but it made it simple for her to identify extinct Ice Age mammals when they came prowling down the beach in front of her.

In a state of shock, her mind instinctively started pulling facts from the endless college courses she'd taken. Sabretooth *cat* would actually be the correct term for the animal. From the extinct genus of *smilodon.* It wasn't really related to tigers, although its coat had a shaded pattern of streaks and spots to help it blend in with the surroundings.

Approximately seven hundred pounds. Short-ish tail. Built more like a bear than a modern lion. Thought to use their massive fangs to pierce the skin of their prey, so they'd bleed to death...

Warren gave a supersonic scream of pent up terror, interrupting her mental checklist of facts. Before Lucy could warn him not to move, he took off running into the forest.

The cat took off after him.

"Warren! Damn it!" Against her better judgment, Lucy headed into the forest. "If you run, you're going to make yourself prey!"

Except, he already *was* prey.

They both were.

God, what the hell was happening here? Even a polar bear would've made more sense. Sabretooth cats had been extinct for about nine thousand years. There couldn't *possibly* be an actual living specimen on this island.

It was hard to misidentify the eight inch long fangs jutting down from the animal's upper jaw, though. What the hell else could it *possibly* be? Lucy's mind was racing, trying to come up with a halfway reasonable explanation. Maybe it was some kind of genetic experiment. Maybe this whole place was like the *Island of Dr. Moreau* or something.

"Warren!" She'd lost sight of him in the woods. "Warren, if you can hear me, try to get up a tree!" The mountains in the middle of the island grew bigger as she pressed forward. Perfect. She was headed *towards* a smoldering volcano to find a guy who'd tormented her throughout her teenage existence. That made even less sense than the sabretooth. At least, she *wanted* to see the cat, again. The animal was a legitimate miracle. She hoped to God Warren didn't hurt it.

"Hellllp!"

His voice sounded like it was coming from her left. Lucy switched direction, even though she had no clue what she was going to do once she found him. How was she going to stop a gigantic carnivore from devouring that moron? She didn't want to harm the cat, but she couldn't let Warren die.

Well, *theoretically* anyhow.

Hopefully, she wouldn't have to choose between them, because it would be a tough decision. First off, she was a vegetarian, so killing animals was kinda a no-no. Secondly, the sabretooth really would contribute more to the world than Warren. Even his eternally disappointed parents would've agreed with that. The Pleses had never gotten over Warren's failure at that damn homecoming game. Maybe she could just scare the cat away.

Scanning around for some kind of weapon, Lucy finally decided on a fallen branch from one of the bizarre piney-palm trees. It was sturdy and thick… and would do absolutely nothing to stop a hungry tiger. Who was she kidding? She couldn't scare this thing even if she wanted to.

"Moose-y!"

"I should just leave him to be cat food." Lucy muttered, ducking through the dense foliage.

She could hear a river somewhere off to her right. Water sources would attract all sorts of animals. Every muscle in her body was tensed against possible attack. As much as the sabretooth fascinated her, there was no getting around the fact that it was an apex predator. Where it came from seemed a lot less important than it being here *now*.

The damn things hunted in packs. In fact, Lucy had written her thesis on sabretooths' social behavior, so she was kind of an expert on just how effective they were at killing in groups. More could be stalking her, right now. She swore she could feel yellow eyes watching her as she closed in on Warren's position.

Turns out, she was right. Sort of. Both Warren and the sabretooth were staring at her when she made it to the clearing.

…And both of them were ankle-deep in a sticky black swamp.

The tar pit was a wide asymmetrical stain seeping up from the ground. There was a thin layer of water and dead leaves collected on top of it, unable to drain through the gooey asphalt. Animals (and Warrens) could easily lumber into it, thinking it was nothing but a shallow puddle, and stay there until some museum team excavated their bones a few millennia later.

"I'm stuck." Warren said weakly.

"You idiot." Two inches of black sludge could incapacitate a cow and he'd somehow waded out into the middle of it.

The sabretooth gave a roar of fury and fear. It seemed like it must have leapt at Warren after he was trapped and landed in the tar itself. The cat was lodged in the pit about ten feet away from him, black gunk in its beautiful golden fur.

Lucy felt a lot worse about the sabretooth being imprisoned than Warren. It was an extraordinary survivor of another age. A paleontological marvel. Just *finding* it guaranteed that colleges would be lining up to give her a Ph.D. More importantly, this majestic creature could add *so much* to their body of knowledge. Studying its behavior would revolutionize everything they knew about the Ice Age. It was the most important scientific discovery of the century.

Already, she was thinking of ways to save it.

"You have to get me out of here!" Warren ordered when Lucy kept staring at the cat.

"Do you understand what this is?" She whispered in awe.

"Yeah! It's a goddamn lion."

It was the size of a large lion and had a tawny-colored coat, but even Warren should've been able to see that this was no ordinary animal. "This is a sabretooth! Look at its teeth."

"*Who cares what it is?* Just find a rope or something!"

"Moron." She muttered again and tried to focus on saving his worthless ass. The rope wasn't happening, unless she weaved one out of vines, so she extended the branch to him. It was too short. Lucy let out a frustrated sigh. "How did you even get out there?"

"I don't know! I was just running and then I was caught. *Do* something."

"Can you really not understand how important this animal is?" Lucy demanded as she hunted around for a longer stick. "Sabretooth cats lived during the Ice Age. The *Ice Age*, Warren! It's like finding a wooly mammoth wandering around."

"I. Don't. *Care*." He shouted, spacing out each word for emphasis. "All I care about is getting free and going home. Away from cruise ships and volcanoes and lions and sharks and..." His rant ended in a wheeze. "Guys with spears."

"Guys with spears?" Lucy echoed. "What the hell are you...?" She stopped short as guys with spears stepped into the clearing and surrounded them.

There were six of them, decked out in loincloths and necklaces made from teeth. All of them were blond and built like MMA fighters. Maybe it was the sabretooth sighting talking, but they looked a hell of a lot like... cavemen.

Lucy gaped at them.

They gaped back.

For a long moment, there was nothing but the sound of the sabretooth thrashing to get free of the tar and the howl of the wind through the mutant trees.

Then, in some kind of cult-y unison, all six of the men fell to their knees and started praying towards the sky. And the volcano. And Lucy and Warren. Insanely enough, she recognized some of the words they were spouting from her dreams with Rhawn. What was *happening* here?

"What... the... fuck?" Warren asked blankly.

"I don't know." Lucy swallowed, trying to wrap her mind around this craziness. "I think... They might believe we're —like— deities."

Warren's eyebrows soared. "For real?"

"I think so." *Thinking* was all she could do at the moment, but none of her thoughts made much sense. Try as she might, Lucy just couldn't get the facts to form any kind of logical picture. "I'll try to explain we're not, but I'm not really sure how to..."

"Are you crazy?" He interrupted, his face suddenly alive with crafty ideas. "Didn't you see *Ghostbusters?* When someone asks if you're a god, you say *yes*."

"You want to impersonate the *gods* of these heavily-armed men? You really think that's a good idea?"

"You got a better one?" Warren didn't bother to wait for an answer. "Hey you." He pointed at the largest man, who gazed up at him in something like awe. The guy seemed to be the leader, with long blond dreadlocks and the biggest necklace of all. It looked like a giant tooth. "That's right. *You*, Conan. Go find me a rope before I zap you with a lightning bolt, ya know?"

Chapter Three

Within two seconds of spotting her, the caveman's hand is already finding its way under the the hem of Lucy's nightshirt. He touches places no one else has touched and she's super-duper fine with that. Considering what his fingers are doing in those places, she's sure not going to object.

Lucy arches against him, sending him a grin. "Hi, caveman." She says teasingly.

His gaze roams over her face, as his hands roam over her body. She can see him working through her words, trying to figure them out. Intelligence and desire battle in his incredible brown eyes.

"Hi." He whispers back.

The caveman might not understand English, but he's smart enough to piece together her familiar greeting and return it. That is amazing. Way better than she could do with his language. Lucy beams, impressed with how bright he is.

He smiles back at her like she's the most special girl in the world.

Rhawn and Lucy's Dream- Thirteen Years Ago

For generations, this day had been prophesized. For generations, people had been both fearful that they would live to see it come and inspired by the thought of witnessing it for themselves.

Yet, this generation was chosen.

All their legends had been leading to this. All their hopes were pinned to it, especially as the shaking grew worse and the island sank deeper into the sea. This was the moment of their destiny.

The final battle between good and evil.

The Clan gathered in reverent excitement, their eyes bright as they gazed at the gods. Finally seeing them was all the Clan hoped for and all that they dreaded. It showed them that the myths were true. Here at the end of time, this man and woman would battle for the souls of all.

For better or worse, the *Ardin* had arrived.

"They are here!" Skoll called, leading the group of men who'd found the gods. He held his spear above his head, the massive tooth pendant at his throat glinting in the sun. "We are saved!"

Rhawn barely heard his shouting. Skoll was an ass, so it was second nature to ignore him even on days when the world *wasn't* ending. Really, though, it wouldn't have mattered who was talking. From the second he saw the female, Rhawn wasn't able to process anyone or anything else.

Blaming Rhawn for the latest shaking, the Clan had confined him in one of the smaller caves while they debated whether or not to execute him. Skoll argued it would be safer to remove Rhawn from their midst, once and for all. Many agreed. Meanwhile, Anniah, daughter of the chief, argued that the gods would be angered if they harmed him. After all, Rhawn was the one who received their visions. Perhaps they had plans for him, beyond the Clan's understanding. Many people agreed with that, too. Sometimes the same people agreed with both ideas.

There was so much fear in the Clan these days, most of them would agree with anything.

Unsure of their correct course, they'd finally compromised on locking Rhawn up. The Clan had fashioned bars from thick bamboo and fastened them over the entrance, trapping him inside. It was pointless and stupid, like much of what they did. He went along with it, because he had nothing else to do. Until now. Until *her*.

Rhawn staggered to his feet, gripping the bars as he gazed out at the woman.

The Destroyer.

Lucy.

Her hair fell in enchanted dark waves, her body so much lusher than the thin and muscular women of the clan. She was dressed in the clothing of her magical world, her nails still tipped with the nearly-black paint. Around her neck, there was a necklace of sparkling green beads that must have been more costly than anything else in creation.

Only someone with the brainpower of a rock could look at her and not see she was made to lure men to their doom. But, Rhawn had never been a man of much intelligence.

To him she looked... perfect.

The punch of desire nearly sent him to his knees. His mind was whirling, trying to process what shouldn't be. How could she be standing right in front of him? It was impossible. His body didn't give a shit about 'possible,' though. It just wanted to get closer to her. Every instinct in him clambered at him to grab her. To throw her over his shoulder and carry her back to his cave. To Choose her before another man could steal her away.

She was real.

The backs of his eyes burned and he squeezed them shut, whispering a prayer of thanks. This wasn't a dream or a fantasy. Whatever happened next didn't matter. His mate was standing ten feet from him, beautiful and alive.

She was *real.*

"Holy goddamn frigging hell on a go-cart." The Savior said in the language of the gods. None of the Clan could understand his words, except for Rhawn, and even he wasn't sure what they meant. It might have been a prayer, but who did gods pray to? "These freaks are living in caves, Lucy. No wonder they smell so bad, ya know?"

"Shut up and try to look divine." The Destroyer hissed back, but she wasn't really paying attention to the Savior. Her eyes traveled up and down the small valley, cataloguing the caves carved into the stone walls. "This isn't right." She whispered. "Where are we?"

"We're in a *National Geographic* special." The Savior told her. "Like one of those tropical islands where the natives worship Coke bottles."

"No, it's not that." The Destroyer shook her head, something like fear on her face. "No way."

Perhaps she knew her time was drawing to a close. If the stories were true, and thus far they had been completely accurate, the Destroyer and her followers were doomed to die on this island. She must sense that. No wonder she was afraid.

Rhawn wished he could move closer to her and ease her terrified expression. She hadn't spotted him yet. Despite his size, Rhawn was good at not being seen, especially locked in his cell. He gazed at her, wondering if she would know him. Gods, but he knew her. The woman was even more gorgeous than she'd been in his dreams. Looking at her, he remembered every inch of her body. The soft glow of her eyes meeting his. The radiance of her smile.

The feel of her lips.

His soul was truly damned, because all Rhawn could do was stare at her and *want*. Many things fascinated him, but sex was right at the top of the list. He rarely got a chance to experiment with it, but now he could think of a thousand different ideas he wanted to try out with Lucy. He knew her arrival signaled the end of the world and he still wanted to roar with triumph.

Several people edged away from his cell, uneasy at the sight of Rhawn's predatory grin. Even with the bars separating them, he tended to scare people.

"Why 'no way'?" The Savior asked Lucy. "What else could these freaks be except a primitive, lost tribe of Aruba or some shit?"

"There are no primitive, lost tribes of Aruba." Lucy snapped. "Are you really that stupid?"

"Well, you explain it then!"

"I *can't* explain it. That's the problem. *No way* does any regular island have an erupting volcano, living sabretooth cats, and a whole village of cavemen, but no anthropologist, biologist, geologist, zoologist, or paleontologist in sight. No *way*." Her words came out so fast that Rhawn had a hard time differentiating one from another.

"Maybe this place is undiscovered." The Savior tried, but not even he seemed to believe it. "Like Robinson Crusoe or something."

"Undiscovered?! It had to be close enough to the path of our cruise that you and I *swam* to it. How could it possibly be undiscovered?"

"So it's gotta be Aruba then. Just like I said."

"No, it's *not* fucking Aruba." Lucy leaned closer to him and lowered her voice. "Something is *wrong*, Warren."

His eyebrows drew together. "Like more 'wrong' than us sinking and getting kidnapped by refugees from *Quest for Fire?* Because how much more 'wrong' can...?"

She cut him off, sounding almost frantic. "Like these plants," she pointed to the *um'nah* trees, "they don't *exist. That* kind of wrong."

"You're goddamn crazy, you know that?"

"I hope I *am* crazy, because the alternative leaves us in even deeper trouble."

"Hey, at least I'm out of the tar pit, so..." The Savior trailed off as he spotted Notan. "Super. Who's this Yoda guy now?"

The chief came down from his cave, leaning heavily on his cane. There was no mistaking he was in charge. The rest of the Clan moved aside so he could pass.

Notan gave the gods the traditional blessings and praises of the Clan, liberally sprinkled with beseeching calls for mercy and benevolence. It went on for a while. Even Rhawn was impressed with the eloquence of the oration. He could only imagine how long it had taken Notan to compose and memorize it. He must have been working on it for ages, anticipating this moment and how it would be remembered for all time.

The gods responded to the carefully worded speech with blank stares.

Notan deflated in frustration. "Rhawn, the Accursed." He wheezed, seeing that they had no idea what he'd just said to them. "You understand their sacred language. Translate my words."

Rhawn braced himself as everyone turned to look at his cell.

Instantly, he felt the Destroyer's attention fall on him. She drew in a sharp breath, like she was the one amazed. Her green gaze met his and he lost all ability to think. No one else ever stared into his eyes. It was like a physical touch.

How could she be so evil and so... *perfect?*

"Hi." He said quietly. It was the way she always greeted him in the dreams and he saw her lips part in recognition.

The Savior didn't seem to hear the greeting. He glanced at Lucy, then over at Rhawn, and then back again. "You know this shirtless giant, Moose-y?"

"I dreamed of him." Her lips barely moved, all her attention on Rhawn.

The Savior didn't like that. "You dream of half-naked criminals? He's all locked-up in caveman jail! Jesus, even you could do better." He sent Rhawn a glare, his body shifting so it was closer to the Destroyer. He placed a hand on her arm, like he was trying to protect her.

Rhawn's gaze narrowed in response. Did the Savior want Lucy for himself? Rhawn's fingers tightened on the bars, wanting to drag the Savior away from her small body. This woman was his.

...Even if she *was* evil.

For her part, Lucy didn't even seem to notice the other man. Instead, she gazed at Rhawn like he was a ghost. Had she not known he really existed? Wasn't it her who sent the dreams?

The Savior glowered between them, as if he sensed Rhawn's resolve and Lucy's confusion. At a loss as to what to do, the other man settled for pointing a finger at Rhawn. "Dude, you leave her alone." He ordered.

Rhawn's jaw ticked. He would not surrender Lucy to this man or any other. Not without a fight that left him victorious or dead. It didn't matter that the Savior was a god, Lucy belonged to Rhawn and he would not give her up.

Ever.

"Rhawn, have you done something to anger the Savior?" Notan demanded, seeing the male deity's scowl.

"He believes the Destroyer favors me." Rhawn answered, his eyes on the dark-haired male god. He disliked the Savior on sight, which just went to prove that his soul really was lost. Seeing the man's hand on Lucy's arm caused Rhawn's jaw to clench. "He is... displeased."

The Clan began murmuring amongst themselves. No one seemed very surprised that the Destroyer would single him out or that the Savior would despise him for it. Rhawn *did* have "Accursed" after his name, after all.

"Now, what are they jabbering about?" The Savior demanded.

"Say something to fix this, you fool." Notan snapped at Rhawn. "The Savior is the only one who can help us and you've already angered him! Repeat each word of my speech, so he knows of our humble thanks and obedience."

Rhawn barely glanced his way, his attention on Lucy. "You've locked me in this cage because you think I'm cursed. What makes you think I will help any of you?"

"You'll help us or we'll kill you right now!" Skoll bellowed back.

Rhawn snorted. "If you planned to kill me, you would have done it long ago. You're too afraid of what you might unleash. What if I am in league with the darkness?"

Skoll's jaw ticked. He looked over at Notan. "We do not need Rhawn. If we kill the Destroyer now, all this will end."

"Kill the Destroyer?" Notan scowled. "We can't. She is all-powerful. Only the Savior can strike her down."

"She is smaller than we thought she'd be. Weaker. If we can stop this before he even *has* to slay her, wouldn't that be better? We can at least try to..."

"I will speak to the woman." Rhawn interjected, before anyone started buying into Skoll's line of reasoning. "Attempting to harm her will do nothing, except trigger our destruction. Gods may look weak, but it is all part of their ruse." He glanced at Notan. "You may hate me, but you know I do not wish to see the island sink. I will translate your speech and we will follow the rules of the *Ardin*. It is the only way we will survive."

"Father, let Rhawn try." Anniah urged.

The old man wasn't completely convinced, but he

relented. "Use my *exact* words. It must be precise."

"Of course." Rhawn lied and switched to the language of the gods. "Welcome." He said shortly. The leader had said a lot more, but that was close enough.

The Savior and the Destroyer both stared at him.

"Holy shit! The big one can talk." The Savior blurted out and looked at the woman. "Did you know these Cro-Mags could talk?"

The Destroyer ignored him, still gazing at Rhawn. "Who are you?" She asked quietly.

His eyebrows drew together. She didn't know who he was? How could she not know, given their history? It was… annoying. Hurtful. "I am Rhawn. I told you this, remember?"

"Oh, I remember." She gave a high-pitched laugh that sounded close to tears. "I just wanted to double-check when I was –ya know– conscious." She ran a hand through her hair, looking on the verge of collapse. "Jesus, I never should have RSVPed for the stupid reunion. *That's* what started all this. I'm losing my mind, because I wouldn't just walk away from the damn cruise ticket. What was I *thinking?*"

She was a being of unimaginable power and cruelty, but Rhawn's heart flipped over as he saw her fighting back tears. He moved as close as he could to the bars, instinctively wanting to shield her. By nature, he always wanted to protect, although no one ever desired his help. "It will be alright." He soothed. "I promise you, Lou-cee."

The Savior slanted him another glower and pulled the woman closer, blaming Rhawn for her upset. "Stay calm and let me handle this, alright, Luce? I can talk to people. Even the primitive ones." He refocused on Rhawn and squinted in deep concentration. "Me. Warr-en." He put a palm flat on his chest, speaking veeeerrryyyy sllllooooowllllyyyy. "Me *friend*." He gave an exaggerated nod.

Rhawn bit back a snarl. Gods, had he really spent his life praying to this moron? "I understand your language." He said flatly. "You can speak in a normal way."

"Ask him if he's come to save us." Tammoh, one of the

Clan's best hunters, called.

"How will he bring us to our new lands?" Someone else demanded. It sounded like Ctindel's mate, Jenda.

"When will he fight the Destroyer?" The final question came from Skoll and everyone grew quiet again, waiting for an answer.

Rhawn's eyes flicked to the woman, again. She was in no condition to fight. Skoll was right; they could probably kill her right now. For whatever reason, she looked to be in a state of shock. Her body shivered so badly, he was surprised she was still on her feet.

Obviously, this was the perfect time for the Savior to strike her down.

Warr-en could easily end the *Ardin*, right now. It was the best strategy. All Rhawn had to do was point that out and this would all be over. Everyone would be safe. His gaze met the Destroyer's, again. Her eyes were damp with tears and confusion. She looked up at him like she was lost. Like she needed protection and he was someone worthy to give it.

Rhawn's mind raced for a beat. "We cannot have the battle, yet." He heard himself tell the Clan, once again proving his mental weakness. "The Savior tells me we must first," he hesitated. Shit. What would stall them? "...have a feast."

Notan's bushy gray eyebrows compressed. "A feast?"

"Yes." Rhawn raised his voice so everyone could hear and gave into his worst impulses. Siding with evil shouldn't fill him with so much satisfaction, but he could not allow Lucy to be harmed. She didn't seem capable of defending herself, so he would do it for her. "He is Warr-en, the Mighty!" Rhawn gestured towards Warren with an expansive hand. "He has come to save us!"

Anniah, Notan's daughter, gave a happy cry, clapping her hands together. As the Clan's healer, she was an intelligent woman. Still, she gazed at Warren with the delight and wonder of a child presented with a magic trick. She wasn't alone. Everyone was excited to have the Savior presented to them, at last.

It made Rhawn's plan easier.

"Warren is gladdened by our welcome and by Notan's great words." Notan preened at that and Rhawn marveled at how simple this was. He should try lying more often. Perhaps he had a talent for it. "The god wishes to see us celebrate his arrival. The festivities will give him the strength he needs for his coming victory."

This time the whole Clan cheered.

The Savior frowned in confusion as dozens of people rushed forward to genuflect at him. "What the hell...?"

"They wish to honor you." Rhawn told him and saw the man grow more arrogant.

"They do, huh?" Warr-en smirked over at the woman. "You hear that, Moose-y? They wish to honor *me*." He tugged on her sleeve when she didn't respond. "Lucy, did you hear that? Finally, I'm getting some recognition, ya know?"

She batted him aside.

Rhawn suppressed his pleased smirk. "We have food and offerings for you, Warr-en. The Clan has long awaited your arrival. You must go with them and rejoice."

The Savior forgot all about Lucy, as the Clan's women surrounded him. The god's eyes went to their uncovered breasts and stayed there. "Offerings?" He repeated, looking intrigued by Rhawn's words. "Like a party? For me?"

"For you." Rhawn agreed. "All we have is yours. You are the Savior of our people."

"I am?"

"Yes. Only you can lead us."

"Really? Leading? Me?" The Savior didn't seem so certain about that. He was *very* interested in the half-naked women fawning at him, though. "But right now, we're just having a party, right?"

"Correct."

"Awesome." The Savior smiled and wrapped an arm around Anniah without even seeing her face. "Well, let's start with the honoring, then!"

Clan lifted him up onto their shoulders, carrying him towards the caves, chanting "Warr-en! Warr-en!"

The god waved at them with haughty condescension. Rhawn really was a fool.

He would be doomed if he worked against the Savior. He knew that. The man was a lack-wit, but he was the only hope for the world. It was pointless to help the Destroyer spread her evil. He should be doing everything possible to help *the Savior* win this battle. At the moment, though, he found he didn't care about the fate of the world. Lucy would live for another day. That was all that mattered.

Rhawn looked over at the woman and saw that she was still in a daze. "Lou-cee." He called, trying to gain her attention. He held a hand out to her through the bars, wanting her to come closer. "Lou-cee, you must listen to me... *stop!*" He bellowed the last word in the Clan's language, not that it did any good.

Skoll grabbed her by the arm, dragging her towards Rhawn's cage. He towered over Lucy, his huge body dwarfing hers, as he hustled her forward. Her feet automatically tried to find traction, digging into the dirt. Skoll was so large, he simply lifted her up and carried her the rest of the way.

"You son of a *tandar*." Rhawn gave the bars a furious shake. "Get your hands *off* of her!"

"If it was up to me, both of you would be tossed into the tar pits to die!" Skoll opened the cage door long enough to throw Lucy inside.

Rhawn caught her before she could hit the dirt. She was drenched to the skin, like she had been in the sea. His arms wrapped around Lucy, sheltering her from Skoll and from the wind. Still in a daze, her body instinctively curved into his.

A perfect fit.

Rhawn closed his eyes for a beat, overwhelmed that he was holding her, at last.

"Do what you want with her for now." Skoll sneered, seeing Rhawn's awed expression. "Gods know, no other woman will have you in the light of day, so you might as well take advantage of the situation. Come morning, she'll be facing the *Ardin*, anyway."

Rhawn glared at Skoll. "The end of the world is already

upon us. Why do you wish to hasten your own demise?"

"I'm not afraid of you, Accursed One." Skoll stepped inside the cage, trying to intimidate him. "You will be dead long before I am, now that the Savior is here. There is no way your bitch will be able to..."

Rhawn slammed Skoll's head into the cave wall.

The other man gave a choked cry and then toppled over, splayed out on the dirt. Rhawn frowned. He hadn't *meant* to do that. Not exactly. He'd simply taken one of his hands off Lucy, reached over, and grabbed Skoll by the neck. The next thing he knew, the man's skull was ricocheting off the rock.

Why did these things always happen to Rhawn?

He made an irritated face. Attacking Skoll was probably going to cause him no end of trouble. Not that he'd had much of a choice. It took a lot to rouse Rhawn to violence, but, once it started, he was damn good at it. Every instinct in his body told him to kill anyone who threatened this woman. Really, Skoll was lucky to get off so lightly. He'd wake up. Eventually. That was more than he deserved. No one else in the Clan would see it that way, but it hardly mattered.

Nothing mattered but his mate.

Dismissing the man from his thoughts, Rhawn focused on Lucy.

The rest of the Clan seemed to have forgotten her existence in their revelry. Even the guard stationed outside of his cell had headed off with the Savior. Meat had been scarce for so long that a feast was an unheard of indulgence. Since Notan refused to consider Rhawn's "unholy" source of food, everyone else in the Clan was half-starved. The festivities his lies just created would use the last of their stores. But, between the food and the Savior, they would be distracted for hours.

Rhawn weighed his options and then shrugged. He was done being a prisoner. "Lou-cee?" Her odd name tasted exotic on his tongue. "Look at me." He tilted his head down to meet her huge eyes. "I am going to take you to my cave? Do you think you can walk?"

"Yeah." But the word was so faint that he didn't believe it.

"Are you ill, goddess?"

"Maybe I'm ill." She agreed vaguely. "Maybe I'm really, really..." Her legs gave way and she didn't seem to notice.

Rhawn supported her weight, growing concerned at her stupor. "Lucy?"

"Where am I?" She whispered and Rhawn knew she wasn't talking to him. "Where the hell *am* I?"

"You are here." It was the only thing he could think to say. "You are with me." Rhawn lifted her up against his chest and he could feel her body shaking. For a woman destined to change the world, she weighed nothing, at all. "You know me, Lucy. Since I was little more than a boy, you've been in my dreams. You say you've dreamed of me, too."

She didn't respond to that. Instead, Lucy's face turned into the curve of his shoulder and she hung on like Rhawn was the only real thing in the universe. He rested his cheek in her hair, briefly closing his eyes. Emotions flooded through him, deep and real, carving out huge spaces inside of him. Spaces that only Lucy could fill. Spaces that would collapse him into nothing if she ever tore free and left him empty again.

The Clan didn't have a word for such feelings, but Lucy's people did.

Love.

Rhawn loved her. He always had. All his life he'd been waiting for this small girl to arrive and now he'd finally been handed his future. He didn't know why or how she was there, but he knew he could never let her go.

Lucy was his mate.

"You are safe." He whispered, breathing in the magical scent of her skin. "I will keep you safe. Always. *Vando*."

She silently shivered in his arms, not responding to the assurance. She seemed so vulnerable in this state. Why didn't a goddess protect herself better? What could scare a being of her power?

Not sure how to help her, Rhawn headed out of the cell. He stepped over Skoll's unconscious form as he left, slamming the bamboo gate closed behind him. He would not waste another moment on that asshole when he finally had his woman in his arms. Rhawn might be an idiot, but he wasn't *that* big an idiot.

"Lou-cee?" He carried her back to his cave and set her down on the thick pelts of his bed. "Are you in need of something?" He crouched before her, trying not to remember how amazing she'd looked there in his dreams.

Naked... Warm... Smiling...

Kissing.

Damn it, he was remembering.

He wasn't sure how to care for a woman. Nobody had ever entrusted him with one before. They seemed delicate. He decided to go with the most obvious need and quickly got to his feet again. "Have some water." He grabbed a shell cup and pressed it into her hand. She frowned like she had no idea what to do with it. "Drink." He prompted and nudged it towards her mouth.

Still in a fog, she obediently sipped the water.

"Good." It was wrong of him to enjoy her presence so much. The woman was troubled and evil and a goddess... But, she was also so beautiful that he had to force himself not to stare. She was in his cave, sitting on his bed, and he wanted to keep her there. Luckily, she didn't seem eager to leave. She didn't seem aware of her surrounding, at all.

Shivers continued to course through her body, as she huddled against the wall. Maybe she was cold. The cave seemed downright balmy to him, but she was very small and wet. He wasn't sure if gods contracted illnesses, but he wasn't taking any chances. Rhawn set about making a fire to warm her. When even that didn't stop her dazed shaking, he frowned and started removing her damp clothes.

"Have you been in the sea?" He asked her, trying to figure out why she'd do such a foolhardy thing. "That is a very unwise pastime. *Jigons* lurk below the surface of the water.

You must be more careful."

The woman didn't seem to hear him. She sat still as he peeled off her strange garments, lost in her own thoughts. Tears were running down her cheeks and breaking his heart.

"It will be alright." He soothed. "It will all be alright, goddess. I promise you."

If it wasn't for the dreams, Rhawn wasn't sure he could've figured out how to unbuckle and clasp all the different fastenings of her clothing. Even knowing how they worked, it was a challenge. Rhawn had always been good with his hands, though. He released a shuddering breath as he uncovered her smooth body. It was impossible not to stare, so he didn't even try. The woman was his mate, after all. He could look at her all he wished. And *oh* how he wished to look. He'd waited forever to find her. Now that she was here –gods!– it was hard to even think in the face of such perfection. He wanted to lay her back and...

No.

Shit.

He shook his head to clear it and wrapped her in his heaviest furs. Having a woman meant caring for her. Lucy seemed completely lost. This was not the time to think of anything beyond her need for security. He carefully bundled her up and touched her hair. "You are safe here with me." He murmured. "Fear not."

Time passed.

He waited for the woman to say something. And waited. And waited.

Finally, just to keep his mind off her flawless (and naked) body, Rhawn began preparing dinner. He assumed even a god needed food. When he set the wooden bowl of meat stew in front of her, though, she ignored it. Luminous green eyes looked sightlessly at the wall. At all the paintings of her world. She seemed mesmerized.

"Lou-cee, you must eat." He prompted after a while.

They'd been sitting in silence for so long that he didn't expect her to answer... And she didn't. She didn't even look his way. Rhawn sighed and took a bite of his own meal. This was pointless. How was someone forsaken supposed to comfort a goddess? Why would she even *want* to talk to him, when she…?

"It's pronounced Lucy." She whispered, interrupting his thoughts. "One word."

Heartened, Rhawn tried to say it the way she did. "Loose-y. Louchee." Gods, their language was difficult sometimes. "*Loooocy.*"

"Close enough." She finally glanced his way and said the last thing he expected. "Are you going to get in trouble for hitting the blond guy and escaping that cell?"

Yes.

"No." He lied. "It will be fine."

She didn't believe him. "I'm sorry. I kind of lost it for a minute there. I didn't mean to drag you into this mess."

"Skoll brought it upon himself. I will not let anyone harm you."

"Thank you." She whispered.

Rhawn shrugged the matter aside. She did not need to thank him for taking care of her. It was his right and duty. "Eat. You will feel better."

Lucy let out a shaky breath and reached over to pick up the bowl of meat. "What is this?" She gave it a tentative sniff, then quickly reared back. "Jesus."

"It's the last bits of the last mammoth we hunted."

She gave a semi-hysterical laugh. "Well, that explains the smell." She set the stew aside and covered her face with her hands. "Okay, forget the acting calm shit. The meltdown's happening. I can't stop it, because I can't deal with this. I can't! How am I supposed to deal with this?"

She was upset over the *Ardin*. She knew she would lose.

Rhawn hesitated, weighing his options. All of them seemed bad. "The Savior seems fond of you." He finally told her, because it was the best way to keep her alive. Maybe she could still change her ways. Maybe there was still time. "If you give up your cruel plans and join him, I do not think he will harm you."

Rhawn might try to harm the Savior if the man tried to take the "joining" too far, though. Gods, he really detested that man.

"The who?"

"Warr-en. The Savior."

"*Warren?* A savior? Are you kidding me? That putz couldn't save a CPR dummy."

Rhawn wasn't sure what that meant, but it sounded like blasphemy.

The woman didn't seem to fear divine retribution. Whatever emotion existed between unfocused agitation and a wild sense of purpose, she was clearly feeling it. "Look, I don't understand what's happening and I'm thinking you do. So tell me. *Now.* How did I get here?"

"I do not know." The mysteries of the gods were far beyond his understanding.

She curved her arms around her body, like she was trying to hold herself still. He could hear her teeth chattering. Rhawn automatically reached out to touch her shoulder in comfort, but she shied away.

Of course she did.

He sighed and dropped his hand.

"Who are you?" She asked again.

"I am Rhawn." For no reason he could imagine, he began to worry that he was intimidating her. The woman was a goddess who could probably kill him in ten thousand magical ways. Aside from that, any other male in the Clan would *want* their women intimidated and compliant to his every demand.

That was not what Rhawn wanted, though. He wanted Lucy to want him back.

To welcome his touch.

He crouched down again so he was at eyelevel with her and made his voice tender. Obviously, she hadn't understood him before, so he repeated the words more slowly. "You know me, Lou-cee." He repeated quietly. "I dreamed of you. Many times. You dreamed of me, yes?"

She bit her lip. "Yes." She whispered.

"What did you dream?"

Her eyes flashed away, her cheeks coloring. "I don't remember all of them." She muttered and he knew she'd dreamed the same things he had.

"*I* remember all of them." He said quietly. "I remember everything. I remember the very first night I saw you. You were very young and in a strange red costume..."

"God, why does *everything* always go back to the fucking prom dress?"

Those words meant nothing to him, so he kept going. "I remember how amazed I was to see you and how much I wanted you." And it was not a fraction of how much he wanted her now. "I remember knowing you were meant to be mine."

"I remember your hands going places that I didn't let my prom date touch." She said sourly.

Rhawn's mouth curved. "I remember that also." He agreed.

"This is crazy, you know that?" She swiped a hand under her nose.

"Yes."

She glowered at him, not satisfied with that calm reply. "You're really real? You're *sure*? You're really a real caveman?"

She often called him that. He could piece together it meant a man who lived in a cave. Therefore, it was true of him. "Yes." He agreed simply.

"That's all you have to say? Just 'yes!' Really? *Really?*"

"Yes." He couldn't think of anything to tell her except the simple truth.

Her eyes narrowed at him. "Fine. Well, how the hell is it possible that I dreamed of you, then? Explain it to me."

"You didn't dream of me. I dreamed of *you*. I dream of your world every night." He gestured to the art on the wall.

She didn't even glance at it. Her eyes stayed on him, as if she was afraid to look away. "My *world?*" She swallowed. "Which is different from *this* world?"

He nodded.

"That's what I was afraid of. Unless maybe you're just confused or…" She shook her head, still looking stunned. "Alright. Let's start simple: Do you know the name of this island?"

"No'wanta-hoan." How would that translate into her words? "Mother of the Clan." That was close, although not exact. There was subtler meaning of this land being a first stop on a greater journey, which was being lost in her language.

"Do you know *where* the island is?"

He had no clue how to respond to that question, so he just pointed down. The island was beneath their feet. For now, anyway. Very soon, it would sink into the Infinite Sea.

"No. I mean where is it in relation to *other* islands."

Rhawn squinted in confusion. "There are no other islands."

"There must be." She wiped her eyes and gestured towards the ocean. "What else is out there?"

"Nothing."

"*Nothing?*"

"There is nothing but water. That is why we've awaited the Savior." Rhawn wasn't sure why she didn't know all this already. "He will lead us to a new home."

The Destroyer watched him for a long moment, as if waiting for him to change reality. "Hang on… You think *Warren* is going to take you to the Promised Land? Wow! And I thought *I* was screwed." She ran a hand through her hair, not noticing the way his eyes followed the move. Thick black strands fell around her shoulders and it was the closest he would ever get to true magic. "Trust me on this, okay? Warren is not going to 'lead you' anywhere you want to go."

Deep down Rhawn suspected she was right. Still, loyalty to his people had him straightening to his full height. He always tried to be a good member of the Clan, even when all his instincts told him it was pointless.

"You say that because you know he will triumph." He decided, crossing his arms over his chest. "You say it to make me doubt the truth."

"I say that because I know Warren's an idiot." Lucy

corrected. "His GPA started with a zero. But, whatever." She flicked the Savior aside like he was nothing but a *movaha* fly. "If you want to listen to the Messiah of Used Cars instead of me, *fine*. I'll just leave here on my own." She looked out the opening of the cave, towards the jungle. "There's gotta be *something* on this island."

"Wolves."

She turned back to frown at him. "Wolves?"

"Wolves are on this island." He did not want her to go, so it seemed wise to list all the hazardous obstacles she might encounter. "Also long-tooths, *tandar*, mammoths, and *boga*. You saw me when I was sick from a *boga* bite, remember? It is not pleasant. Few rodents are. It would be very dangerous to leave."

She stared at him. "You really have mammoths here?" She finally whispered. "I know you said that crap about the gooey stew, but you have like... *real* mammoths? The kind of mammoths that have been extinct for *ten thousand years? That* kind of mammoths?"

Rhawn frowned, not understanding the question.

She gave up on the idea of walking off into the forest, a dazed look on her face. "Do you know what year it is?"

"I'm unfamiliar with this word."

"What word? *Year?* You don't know what a *year* is?" He shook his head, ashamed of his stupidity.

"How do you keep track of time here?" She pointed to the sky. "With the sun or something?"

"We count the moons' passages."

"Right. Good. So what is today on your calendar?"

"The third cycle of the red moon adjoining the yellow in the ninth rotation of Tnatun."

Lucy looked frustrated by that news. "Great. Very helpful." She sighed. "I guess that explains why you'd tell me we had the dream on the same day every year and I'd say we didn't, huh? We're on different schedules here." She rubbed her forehead. "Let's try this an easier way. Do you know what CNN is? Peanut butter? Converse sneakers? Mickey Mouse?

Anything that even *hints* of the modern world?"

Rhawn perked up. "I've seen the Mouse King in my dreams. He is worshipped by children who sing. I suspect he is luring them into his lair to devour them." He nodded, thoughtfully. "As I said, rodents are deadly creatures."

The Destroyer closed her eyes and seemed to brace herself. "Do you know what *Earth* is?"

"Yes."

"You do?" She exhaled in relief. "Thank God, because..."

Rhawn kept going. "It is the distant land of the gods." He gestured towards the sky and the far off world where they dwelled. "It is part of Newyork, I think."

"Aw... shit." She whispered in defeat.

He hated the feeling of dread that crawled through him. "This is the wrong answer?" He guessed dismally.

"You have no idea how wrong that answer is, caveman."

Rhawn wasn't surprised. He looked down at his meal. Why couldn't he be smarter?

"Hang on... What are *you* eating?" She demanded suddenly. "Is that lobster?"

Uh-oh.

"The food on the island is running low." He defended, used to the criticism, but not wanting her to think less of him. No one else in the Clan would eat from the Infinite Sea. It was forbidden. "I am bigger than the others and I need more than the rations Notan provides." He was the largest one on the island, something Skoll hated. "It serves no purpose to starve when there are plentiful resources..."

The Destroyer cut him off. "So, you give me *this*," she gestured towards the precious bowl of meat, "and you're eating *lobster?* For real?" Green eyes bore into his, accusing and beautiful. "You're a hell of a host, you know that? I get rancid mammoth and you get *fresh lobster!*"

It took him a moment to realize she was angry at him for giving her the better meal. Rhawn had no idea why. Hesitating for a beat, he took a chance and held out his bowl of shellfish.

"*Thank* you." She grabbed it for herself, still looking pissed. "Unbelievable. Why don't *you* eat that gross stew?"

Rhawn blinked. She wished to switch food? Unsure of what would please her, he picked up the mammoth and popped a piece into his mouth.

"No!" She leaned forward to smack the bowl from his hand. "God, don't seriously *eat* that! It looks terrible and smells worse. Here. You take the mutant-sized lobster back. I was just making a point. I don't even want this." She tried to return it to him.

He shook his head. "It is good. You should eat it and keep your strength up."

"No thanks. I'm a vegetarian."

"That word is unfamiliar to me."

"It means I don't eat meat."

"You do not... eat... *meat?*" He repeated slowly, trying to make sense of the words. It was useless. They were pure nonsense.

"Well, I'm not –like– setting fire to steakhouses or anything crazy militant. I just prefer to skip the part where cute, fuzzy things die for my dinner. I like animals too much to kill them."

He squinted. "What if the animals are trying to kill you?"

"Why?" She shot back sarcastically. "Did this lobster attack you or something?"

"No. I did not give it a chance to."

She glowered at him. "Look, let's just sit here and silently think of reasons why none of this can really be happening, okay? It's just an incredibly strange and vivid dream."

"I do not think it is. I have many dreams, but none of them are *this* strange."

"Did I ask for your opinion?" She watched him break open a lobster claw and frowned. "I don't suppose you have any sesame bagels around here, right?"

"That word is unfamiliar to me."
"How did I *know* you were going to say that?"

Chapter Four

"Hey, caveman? You okay?"

Rhawn forces his eyes open, although he is unsure how he could have closed them inside a dream. His whole body hurts. The boga *bite will kill him*. He's sure of that. The rodent's fangs always mean an agonizing death. But something is pulling him from the waiting darkness.

Something important.

He tries to focus on the voice calling him and is so grateful when he sees it's the woman. He would not want to leave this world without seeing her again. This is why he's been fighting so hard to stay alive. Because he knew she would come this night and she is all that he cares about. All that he regrets leaving behind.

"Are you sick?" She demands, looking concerned. "What happened?"

He ignores her questions and tries to tell her what's important, but his thinking is so muddled he cannot recall any tender words in her language. He's trying to learn it from his dreams, but it's difficult.

"Vando." He mutters instead. She will not understand the Clan's tongue, but he needs her to know how he feels. He has so little strength left. "Vando."

"Huh?" She looks worried. One cool hand presses against his forehead. "Geez, you don't look so good, sweetie. Your skin is all greenish."

That is one of the symptoms of a boga *bite*, so he is not surprised. The green hue is a signal of death and pain. There is nothing that will stop it from claiming him, now. His eyes drift shut and he forces them open again, frightened that she will disappear if he falls asleep.

Except, can *you* sleep in a dream? That makes no sense, but he is so tired...

"Caveman?" She lies down beside him, looking scared as he begins to drift off. "No! Don't do that. Don't sleep. Keep looking at me." She pulls the furs around his shivering body. "You have to concentrate. How can I help?"

"Stay with me." He whispers. That is all he wants. If she is here, he can fight the darkness for a little while longer.

She hugs him, her gentle hands smoothing back his hair. "I will, caveman. I'll stay right here beside you. You just stay with me."

Lucy and Rhawn's Dream- Twelve Years Ago

Rhawn stared at the rising sun. He'd been standing at the entrance of his cave for hours, waiting for someone in the Clan to come looking for the woman. It only made sense that they would try to defeat her while she slept. At least, it made sense to *him*. Why not try to catch her unaware? Obviously the others were more interested in feasting with the Savior than launching a surprise attack, though. Not even Skoll had returned to continue their fight.

The Clan was so confident that Warren would win that they were already celebrating. No one had bothered Lucy all night, which should have given her time to regroup. For once, Rhawn was glad he thought differently than the others.

All the teachings of his life told Rhawn it was imperative that Lucy fall, but a much deeper instinct was screaming inside of him to protect her. It told him to keep her safe, no matter the consequences. He did not accept that she was evil. She couldn't be.

Shit, maybe he really was an idiot.

Rhawn's eyes drifted over to the Destroyer. She'd fallen asleep on his bed. Her knees were pulled up to her chest as she huddled against the cold. Apparently, Newyork was warmer than the island, because she didn't seem accustomed to this weather. Frowning, he headed over to pile more furs on top of her. The early morning temperature was mild, but she was so delicate.

Rhawn's palm brushed her hair as he rearranged the pelts. Had he ever touched anything delicate before? He didn't think so. Gods, he wanted to touch her everywhere, finding every delicate spot on her delicate body. Her bones seemed half the size of his. Her skin soft and easily bruised.

He was going to have to be so careful when he took her.

Green eyes fluttered open, catching his, and Rhawn promptly lost the capacity for thought. He could not even drag air into his lungs. She was the most beautiful creature he'd ever seen. Every beat of his heart was for her.

His mate.

Stupid or not, he believed it with an unshakable conviction.

"This isn't another dream, is it?" Lucy said.

Rhawn frowned, uncomfortable that she'd woken up and found him staring at her. Mate or not, revealing weakness to this woman would be a huge mistake. It was impossible to even imagine all the wicked things she could do to him. ...Although the more salacious recesses of his mind were certainly coming up with some interesting options.

"No, it's not a dream." He ducked his head, so he wouldn't have to maintain eye contact. "You are awake."

"Wonderful." She rolled onto her side, so she faced away from him. "And of course you look like you just stepped out of a Tarzan movie, while I don't even have a toothbrush. I just... can't."

His frown grew deeper at her listless voice. Lucy had sounded that way when they finished eating the night before and told him she was going to sleep. Well, she'd briefly showed a flair of emotion when she'd told him to spend the night on his side of the cave. Rhawn had seriously considered arguing that point, but Lucy watched him with so much apprehension that he'd feared she might bolt if he said the wrong thing.

Even for someone who was chronically dumb, it seemed far wiser to say nothing at all.

Rhawn had silently settled against the far wall, trying to look as harmless as possible. Lucy had nodded in satisfaction at his acquiescence, feeling in control. Lucy *liked* to feel in control. He knew that it was important to her, so he willingly provided it. She'd pulled her own clothes back on and settled down on his bed, secure in the knowledge that he wouldn't touch her.

And he didn't. Any other man would have pushed his

mate for more, but no other man had a mate like Lucy. She was a difficult woman. With her, things were never going to be normal or easy. And so a girl half his size took over his bed, like she had every right to it and fell quickly asleep. Trusting him to protect her.

It was baffling. No one had ever trusted Rhawn to protect them before. Like so much else about Lucy, the wonder of it slipped past his defenses. He still wasn't sure how to deal with such a strange being, but the last thing he would ever do was harm her.

...Even if she was evil.

Rhawn studied her back and had no idea what to say. "You are still upset." He finally surmised.

Lucy gave an incredulous scoff. "No kidding." She pulled the pelt up over her head. "Go away. I plan to *stay* upset until the twenty-first century rolls around, so try to keep it down, okay?"

"You should awaken and prepare for the *Ardin*." He pressed. "It's vital." If Warren caught her off guard, he could defeat her without a fight. Even if the woman was destined to lose, the battle should at least be fair.

Rhawn's jaw ticked.

He couldn't tolerate the idea of Lucy being defeated. For so long he had dreamed of having his woman and, now that she was here, he was desperate to keep her by his side. Evil or not, she was *his*.

What was he going to do?

"I'm not preparing for anything except maybe a psych evaluation." Lucy muttered. "Either the whole world's gone crazy or I have. I'm not sure which I should be hoping for, but I'm staying in bed until I decide."

Rhawn wasn't completely clear on what a "psych evaluation" was, but he understood that she was distressed. "You should not give up before you even begin the fight. That does not seem like you."

"Because you know me so well, right?"

"Yes." The word was certain.

She was quiet for a moment. Then she turned to face

him again, looking more serious. "I don't think anyone's ever known me." She told him, sounding very small.

"I know you." Rhawn said firmly. "I look in your eyes and I *know* you are a part of me." He shook his head, frustrated that he couldn't articulate his feelings. He didn't know the right words to describe the connection he felt to this woman. Not in any language. "You know me, too. I *know* you do."

She stared up at him and gave a tiny nod.

Relief washed over him at the admission. "And you can be saved. If you simply forsake this path, all will be well." If she wasn't evil, the Savior wouldn't kill her. She could stay with Rhawn and he could finally be...

Happy.

Gods, this woman was the only being in the universe who could ever make him happy. He saw that so clearly.

"I think it's gonna take a little bit more than some kind of born-again thing to turn this mess around." Lucy sat up, pushing the hair back from her face. "Look, I have to get out of here. I *have* to. You have no idea how close I am to a complete freak out. I can't deal with this shit. I'm not supposed to *be* here."

"Of course you are." Her presence was the only thing that made perfect sense to him. "From the moment you and I were born, we were fated to be in these spots."

She squinted at him. "You seriously believe that?"

"I know it." To Rhawn, there was simply no other explanation. Her being here with him was exactly the way it was always meant to happen. Now he just had to figure out how to keep her alive and save the world from her wicked schemes. "Here." He held out a bowl full of *shanee* that he'd gathered for her. "You must eat."

She hesitated, clearly not recognizing the delicacy. "What are they? Some kind of flowers?"

"They are a fruit." He jiggled the bowl enticingly, so she'd take one. "Please. I do not want you hungry."

"They're food? You're sure?"

"Yes." His mouth curved. "Food that is not meat."

That made her smile, as he knew it would. She obligingly popped some fruit into her mouth, without even demanding that he eat one first. He liked that she trusted him. Given her difficult nature, he'd expected far more resistance. "These are good, actually. Kind of like ..." She stopped short, her eyes falling on the wall like she was seeing the art for the first time. "Is that a hang glider?"

Rhawn turned to look at the drawing that had caught her attention. "I don't know the name you have for it. I saw it in a dream."

"It's a hang glider." She glanced at him. "You *made* a hang glider?" She gestured to the drawing beneath it, where he'd been working out a building plan.

"I am gathering the supplies to create one. Yes. The sail of your *han- gly-der* is difficult to create, though. I find that the skins are too heavy to..."

"You're *building a hang glider*." She interrupted incredulously.

Rhawn had no idea why she was so interested, but he nodded.

"Jesus. You're like a prehistoric *inventor?* Is that it?"

His brows drew together, unsure if that was an insult or praise. "What is an inventor?"

"Someone who has ideas and then builds them." Her eyes traveled over the cave walls, taking in the other drawings he'd done. "My God. You really do dream about Earth every night, don't you?"

"Every dream I've ever had has been of you and your Earth. Sometimes I feel like I've spent more time in your world than in mine. The rest of the Clan often despairs of it."

Lucy's gaze met his. "I've never really fit in anyplace, either. People are always telling me I spend too much time reading about the past and not enough time in the present. Then, I tell them to shut up and I buy some more books."

He couldn't understand why she wouldn't love Newyork. "If I lived in your world, I would do nothing but explore its wonders. You are surrounded by so many amazing things." He waved a hand around to indicate the walls full of pictures. "Every day there is something new to experience. On this island, we endlessly see the same rocks and trees and sand. But, you could do so *much*."

She glanced back at the drawing. "Sometimes there so much we *could* do, that we don't do much at all. New York can be a very lonely place."

He hesitated, struck by her sad tone. "You have no Clan?" He knew what it was to be alone and he didn't want that for her. Of course, he didn't want her surrounded by others, either. Well, other *men*. The idea of it bothered him deeply.

"No. My parents were killed when I was a baby. I was raised by my grandparents and, when they died, I was on my own. The school psychologist suggested those experiences made me untrusting and antisocial."

If that meant that she was a prickly, difficult little creature, then he would have to agree.

She arched a brow, like she was reading his mind, and ate some more fruit. "Still, I don't think I'm the only one ranking low on the popularity polls. I get the vibe that you're more Mary Ann and less Ginger, here on Gilligan's Isle."

He pieced together about three words of that statement, but it was enough. "I am the most reviled man in the Clan." He admitted. "They call me Rhawn the Accursed."

"Catchy." She didn't seem overly terrified of his shameful admission.

Rhawn took a deep breath. "They hate me because I am stupid."

"Oh, obviously." She glanced back to the measurements for the han-gly-der that he'd worked out on the wall. "So many cavemen understand how to calculate fractions."

Rhawn kept talking, not wanting to dwell on his lack of intelligence. "Also, I dream of your world and its magical creations. No one but the gods should ever look upon Newyork's perfection."

"Perfection? You've clearly never dreamed about a

Brooklyn cab, have you?"

He ignored that. "And then there are my eyes."

Lucy frowned. "Your eyes?" She repeated blankly.

Rhawn nodded, confused by her confusion. "They are brown."

"Yeaaaahhhh." She drew out the word, clearly still at a loss.

"No one else has *ever* been born with brown eyes." Everybody knew this. "Eyes should be blue, gray, or green. Brown eyes are surely a mark of disfavor."

"That's ridiculous. Lots of people have brown eyes where I come from."

That drew him up short. "They... do?"

"Yes." Lucy gave him a slight smile, polishing off the rest of the *shanee*. "Trust me. Your eyes are beautiful." She looked him up and down. "In fact, everything about you is very, very *not* disfavored."

Rhawn stared at her. Nothing in his life prepared him to answer such a bizarre statement.

Another quake occurred before he could think of a response, the ground beneath them trembling. It was just a small rattle and it passed quickly. Rhawn barely noticed. Everyone in the Clan had grown used to the minor shakings.

Lucy hadn't.

She leapt up, nearly falling over as the island moved. Rhawn quickly stood, catching hold of her. Her body fell into his arms and her hands grabbed onto his shoulders. She pressed against him, small and soft and... perfect. She felt perfect. Like she was meant to fit against him. Like he was meant to hold her.

His mate.

For one heartbeat, it seemed that Lucy felt it, too. Her eyes flashed up to his and then quickly away. She gave her head a shake and shifted back from him. Balancing against the wall, she turned towards the cave entrance. In the distance, black smoke poured from the top of Uooloa.

"My God. It's really going to erupt, isn't it?" She breathed.

For a deity, she asked many questions that seemed obvious.

"Of course." Rhawn moved closer in case he needed to steady her through any aftershocks. ...And because he loved the scent of her skin. Even if he hadn't known she was the Destroyer, he'd know she was magical from the way she smelled. It was divine. "Very soon, Uooloa will sink this island. Your arrival will set it aflame."

She met his eyes again and his chest tightened in longing. He would never get used to the way she looked right at him. The Destroyer was no doubt accustomed to gazing at horrible things, but, for Rhawn, it was nothing short of a miracle to have someone gaze into his hideous eyes and not cringe.

Rhawn began to think thoughts he shouldn't think. Which wasn't unusual, but rarely had they been *this* stupid.

When he began to ponder an important puzzle, it consumed his mind until he solved it. ...And nothing was more important than Lucy. She was meant to be his mate. He knew that she would not have Chosen him herself, but the law still gave him the right to Choose *her*. If she were a normal female, he could just challenge the man she belonged to and win her for himself.

But, who did you have to challenge to claim a goddess? Warr-en, the Savior perhaps?

"Alright, let's focus on the real problem here." Lucy seemed to be trying to calm her panic. "I'm a pragmatic person. I'm pretty sure all of this crazy shit is really happening, so I'll deal with it. I *will*. I don't have a choice, so I'm going to deal. It *will* be dealt. Alright?"

She was only trying to convince herself, but Rhawn nodded anyway. She clearly wanted an answer.

"Good. So, I'm just going to stay calm and be practical and take it one crisis at a time." She continued in a carefully steadied voice. "Okay. Now, of all my present dilemmas, that volcano seems like the most pressing. Actually, it's *both* our dilemmas. I'm never getting home to my tiny apartment and the cute little dog I'll someday adopt, if I'm a charcoal briquette. Meanwhile, you've got a scenic view of Mordor out your front door." She pointed to the mountain. "Oceanfront or not, it's just some really lousy real estate, Rhawn. We *both* need to get away from here. You with me so far?"

Rhawn wasn't sure what answer she sought. "The Savior must lead us to safety." He reminded her. "Only he can find the way."

"If you knew Warren you'd know that isn't real likely." She scoffed. "Even with a GPS, a map, and guide dog, I wouldn't trust that doofus to lead me down the street. You, on the other hand, I trust."

His heart flipped over.

"I can't explain the dreams and I don't even want to. Maybe they're real and maybe it's all a hallucination. Right now, it doesn't matter to me." Brilliant green eyes met his. "You – *real* you, right here– protected me earlier, you speak English, you know this place, and you're the only one here sharp enough to skip the chanting. All *major* points for you."

That made him happy. "Points are good?" Rhawn liked rewards and he rarely received them. "And you're just giving them to me?"

"What?" She shook her head. "Whatever. Pay attention, alright? You're a smart guy. *That's* what I care about. It makes you my best hope for survival. We need to work together."

He shook his head, caught off guard by the idea. Rhawn had never been called smart. Never been anyone's "best hope." Never had anybody trust him. Not ever. No one ever wanted his protection or to "work with" him. Even if Lucy only planned to fool him into committing vile acts of heresy, he was a little intrigued by her flattery. She could recruit far worthier men. Still...

"I can't help you win the *Ardin*." No matter how perfect she seemed or what "points" she offered, Rhawn wouldn't assist with her malevolent plans. He did his best to live with honor. While he wished for it to be a fair fight, he couldn't help her achieve victory and doom the world. He couldn't do that. *Wouldn't* do it. Absolutely not.

...Probably.

Lucy's jaw tightened. "Oh, you *are* helping me." She warned. "You've seen me naked, caveman. You owe me."

Rhawn stifled a wince. Dwelling on the perfect curves of her body didn't exactly inspire him to resist her evil influence. "I won't be a party to your schemes." He muttered. "I wish for you to *forsake* them and to..."

She cut him off. "Fuck that, Rhawn! You're helping. You saved my life earlier, so it would be pretty dumb of you to just waste all that effort."

"I told you I *am* dumb and I did nothing to save your life."

Rhawn tried to turn away from the impossible color of her eyes, but she wouldn't let him. Just like in the dream, she moved her head to the side, keeping her gaze locked on his. It was as if she'd caught him in a snare. Rhawn helplessly stared back at her, his heart hammering.

"You *did* save my life." She insisted. "You're the reason I got off the ship in time. You told me the *Arden* would sink."

"The sinking *is* the *Ardin*. It is the end of the world."

She looked baffled. "Come again?"

How could she not know a prophesy that she was a part of? Rhawn was beginning to feel as confounded as she seemed. Perhaps he was not smart enough to converse with a god. Once again, he decided to go back to basics.

"During the *Ardin*, the Savior will bring all the worthy to a new homeland. The Destroyer will sink the island with the eruption of Uooloa." He gestured towards the volcano.

"I don't think an island *can* sink outside of a Hollywood effects studio." She seemed uncertain, though. "It could get blown apart, I guess. Or maybe geology just works differently in Ice Age dimensions." She shook her head. "I mean, how could we possibly know what kind of plate tectonics you guys have going on around here?"

Rhawn had no idea what she was talking about. "This island will vanish into the waves." He repeated firmly. "This is all foretold in the myths."

She held up both palms. "So, however it happens, this *Ardin* thing is your doomsday and *Warren* is the Savior of it? *That's* what you're saying?"

"Yes."

"Which makes me...?"

"The Destroyer." Rhawn needed to remember that. "You will bring about our end." He forced himself to move back from her. "And I will not help you, no matter how much I wish that..." He trailed off and finally turned away, unable to look at her beautiful face. He couldn't aid her in sinking the island, but Rhawn could also never see this woman harmed. Not for any reason.

So what was he going to do?

Lucy seemed more mystified than ever. "I'm not going to destroy anything." She said in a voice that sounded almost vulnerable. "I just want to go home and I think you can help me get there. You and I are... connected somehow. I can sense it and so can you, Rhawn. You told me so."

He shut his eyes. She was right. He did sense it.

Rhawn still shook his head, his heart breaking. "No matter what I feel, I cannot help you win this battle." He whispered. "If you succeed the world will end." It might kill her too for all he knew. He could never allow that. "Warr-en is our only hope. You must join his cause."

"Did you *meet* Warren?! You can't *possibly* think that's true."

He tried to believe in the legends, but the incredulity in her tone cut down to all his secret doubts. Rhawn always questioned when he should surrender to faith. It was why Notan was forever telling him he was stupid. Smart men understood without having explanations. You didn't need proof to *know*. The truth was evident to all worthy of seeing it.

"Everything else the prophesy predicted has come to pass." Rhawn pointed out, refusing to admit his failings. "Why would the end be any different?"

"So you want me to die?"

"*No*." He roared and then quickly lowered his voice.

"You twist my words." The last thing he wanted was this woman dead. The thought of existing without her was unimaginable. Rhawn scraped a hand through his hair and tried to think of a way out of this mess. What he knew was right warred with his instincts to protect her.

Lucy was *his mate*.

Never before had he been so sure of anything. When he looked at her, everything felt *right*. What did that mean? Was this some sort of test that he was failing?

...Or was he *supposed* to keep her safe?

Maybe this was why she'd been brought to him. Maybe he could get her to see reason and not doom the world. Maybe he could tap into the good he saw inside of her and dissuade her from this terrible plan. He latched onto that desperate idea like a drowning man with a *nutyh*.

"I'm not twisting anything." Lucy retorted. "And I'm not going to doom the world, Rhawn." Every time she said his name, he felt a jolt in his stomach. "Your prophesy is wrong. I'm not the Destroyer. I'm *not* evil." She sounded so convincing and so *sure*, as she leaned closer to him. "This is very simple. Who do you want to back in this apocalypse: Me or the guy who flunked so many classes, he could drive to eighth grade?"

Rhawn had no idea what "drive" meant, but he understood the gist of that comment. Did he honestly believe that Warren could ever defeat this woman? Against his will, Rhawn's gaze met hers again and he saw the resolve burning in her eyes. Vulnerability was replaced with boundless determination. She would fight until the end and she would triumph. The Clan couldn't stop her. Warren couldn't either.

The woman was so damn *bright* she could defeat all who opposed her.

Lucy would win this battle. For good or bad, she would change the world. Nothing could stop that. It seemed Rhawn had to either kill her or work with her. ...And nothing in this world or any other could *ever* make him kill his mate.

The best he could do was try to mitigate the Destroyer's destruction.

Chapter Five

He can scent her arousal.

It's a heady fragrance and his body responds instantly. Rhawn's hand slips between her legs, wanting to feel the moisture he knows is there. His fingers press open the folds of her body, learning her texture and shape. Slipping deep, amazed at the heat. Rubbing at a spot that seems to be straining for his attention.

She gasps, her hips thrusting against his hand.

He's never seen another woman react as she does and Rhawn has seen many couplings. Clan members often mate within view of each other. The men like to show their dominance over the woman and the women vie for the strongest men.

He would remember if any of them responded like this one does, though. She is an equal partner in their passion. Her body is flushed and wet and moving over his fingers like ripples of water. If any other man had ever accomplished something like this with a woman, he would still be bragging of it. Usually the female silently endures for a few moments as the male finishes. Until this woman, Rhawn thought that was the best anyone could hope for from a mating.

He's never been so glad to be soooo wrong.

Lucy and Rhawn's Dream Eleven Years Ago

Warren loved being a god.

Half-naked women fed him a bounty of food, while some strong smelling fermented drink flowed freely. He lounged back on a pile of skins, grinning like an ass, as he was fawned over. His hands fondled and his smug laughter boomed. He'd taken over the community's largest cave, indolently basking in all the attention. Obviously, it beat the car lot all to hell.

Just when Lucy thought she'd hit rock bottom on her frustration with the guy, he somehow managed to dig the hole even deeper.

"Warren." She loomed over him, ignoring the terrified

looks the Clan members were shooting her. "We need to talk."

"'Bout what?" He asked with his mouth full. No smelly mammoth for him. He was chewing on what looked like a supersized chicken leg.

Lucy had a brief flash of curiosity about the kind of animal it had come from. Some kind of teratorn, probably. The fearsome birds had wingspans of a dozen feet and looked like a combination of a California condor and a gigantic vulture. They'd been prevalent during the Ice Age, which made sense since everything around here seemed to be circa the Pleistocene epoch.

Actually, no. None of this made any sense, at all.

"About *what?*" She echoed. "What do you *think* I want to talk about, Warren? We need to get out of here, unless you want to spend the rest of your life on the set of *One Million Years B.C.*"

"Hey, it could be worse, ya know? I mean Raquel Welsh was majorly…" He trailed off, his expression darkening as he spotted Rhawn by the cave's entrance.

The caveman had followed her to the party. Lucy wasn't sure if it was to protect her or protect the others *from* her. Everyone else on this island seemed poised to run the second she murmured "boo!" in their direction. His expression remained frustratingly unreadable, so she wasn't entirely clear which team he was backing.

She had the feeling Rhawn was going to be the deciding game piece, though. He was the only one here with the brains to screw her over. If he joined up with Warren, she was doomed.

"You know, that Bigfoot stalker of yours is the one we *should* be worried about." Warren muttered. "You see how he's the only one here not treating me like royalty?"

"That's because he's the only one here with an IQ in the positive digits." Still, Lucy glanced over her shoulder and caught Rhawn staring at her.

She had no idea how anyone could think his eyes were a curse. They were a deep, pure, chocolate brown surrounded by incredibly thick lashes. He had the most beautiful eyes she'd ever seen. *Obviously,* he did. Every single part of the man was insanely gorgeous, from the shiny length of his blond hair, to the stunning angles of his masculine face, to the massive expanse of his bare chest. Looking at him, though, she felt more than just the punch-in-the-gut physical attraction. She felt... a connection.

Like they somehow belonged together.

Those dreams weren't a fluke or a hallucination. This man's fate was linked to hers. Lucy believed that and she didn't even believe in fate. For better or worse, the two of them were in this together.

...And Rhawn *clearly* thought it was for worse.

He watched her with wary confusion, braced for the evilness to start. Lucy arched a brow at him and he quickly dropped his gaze. Because, of *course*, the big, hot, caveman she'd been having sexual fantasies about for fifteen years would be socially introverted. And be certain that she was the antichrist. And be planning her losing showdown against Warren. Because, that was just how things worked when you were Lucy Meadowcroft: Unluckiest Girl in the Universe.

Un-frigging-believable.

Anger worked better than fear and Lucy embraced it. Luckily, being infuriated was second nature to anyone who worked in retail sales. Maybe she was stuck in the past or in another dimension or on a distant planet, but that didn't mean she was just going to *accept* it. Hell no. She was going home or she'd end the world trying.

"I just don't like that guy." Warren muttered, his beady eyes still fixed on Rhawn. No doubt he was thinking of all the football recruiters who would've killed to have a six and a half foot caveman on their team.

People like Rhawn didn't sell cars. They collected them. They didn't work in bookshops. They posed on the covers. He was like a golden statue come to life.

That annoyed her, too.

Lucy turned back to Warren and made a face as some topless girl fed him pink grapes. "I don't care what you think of

Rhawn, he can help us." The same instinct that told her to get off the boat told her that Rhawn was her ticket out of this mess. "In case you didn't notice, Rhawn is helping me."

She hoped.

"Well unless he's helping you find a freaking sat-phone, I don't see how anything that primate does is going to save our asses."

"Do you really think there are *satellites* around here? Really?"

"Well, there's gotta be something!"

"Warren," Lucy broke it down as simply as she could, "there are only two possible explanations for where we are, right now. Either we're not on Earth or we're not in the present." She'd spent all last night working it out and, as crazy as it was, it was the only thing that made sense. "Personally, I think we're in another whole world. This place has a lot of the same characteristics of our Ice Age, but it's not exactly the..."

"You're fucking crazy!" Warren had always been a belligerent drunk, as many a high school party host found out when he trashed their parents' house. "It's all *crazy*!" He staggered to his feet, dislodging a half-naked worshiper with blonde braids.

The girl was clearly crushed by his desertion. She looked like one of the waif-y creatures who frolicked through makeup commercials; all long limbs and unattainable skin. Like most of the women here, she wasn't wearing a top. Several strands of shiny stones were draped around her neck, serving as her only chest covering. Rather than being sexual though, it just made her seem like some kind of uninhibited wood nymph. It was annoying as hell to be around someone so fucking adorable when Lucy hadn't even brushed her hair in twenty-four hours.

America's Sweetheart turned to Rhawn with weepy blue eyes, saying something sad.

He sighed and responded in the Clan's language.

Lucy looked between them with a frown, not liking their familiarity. "Who's that?" She demanded. Damn it, that girl was way too thin and pretty to be near Rhawn.

"Anniah, our Clan's healer. She is Notan's daughter. She worries that she's done something to displease the Savior. I've told her no. He's just an ass."

Lucy didn't really care if Warren hurt Sheena's feelings, although you'd think a kinda-doctor would have better taste in men. Anniah seemed inexplicably smitten with Warren. Jesus, that was a prehistoric talk show waiting to happen. Just so she stayed away from Rhawn, Lucy didn't much care, though.

"You never dreamed about *her*, did you?" Lucy demanded, worried that this girl might be more Rhawn's type. Hell, she was a shirtless blonde. She was *every* man's type.

Rhawn met Lucy's eyes and she saw something tender spark in his gaze. "No, goddess." He whispered. "You are the only woman in my head."

"Good." She muttered and relaxed a bit. Lucy wasn't sure about a lot right now, but she was fucking *positive* she didn't want Rhawn fantasizing about another girl. Just the idea had her temper redlining.

Warren barely noticed the byplay or the mascara model blinking up at him like he was Zeus. "We're not on some other planet!" He insisted. "We're *not*."

Lucy didn't have time for this crap. "Where are we, then?" She challenged.

He made an annoyed sound, as if she was the one being unreasonable. "I told you, –like– maybe Aruba."

"You still think we're on Aruba?!" She swept a hand around the terrified cave people. "Does this look like *Aruba*, you oblivious dickhead!"

"Fine! Then, it's just some flyspeck island that gets left off the maps, ya know? We'll walk around the beach until we find a dock."

"Did you ever see *Game of Thrones*, Warren?"

He blinked at the non sequitur "Yeah. Why? Do they get cable here?"

She ignored that. "You know the big-ass dire wolves that sometimes eat people? The ones that are *literally* the biggest wolves ever born? Well, they're real. That type of wolf *actually lived* during the Ice Age and I'm pretty sure they're *still* alive on this island." Rhawn said there were wolves here and Lucy believed him. She was taking an educated guess on the species, given the other Ice Age animals surrounding them. "Now do you *really* want to go walking around, with *one hundred and seventy pound wolves* out there? After what happened with the sabretooth almost eating you?"

"That wasn't a sabretooth!" Warren sounded like he *really* wanted to believe that. "Sabretooths are all dead. I saw it on TV."

"Except we almost got eaten by one yesterday." Lucy shot back. "Do you understand what kind of creatures lived during the Ice Age? Wooly rhinoceros covered Europe. Armadillos the size of VW bugs were in South America. There was a fucking *American camel* roaming around Arizona. The biggest, weirdest stuff you can imagine actually existed back then and some of it's here on this island."

"I do not know of an insect called a 'vee-double-u' or what a 'rhi-noss-er-us' might be," Rhawn interjected quietly, "but the camels are no longer here. We hunted the last of them several winters ago."

Warren shook his head, refusing to believe the truth. "Bullshit."

"No, it's true. Their meat was quite a delicacy, so..."

Warren ignored him. "*Bullshit,* Lucy! There aren't any extinct creatures on this island. It's i*mpossible.*"

"What animal does that come from, then?" She pointed to his dino-sized chicken leg. "Name *one* possibility."

"I don't fucking *know*, alright?" He threw it aside. "But, any minute, rescue teams will be coming for us and..."

"No one is coming for us." She interrupted. "We have to get out of here ourselves."

"You're the one who said we couldn't leave this island, because it's surrounded by goddamn *Jaws*, remember?"

"I said we couldn't *swim for it*, because of the sharks. I didn't say we should start making houses out of coconut shells or something. We can't just *sit* here, Warren."

"You do what you want. I'm not going anywhere."

It was hard to say if he was refusing to leave just because she'd suggested it or if he'd actually convinced himself staying put was the best plan. Seeing as how the *Clan of the Cave Bear* thought he was some kind of Savior, though, she needed to get him on board with reality.

"Warren, there's a *volcano* out there. We. Have. To. Go." She carefully spaced each word.

Notan said something to Rhawn, apparently demanding a translation of the bickering.

Rhawn's gaze flicked over to Lucy again and then quickly away. Whatever he told Notan in the Clan's language seemed to agitate the guy even more. The chieftain gestured towards Lucy and proclaimed something with righteous fury.

She flicked him off, just because she could. The guy bugged her.

Rhawn's eyebrows soared, apparently recognizing the gesture and boggling over the fact she'd use it on the chieftain.

"You're having some kind of PMS freak out." Warren told Lucy with his typical level of tact. "Just let me handle this, okay? It seems pretty clear they like me *way* more than you. I'll talk to these hillbillies and they'll get us to some kind of radio and we'll go home."

"Warren..."

"You won't change my mind, so shut up." He interrupted. "I'm staying right *here* until help comes, where it's safe and warm and chicks with big knockers feed me fruit."

"Good plan. And you'll be a hell of a lot warmer under six feet of molten lava."

"*The rescue team will be here before that happens!*"

All around them the Clan grew quiet, watching them shout at each other. Dozens of identical sets of blue eyes switched back and forth between them, growing more and more wary.

Notan snapped another translation order at Rhawn.

This time, Rhawn ignored him. He straightened away from the wall, his gaze fixed on Warren, as the "god" loomed over Lucy. Brown eyes were cataloging every move he made, waiting for Warren to take another step forward. "The Savior has been drinking, Lucy." At least, Rhawn had figured out how to pronounce her name. "Do not get too close to him."

"You shut the hell up, too!" Warren jabbed a finger at him and almost overbalanced. "No one asked for your opinion, Krull."

"The woman is not a threat to you." Rhawn told him quietly. "Not at the moment. There is no need to try and intimidate her."

"That bitch wouldn't be intimidated by a cannon." Warren retorted. "What? You think she's going to fuck you if you act like some hero? Is that it?"

Rhawn's jaw tightened ever so slightly.

Lucy rolled her eyes. "Good thinking, Warren. Piss off the only guy here who knows our language."

"You seriously trust Encino Man here to know *anything?*"

"Over someone too stupid to realize that Caribbean islands don't have sabretooth cats on them? You bet I will. At least, *he's* not an idiot."

Rhawn glanced at her, looking surprised.

Several clan members shrank into the corners of the cave, watching her like she was a demon. Notan said something else, sounding more agitated than before. Rhawn spared him a frustrated look and snapped something back.

"What's he saying?" Lucy demanded.

"He wishes to know if the *Ardin* is beginning. I have told him no." Rhawn headed closer to her. "You should come back to my cave with me, Lucy." He nodded towards Warren. "He is not thinking clearly. You will be hurt."

Lucy's eyes narrowed in sudden thought. "The *Ardin* is the fight thing, right?"

"Yes." Rhawn seemed to make up his mind about something. He took a deep breath and moved so he was slightly in front of her, shielding her from Warren. "Come with me, now. I will protect you from him, no matter the consequences."

"She's not going *anywhere* with you." Warren declared with drunken propriety. "I see the way you look at her. I know what you're thinking. But, –newsflash!– *I'm* Savior of Atlantis. *I* get the chicks."

Rhawn stared at him for a beat, like he was trying not to say something snarky. Trying really, *really* hard. …Then he said it anyway. "And yet she spent the night in *my* bed, rather than here at your side."

Lucy shot him a glare. "Really?" She challenged in exasperation. The guy might be some kind of scientific genius of the Paleolithic, but he wasn't great with the whole "people skills" thing. "You're *really* going to start with that macho shit, Rhawn?"

He glowered at her, irritated that she was irritated. "Do I not get points for telling the truth? You would prefer that I lie?"

"Points?" She echoed blankly. "What are you talking about?" Then she remembered telling him he'd earned "major points" back in the cave. He must have taken her literally. Was he serious? "Wait, you think there's actually a *point system* and you're going to win some…?"

Warren cut her off. "Lucy didn't sleep with you, dude. You know how many guys she balled in high school? *None*." He made a circle with his thumb and forefinger and held it up as a zero. "You really believe she'd turn *me* down a thousand times and let *you* touch her? I was quarterback of the team! Anyone else would've been *happy* to give me a blowjob." He nodded wisely. "I think she's frigid or something, ya know?"

Rhawn's eyebrows arched in something like amusement at that idea. "I think she's *not*." He said with the utter confidence of a guy who'd been making her body do hot, wet things since she was eighteen.

Lucy flashed him a glower. "Nothing that happens in a dream even counts." She snapped, annoyed by the world at large.

"I disagree."

Lucy's eyes narrowed at his smug tone. "Just zip it, Rhawn. And Warren, stop embarrassing yourself. I turned you down because you're a repellant little toad and you know it."

"Yeah, but that was before I became a god. Now you *have* to do what I say and I say you should stay away from him." He pointed at Rhawn.

Rhawn didn't agree with that, either. In fact, he was looking more determined now. "You cannot keep her from me." There was an underlying note of steel to his voice that had Lucy glancing at him in surprise. "And there is no power in this world that can keep *me* from *her*."

"I can do whatever I want!" Warren waved a hand around the cave, reveling in his *Flintstone*-ian empire. "Look at all the people who love me! I'm like the biggest guy on campus, a-hole."

Anniah the wood nymph didn't understand a word they were saying, but she still looked like she agreed with everything Warren said. She frowned at Lucy, clearly annoyed that her precious Savior was so upset.

Lucy rolled her eyes. "You stay out of it, Pebbles."

Rhawn still wasn't backing down from his stupid argument with Warren. "Lucy is unclaimed." He bit off. "I have the right to approach her and not even you can change that."

"Well, *I'm* fucking claiming her, then!"

"You're *not* claiming her." Rhawn snarled, stabbing a finger at Warren. "*No one* will Choose this woman but me. Not while I'm still alive to fight for her."

Lucy glanced at him in confusion. "What are you doing?"

He sent her a quick glance, brown eyes glowing hot. "I'm about to challenge a god for you."

Her eyebrows climbed up her forehead at that bewildering news. "What? Why?"

Rhawn shot her a frown, as if that question was the weirdest thing he'd heard all day. "Because you are *mine*." He said simply and refocused on his pissing-match. "I have waited for Lucy and I will *not* give her up." He took a step forward and Warren took a step back. "In the Clan, you must challenge if a woman is contested." And it sure sounded like he was contesting, even believing that Warren was a supreme being. "Do you wish to challenge me for her?"

Lucy looked between them, amazed that this was happening. "Are you two out of your *minds?*" She pointed at her own chest. "I'm a fucking *person*, here. Neither one of you can just throw a few punches and declare me the prize. I'm not going to…"

Warren cut her off, again. "Yeah, I'll fight ya!" He gave a woozy "bring it on" gesture. "I'll whomp your pretty boy face. Once she knows what she's missing, she'll be the Brooke Shields to my blond guy for as long as we're stuck here in *Blue Lagoon*. I mean, she's not as *hot* as Brooke, but…"

That did it.

Lucy looked over at Rhawn, sick of the chauvinist posturing. She'd deal with this crap herself. "Tell your Clan that the *Ardin* has arrived."

"What?" He spared her a concerned frown. "No. That is a very bad idea."

"*Tell them!*" Lucy bent down to scoop up a stray rock.

Rhawn didn't need to translate her words to Notan. The old man and half the Clan had already fallen to their knees, praying.

Rhawn barely glanced their way, all his attention on Warren. "Lucy, the Savior and I will…"

Warren frowned in confusion, talking right over Rhawn. The guy's constant interruptions were typical and annoying. "What the hell is the *Ardin*…?" He didn't get a chance to finish the question.

Lucy pegged the stone at his greasy head.

Junior year, the school counselor had convinced her to join the softball team in order to pad her college applications. Lucy had been the pitcher. The rock slammed into Warren's skull with a precision that would've made old Coach Leaky proud. The "god" toppled backwards like a cow someone had tipped over in a field and laid there unconscious. Lucy wasn't worried about the long term effects. He was too sloshed and useless to die.

The Clan screamed in panic as he fell.

Anniah scampered over to kneel beside him, checking his wounds.

"Varsity team, baby." Lucy raised a hand over her head and looked at Rhawn who was gaping down at Warren's splayed form. "Uh-ho, guess who just won the *Ardin?*"

His gaze slowly traveled to hers.

Lucy smirked at him. "Too bad, so sad. Looks like your Savior isn't going to be saving anybody, caveman."

"You hit him with a rock." Rhawn sounded stunned.

She made a face at his tone. "So? You slammed that big guy with the dreadlocks into a stone wall, back in that bamboo cage. Compared to that, I'm almost a pacifist."

"But you *hit the Savior with a rock.* That is not how the *Ardin* is supposed to go."

"Well, I'm the evil god, remember? Cheating's in the job description. Now unless somebody wants to try and steal my new throne, I'm in charge." She arched a brow. "Are any of *them* going to stand against me?" She gestured towards the stunned and whimpering Clan.

"No."

"Are *you* going to stand against me, Rhawn?"

Please say no. Please say no.

Lucy would lose if he chose the other side. She knew it. Rhawn was the only one here with the brains to see through her little "god" trip. For so many years, she'd dreamed of this guy. Her instincts and body all told her he was special. That he was here with her for a reason. That she could depend on him. Her mind had a real hard time accepting those ideas, though.

Lucy never had been one to just take things on faith.

Rhawn studied her for a beat. "No." He finally whispered. "I will still try to stop your evil plans, but I am pleased the Savior lost this battle." His gaze flicked to Warren. "The challenge ended when he fell."

Lucy blew out a relieved breath. "Sure did. And I'm the champion."

Those beautiful brown eyes met hers. "I mean his challenge to *me.*"

"Yeah, well, you were doing plenty of 'challenging' yourself." Warren had deserved someone getting in his face, but Rhawn had escalated things pretty fast. "What the hell were you thinking trying to "claim" me or whatever?"

"I was thinking that I've claimed you."

"Well, I'm thinking you're *wrong*." She snapped. "And believe me, we're going to talk about that sexist display, just as soon as I'm done conquering the world."

"There is nothing to talk about. The challenge is decided."

"Just shut up and let me rule my doomed kingdom, okay?" Lucy clapped her hands together in satisfaction. *Finally* something was going right. "So, just to be clear, *who's* Queen of the Isle of Misfit Toys?" She asked her new followers.

"You are?" Rhawn guessed.

"*I* am." She agreed. "Tell the others the good news."

"Believe me, they know." In fact, he had to raise his voice to be heard over their piteous moans of despair.

"Tell them anyway." The only way Lucy was going to survive this was making them all too scared of her to rebel. In a fair fight, Rhawn or Warren or anyone else here could take her down. She *had* to assert herself fast or she'd be dead. "Tell them I'm a wrathful bitch, who will sink them into the sea unless they do *everything* I say."

Rhawn hesitated and turned at Notan. He must have translated her words correctly, because the old man looked appalled. Notan began stammering out long sentences punctuated with expansive hand gestures and beseeching glances towards Drunken Beauty. Anniah was crying, petting Warren's hair. It was all ridiculously maudlin considering it was just *Warren*, after all.

"Warren's lost the battle." Lucy told Notan and, even if he didn't understand her words, he got the meaning behind them. "*I* am your only hope, now."

Rhawn translated that, too.

Notan whispered something that could only be a prayer. Too bad for him, Lucy was the only god listening and she had bigger problems than his stupid apocalypse. Several more people started wailing.

Lucy felt a *little* guilty. Since this was the only plan she had, though, she kept going. On the upside, maybe she hadn't left school and changed the world, but she was the only person in Woodward High's graduating class to become an evil deity.

Top *that,* Taffi.

"Look, I'm not going to throw any of you into the volcano." Lucy promised. "I just want a way *off* this island." She arched a brow at the petrified Clan. "Any ideas, kids?"

"Only the Savior can lead us from here." Rhawn reiterated. "And you have just killed him."

"Oh, he's fine." She flicked a dismissive hand in Warren's direction. "I once saw him take a header off the roof of the gym and still be well enough to sexually harass the paramedic. Forget about him and concentrate. How do we get out of here? There has to be a way."

Rhawn's brow furrowed like he'd never considered the idea before. Or maybe it was just that no one had ever asked for his opinion. "Well," he finally allowed, "there is the *ragan*."

Notan started to say something else, but Lucy waved him silent.

"What's a *ragan?*" She demanded.

Rhawn glanced at Notan, who was making the universal sign for "shut-up, stupid."

"Ignore him." Lucy ordered. "What is a *ragan?*"

Rhawn cleared his throat. "It is a device I invented to fish in. It floats on the water." He pantomimed a bobbing motion in the air, his flattened palm mimicking the waves. "The Clan believes it's wicked, but I can paddle it into the sea and gather..."

Lucy cut him off, her eyes going wide. "Hang on, you're saying you've build a *boat?*"

"I am unfamiliar with this word."

"You sit in it, staying dry, and it moves you across the ocean?"

"Yes. A *ragan*."

"Holy shit! You invented a *boat!* You're brilliant!" She

stepped forward to grab his arm and yank him down for a smacking kiss. It was only meant to last for a heartbeat, but Rhawn had other ideas.

He drew in a surprised breath as her lips met his. A groan vibrated through him and his hand fisted around her shirt, dragging her closer. Lucy's body was jerked against his, her feet going on tiptoe to compensate.

Holy *shit!* Her gasp of surprise was swallowed by his mouth. Within seconds, he'd taken control. His lips opened against hers, his tongue claiming new territory. She'd forgotten he was fascinated by kissing. And surprisingly dominant in bed.

And a caveman.

The taste of him rushed over her like a tidal wave and all she could do was hang on. He shifted his body, somehow maneuvering so he was standing between her and the Clan. God only knew what kind of kinky stuff the cavemen did in their spare time, because Rhawn clearly didn't give a damn about privacy when he wanted a woman. Lucy kind of... liked that. No one had ever wanted her like Rhawn did.

And she had certainly never wanted anyone the way she wanted him.

He lifted her up like she weighed about half of what she actually weighed. The heat of his chest was at her front, and the stone wall of the cave behind her, and she whimpered at the sensation. Every incredible, dirty, fun part of the dreams filled her memory and she wanted more. She wanted *him*. All she had to do was surrender and Rhawn would do the rest. This place was probably in some far-off *Star Trek*-y nebula, so normal sexual mores hardly mattered. Why not let the caveman have his way with her?

It wasn't like Rhawn was a stranger. He was *Rhawn*. She'd known him so long, he was practically a part of her. All those fragmented dreams when they'd gotten so *close*... Lucy could finally have what she'd been aching for. She could feel how aroused he was. The guy was really going to take her right there and no one could stop him. In another moment, not even *she* could stop him.

Bad idea.

Wait… this was a *really* bad idea.

Lucy jerked away.

Rhawn stared down at her, his chest heaving. For once, his gaze stayed locked on hers, his head titling to maintain eye contact when she would've looked away. Up until this point, he'd been pretty accommodating, luring her into believing that she was in control. Now he didn't seem so tame. He stayed within her space bubble watching her intently and Lucy felt very vulnerable.

This guy was not part of a domesticated species. She'd dreamed of him, but could she trust him? Instincts said yes, yes, *yes*.

Panic told her *no* and it was damn hard to ignore panic.

"That was a mistake." Lucy quickly tried to reaffirm her status as a heartless overlord. Flattening a hand on his chest, she gave him a push. "It shouldn't have happened."

He humored her by pretending he felt her shove and took a step back. Rhawn was the biggest, strongest, smartest guy in a world without laws. He could do anything he wanted to her. He didn't *have* to back down for anybody. Certainly not a girl who'd been banned from the health club for her bad attitude. Men in this place didn't woo their dates with flowers and a nice play. They could just *take*. It seemed to be part of their system, so it wouldn't even be breaking any rules.

The only thing protecting her was Rhawn himself. She didn't like that. It made her feel out of control and vulnerable.

"It's alright." He soothed, seeing her nervousness. "I can go slower, just as you like. I won't harm you."

Lucy shook her head and tried to be practical. He might speak in quiet tones, but under the calm façade Rhawn was still a caveman. "You *can't* hurt me. I'm the all-powerful Destroyer, remember? *I'm* the one who does the hurting."

Rhawn didn't look so convinced, all of a sudden. "I *will not* hurt you, Lucy." He reiterated softly. "Not ever. You may still bring on the apocalypse, but I've Chosen you as my own. I will protect you. Always."

Lucy wasn't clear on what exactly that "Choosing"

thing meant, but it didn't sound good. She glowered up at him, hoping he somehow overlooked the fact that she only reached his (really wide) shoulder. "You didn't Choose me, pal."

"I did."

"How?"

"The Savior and I were preparing to battle for you and he fell." Rhawn shrugged. "It was not how I expected things to go, but the outcome was clear."

"That's ridiculous. *I'm* the one who fought him."

"Women can make their preferences known in a challenge. That is what you did." In his mind, everything was settled. "It was a fair contest, Lucy. I have won you and you are my mate." He nodded like he'd catalogued all the pertinent details, made his decision, and now he was just waiting for her to catch up and agree with him.

Smart guys always thought they were soooo frigging logical.

"You can't Choose a god." She decided. "*We* do the Choosing."

Rhawn frowned. "Where is this stated?"

"I just stated it."

The caveman didn't appreciate the randomness of that pronouncement. He reminded her of an engineer, wanting everything in his world to be neat and quantifiable. "Choosing does not work that way." He argued. "There are rules." Rhawn was clearly a rules-are-rules kinda guy. As far as he was concerned, he'd followed them and she was cheating.

Too bad.

"I'm the god. I'm above the rules." She gave a "what can you do?" shrug just to piss him off. She was getting the distinct feeling this "Choosing" deal involved a lot of nakedness and prehistoric sexy times. No *way* was she being that stupid.

No matter how incredibly tempting Rhawn was.

His eyes narrowed, seeing that she wasn't going to budge. "We will speak of this again." He warned.

Doubtful since she was on the first boat outta *Land of the Lost*. No sense in antagonizing the really muscular caveman *too* much though. "I'd rather talk about this *ragan* thing." She arched a brow. "Let's start with how many people it'll hold."

Chapter Six

"I got my master's degree last week." The woman says. "Thanks to these dreams, I'm a certified expert on the Ice Age, now. They inspired me to read everything I could about it and get my degree. You inspired me. I wouldn't have gone to graduate school, if I hadn't met you."

Rhawn is not sure what that means, but it pleases her so it pleases him. "I am glad." He says and shifts her body beneath his. His teeth graze the curve of her neck. She tastes of warm honey and mysteries unexplored. He will never get enough of this woman. The fragmented pieces of dreams do nothing to alleviate his ache for her.

"Yeah," she sighs out and tilts her head to give him better access, "you seriously hold the best study sessions ever."

Rhawn and Lucy's Dream- Ten Years Ago

Rhawn looked down at Lucy as she looked at the *ragan* and saw she didn't look happy.

"That's the boat?" She demanded.

"It's the *ragan*."

"'Cause it looks like the mutant offspring of an outrigger canoe and Huck Finn's raft."

He wasn't sure what those words meant. They certainly weren't compliments, though. Rhawn was used to insults and derision, but he still felt his jaw tick. Ever since he'd Chosen her, the woman had been increasingly difficult. What had happened between them made her feel nervous and less in control. Lucy didn't like it when she wasn't in control. She seemed to be trying to cover her unease with sniping and with imaginary rules that prevented goddesses from being Chosen.

Neither tactic would work. The laws were clear and she was his mate.

He hadn't *meant* to Choose her. Well, at least not *yet*. He was still fairly certain she planned to end the world, after all. But, Rhawn had watched as the Savior tried to take her as his own and something had snapped inside of his already weak mind. He'd known that he could never allow Lucy to belong to another. That he would fight to have her, even if it meant challenging a god.

When Warren fell, it might have doomed the island, but it had given Rhawn what he most wanted. Lucy was his according to Clan law. Now that he'd Chosen her, he'd never see the bond undone. Regardless of how much she protested that *she* was the one who had to perform the Choosing, he knew they were already joined. He felt it. She did, too.

Unfortunately, the knowledge just made her more difficult.

"It's a *ragan*." He told her flatly.

She let out a long breath. "It's not very big. You sure it will float?"

"Yes." This was the first time anyone had ever been interested in one of his creations, so Rhawn found himself wanting her to understand it. To approve. "It took me many attempts, but the *thann* on the sides offer support even in large waves."

"The pontoon thingies?" She pointed to the *thann*.

"Yes. They create stability." Pleased that she was paying attention, he kept going. "The *um'nah* trees naturally float, so they provided the wood. Then I used the tar from the pits as a sealant to keep the water out."

She didn't say anything. She just stared at the *ragan*, her expression unreadable.

Rhawn braced for her to tell him he was an idiot. Everyone else did. ...Except he didn't want her to be like everyone else. If she laughed at him, something was going to break inside of him. Lucy's was the only opinion that mattered.

"It floats." He told her, quietly. "You have my word on it."

Green eyes flicked to him, weighing his promise. Finally, she nodded. "Okay. So, how far can it travel?"

Rhawn didn't know what to make of that question, but he breathed a sigh of relief that she was taking him seriously.

"It would stay afloat over a long distance." He hedged. "Probably, even after everyone aboard succumbed to exposure and thirst."

"That's good enough for me." No one ever had any faith in his ideas, but she seemed to believe in them more strongly than even he did. "You and I are getting off this island. *Now*." She made a face. "And I guess Warren too. I don't want to have to explain to the Alumni Committee why I left the dumbass marooned in *The Land Before Time*." She paused. "Only there are *obviously* no dinosaurs in the Ice Age." She looked around with a stern frown, in case someone dared to contradict her.

No one did.

Rhawn wasn't sure what she was talking about or what she planned to do, but there was one point he wouldn't budge on. "However you plan to escape Uooloa, you must include *everyone*, Lucy. I do not wish my people to die."

"But, they're assholes who hate me and locked you up in a cage. I'm not really in the mood to save them."

"They are my people." He repeated. "*Your* people, now. They became your responsibility when you won the *Ardin*. We cannot leave them here to sink."

Her eyes rolled so strenuously, she probably made herself dizzy. "*Fine*. God, you're such a Boy Scout." She gestured to the rest of the Clan, who were hovering along the shoreline. "Tell them to make more rafts, then." She did a quick headcount. "We'll need ten or so. Like five or six to a boat."

Rhawn's eyebrows drew together in confusion. He wasn't surprised that Lucy agreed to save the others. Beneath her grousing, she had a kind heart. He had no idea how she expected the *ragan* to save them, though. "Why do you wish to build more?"

"So we'll have enough to carry all of us, obviously. Isn't that what you're insisting on?"

Rhawn blinked. She couldn't *possibly* be thinking of trying to cross the Infinite Sea. "Carry us where? There is nothing out there but water." He pointed at the ocean. "We would be sailing to our death."

"That's what they told Columbus."

He was unfamiliar with that word and suspected she knew it. It annoyed him. "If you wish to kill us, you could do it here on land, Destroyer. It would be less trouble."

"If I wished to kill you, I'd just leave you here with Krakatoa." She retorted. "I'm trying to *save* you. And me…. And apparently the rest of these morons."

"What is that bitch saying?" Skoll demanded. He finally awoken from the beating in the cell and he was angry. Angry at Rhawn. Angry at the Clan for not punishing Rhawn. Angry with the outcome of the *Ardin*. And *especially* angry at Lucy.

Everyone in the Clan was upset, but Skoll was one of the few who wasn't bothering to hide it. Even Notan tried to cover his feelings. Skoll brazenly watched Lucy with open hatred, tracking her every move like he was planning an ambush.

Rhawn flashed him a glare and deeply suspected that he'd have to fight the bastard again soon. "She is a god. When she wishes you to understand her words, she will let you know."

Skoll's fists tightened. "You align with evil to protect yourself from punishment." He spat out. "You know that she is all that protects you from execution, Rhawn the Accursed. You should still be locked in your cell, awaiting your punishment, but she set you free and now you are in her thrall."

Lucy glowered over at Skoll. "What's Asshole saying?"

"He doesn't like you." Rhawn told her softly.

"The feeling is mutual." She wrinkled her nose in distaste. "He looks like those movie villains who keep canaries in cages so they can eat them as snacks."

Rhawn kept his attention on Skoll, switching back to the Clan's language. "The Destroyer triumphed over the Savior. That was the will of the fates and you wish to challenge it?"

"I wish to survive. For *all* of us to survive. Be smarter than you usually are and help us get rid of this monster. She favors you, for some bizarre reason." Skoll's eyes gleamed, with rage... and lust. "The men say she did something with her lips on yours. What did it feel like?"

If he knew what Lucy could do, she would be in even more danger than she was now. Skoll would want her for his own, *before* he killed her. The Clan had seen the way Rhawn reacted in the cave. He'd Chosen her in front of everyone, openly challenging the Savior. If Lucy hadn't stopped him, Rhawn would've taken her right there against the wall.

Rhawn had never acted that way before. He'd never been so blatant about wanting a woman or so possessive of one. Of course the other man would be curious about kissing and what magic Lucy held. He was probably going to have to kill at least four of them, before they gave up on the idea of stealing her away.

"She is *mine*." He warned Skoll in a deadly voice. "I don't surrender what's mine. I will dissuade her from her evil plans, but I will not see her harmed."

"Her magic might be all that can revive the Savior." Anniah put in. For whatever reason, the girl was inconsolably worried about Warren. "The Destroyer spared his life, which means she may not be as cruel as we first thought. I was encouraged by the mercy she showed. Perhaps, if we help her find a better way, she will bring him back to us and..."

Skoll cut her off in annoyance. "The Savior is weak." He scoffed. "We have no need for him now."

Some of them men seemed to agree with that. Tammoh stroked his beard, the way he always did when he was thinking. Ugghot exchanged a meaningful glance with his twin brother Uyhot. Ctindel looked over to Notan for guidance.

The old man seemed torn. "We must think on the proper path." He temporized. "The answer will reveal itself when the gods wish it so."

"Warr-en is not weak!" Anniah announced, already knowing the path she would take. "There is *greatness* in him. I see it."

"The Savior lost to a woman, without even putting up a fight." Skoll waved a dismissive hand. "Notan, tell your daughter to let the men decide the best course of action. She speaks nonsense."

Anniah's blue eyes narrowed in his direction. She'd been spurning Skoll's advances since she was a child. The girl had a mind of her own. She was one of the few people unafraid to stand up to her father's second-in-command and it pissed Skoll off.

Notan made a hand gesture, urging his daughter to silence.

"*I'm* protector of this Clan." Skoll continued, jabbing a finger at Rhawn. "If you're not smart enough to see that the Destroyer is manipulating you, maybe she should belong to someone else."

Rhawn stepped closer to him. "Do you wish to challenge me for her?" That was the way the Clan settled disputes like this. The men fought and the winner got the woman. "I stood against the Savior and I will do the same to you, if you seek to claim my mate." Skoll was strong and dangerous, but Rhawn was willing to die to keep Lucy.

They both knew who would win the battle.

Skoll backed off with a scowl. "For whatever reason, *you're* the one she wants and I don't wish to incite her wrath by killing you." He muttered. "Besides, Notan and I have decided that I will Choose Anniah soon."

Anniah didn't look thrilled with that news. She frowned over at her father. Notan studiously avoided her betrayed eyes.

Lucy watched the byplay. "What's this about now?"

"Skoll wishes to take Anniah as his mate and she does not desire the Choosing."

"Well, who can blame her? The guy's a tool." Lucy snorted. "Tell her that I'm changing all the backwards rules of this place and *she* gets to be the one to Choose her mate, now. That'll cheer her up."

"That will start another battle." Rhawn predicted, darkly. "Skoll already dislikes you enough." But he too was angry over the idea of Anniah being forced to mate with a man she detested. Perhaps Lucy was right. Perhaps the laws of Choosing *were* backwards.

Perhaps they *should* change.

"The best option is for you to fuck the Destroyer, so she's compliant and relaxed." Skoll continued, either not seeing or not caring about Anniah's unhappiness. "Then, when she least suspects it, strike her down."

Several others nodded.

Rhawn shook his head. "I told you, I will not…"

"You must do *something*, boy." Notan interrupted. "You've Chosen a vicious demon. We're your people and she seeks to destroy us. You're the only one who can get close enough to stop her."

How convenient that they decided to include him just as he became useful. On some level, Rhawn did relish the idea that everyone knew Lucy was his, but mostly it just pissed him off that they thought he would harm her. Finally, he had a mate and they wanted him to kill her. It went against all honorable conduct for a man to hurt his woman. It was his job to *protect* her.

Lucy was following the conversation with a suspicious frown. "Are they trying to turn you against me?"

"Yes."

"Is it working?"

Rhawn studied her worried face. "No." He said quietly.

She let out a relieved breath. "Good."

Lucy did not seem all-powerfully evil. In fact, mostly, she seemed very delicate to him. A small, fragile being cast down among the hardened creatures of the island and trying to stand up to them. When he'd kissed her earlier, she'd been soft and warm and so damn *welcoming*. It had been like the dreams, only better. For a heartbeat of time, she'd responded to him and everything had been… perfect.

Then she'd panicked.

He felt the moment Lucy began to worry about their size difference. She'd pulled back from him, feminine caution in her eyes. The fear that he would overpower her and take more than was offered. The fear that he *could*. Even as he'd soothed her, Rhawn had known that her reaction was wrong.

Why would a goddess be frightened of a man, no matter how big?

Why would she win the *Ardin* with a rock and not her colossal, unstoppable magic?

Why was she so concerned about getting off the island in *ragan*, when she could ascend back to her homeland of Newyork?

None of it made any sense.

...Unless the woman was far less powerful than she let on.

Intelligent people didn't question. Didn't push. They accepted what was right in front of them. He *knew* that. And still he looked at this woman and his instincts told him she was different than the Destroyer of legends. Given time, he could talk her out of her plan to sink the island. Lucy had a kindness in her. He just needed to keep her safe until she stopped her wicked scheming.

Rhawn weighed his options and decided to stall.

It was the best way to keep Lucy safe, especially if she was somehow weaker than she let on. "The Destroyer wishes for more *ragan*." He told Notan. "She believes they will help us escape Uooloa. Have the men make them and she will be satisfied. At least for now."

"I agree with Rhawn." Anniah interjected. "We should give the Destroyer a chance to do something good, before we condemn her."

"Is that Anniah girl on my side?" Lucy asked, still trying to follow the conversation. "She looks like she's on my side."

"She is grateful you spared Warren's life and is now convinced we should give you the benefit of the doubt. She is urging the others to build the *ragan*."

Lucy snorted. "Maybe she's not as dumb as the rest of the *Croods*. Except for her crush on Warren, of course."

"How can *ragan* help us?" Skoll demanded. "What is the Destroyer planning?"

Rhawn shrugged. "Does it matter?"

"No, it doesn't." Notan swiftly agreed. "We must placate the Destroyer while we wait for our chance to overthrow her." He turned to the other men and started barking at them to gather *um'nah* trees.

"Do I even want to know what they were saying about me now?" Lucy asked.

"No."

"Wonderful. So glad we're wasting our time building life rafts for those clowns." Shaking her head, she started down the beach. "A couple hours as leader and already my loyal followers want me dead. Well, we can just add them to the ten thousand other threats hanging over my head."

"No one will harm you, Lucy. I will not allow it."

She sent him a half smile. "Forget it. I can deal with angry villagers wanting to burn me at the stake. I'm already moving on to the next problem." She pointed at the sea. "Which way do we go?"

"Only the Savior can lead us from this island." Rhawn wasn't sure why she still didn't grasp that, because it seemed like he'd explained it many times. "We cannot leave this place."

"We have to or we'll be Pompeii-ed."

His eyes narrowed, suspecting that she was mocking him. "I understand your language well enough to know that is not a word."

To his surprise, her mouth curved. "Yeah, you're right. I made it up."

"To trick me?"

"No!" She looked surprised by the accusation. "See, there was a volcano above a place called Pompeii. When it erupted, it destroyed everyone in its path."

Against his will, Rhawn glanced towards Uooloa. Smoke poured into the sky, the ominous color growing blacker by the hour. Could *Lucy* really be causing all that? Could this small woman control a mountain?

He suddenly doubted it.

"Pompeii wiped out *everything*. Generations later, when we began digging up the ruins, we found voids in the hardened ash. Just these odd-shaped holes in the rock. No one could figure out what they were." She crouched down to grab a shell and some sand. "Then someone put it together." Rhawn watched as she pressed the shell into the damp sand so it left an imprint. "They were *people*. The voids were the negative spaces left by the citizens of Pompeii when their bodies were covered in ash." She held up the handful of sand, so he'd understand. "Anyone who stays here will just be impressions in the dirt."

He considered that, staring at the ridges the shell left behind in the wet grains. "Even if what you say is true, the Clan will never follow you into the Infinite Sea. They fear it too deeply."

"More deeply than a *volcano?*"

"Of course. There are *jigons* in those waters."

"Which are?"

"Monsters."

She rolled her eyes and brushed her palm off on her leg. "Well, monsters or not, the other members of your Clan are getting in the boats. I'm the god around here and I'm going to save their lives whether they like it or not."

"Why do you wish to *save* lives?" It went against everything the Destroyer stood for.

"What do you mean 'why?' You told me you wanted them saved, didn't you?"

"Yes and you agreed very quickly. You are not an agreeable woman, Lucy. I believe you would have aided them, regardless of my wishes."

She made a face. "Yeah, well, alien cave-dwellers or not, I'm going to try to keep those losers breathing. Maybe I don't always play well with others, but I'm obviously going to help people in trouble."

Rhawn's head tilted, studying her.

She winced as if remembering she was supposed to represent all that was dark in the world. "I mean... I'm going to help them and then... *not* help them. It keeps all of you off balance about my villainy." She cleared her throat, nervously twisting the green beads of her necklace. "Right."

Rhawn's expression softened. "The Clan is yours now." He told her in a reassuring tone. "You should try and win them over, so they will not revolt. Show them that you care and they will follow you."

"Except, I *don't* care. I'm a bitchy, antisocial person. Ask anyone."

"You pretend to be." He corrected. "But I *know* you, Lucy. You are difficult, but you care far more than you let on."

She stared at him for a beat and then she looked away from his steady gaze. Clearly, she wanted a subject change. "Let's refocus, alright?" She skipped the shell out into the waves. "If you had to pick, which way would you sail to reach land?"

"I would stay where we are, because there is no other land out there."

"So you've said. Let's pretend I'm crazy enough to try. What's your best guess on a direction?"

Rhawn's mouth tightened. Why did she not understand? "You could pick *any* direction and it would simply circle you right back here. There is nothing. but. water." He spaced out each word.

Lucy digested that for a moment. "How do you know?" She finally asked.

"How do I know that we are alone in the Infinite Sea? *Everyone* knows this."

"And you don't ever question it?"

Rhawn hesitated. "Intelligent men do not question the truth." He temporized.

"Right." She seemed skeptical of that bedrock tenet of Clan belief. "Didn't you once tell me you thought you were stupid?"

His shoulders straightened with pointless dignity. "Yes."

"Because you question?"
"Questioning is a sign of doubt."
"Smart people don't question and doubt?"
"Of course not."

"Right." She pursed her lips. "Tell me, if no one ever questions or doubts, how is anything ever going to change?"

"Why would we want anything to change?"

"Because you live in caves and worship *Warren*, maybe?" She guessed. "Seriously, this isn't the best of all possible worlds, Rhawn. You say you dream of New York. Now —granted— it isn't paradise, *either*, but at least we have electricity and toilet paper and shoes." She pointed down at his bare feet. "You know how we accomplished all that?"

He shook his head, mesmerized.

"We started by assuming that every idea labeled 'impossible' just hadn't been done *yet*."

Rhawn blinked. "Your world celebrates doubt?"

"If you don't doubt, how can you ever know what you truly believe?"

He swallowed. "Of course you say that. It's your *job* to inspire doubt." Allowing himself to believe otherwise would damn him. He may have Chosen her, but he had to remain on guard. "You hide the truth behind lies men want to hear."

"You *want* to hear you're doomed if you stay on this sinking rock?"

"No, but…"

"So, *help* me then. I don't care what your stagnant Clan thinks. *I* think you're the only guy here who *isn't* a moron. That means you're helping me. I'm a god. You're recruited. Deal with it." She jerked a thumb at the ocean. "Now, which way is off the island?"

"I don't know."

"I'm betting you know *something*." She pressed. "Take an educated guess."

He stared out over the waves, thinking.

"Rhawn," her tone went serious, "I know it seems like a bad idea to just set sail and hope we hit a continent or something. But, whatever the risks out there, it's better than staying *here*. We have to go."

Rhawn was *not* swayed by the way she said his name. He barely noticed that her foreign accent caressed the word and made it beautiful. Not even he was stupid enough to be so stupid.

Damn it.

Lucy's head tilted, maintaining eye-contact when he would've looked away. "Please, Rhawn." She persisted. "Help me."

Rhawn's resistance disintegrated like a pile of sand under the force of a wave. "On this side of the island, there are sometimes purple flowers." He said, unable to stop himself. When she looked at him with that bottomless green gaze, he lost all commonsense. "They wash up on the shore. It happens rarely, but I've seen it."

"Purple flowers?"

"Yes."

"And this matters because…?" Her voice trailed off in a question.

"We do not have purple flowers on this island. So, I've occasionally wondered where it is they *do* grow."

Lucy gave a slow smile. "Stupid, huh? Shit. I *knew* I was talking to the right guy." She eagerly looked around. "Which direction do they float in from?"

He lifted a shoulder in a shrug. "It's hard to be sure."

"But you have a pretty good idea, don't you? You've been out in the water. You know the tides. Tell me."

"Telling you means you will drag me out to sea. Why should I give you information that will lead to my death?"

She crossed her arms over her chest. "Because I'm a god."

"What are your powers?" The words were out before he could stop them. It was often that way with him. Rhawn thought thoughts he knew were wrong and he said things he knew he shouldn't say. He couldn't stop himself, though. He always had to push. He had to *know*.

"It's none of your business what my powers are! Just understand that I can *completely* kick your ass."

Rhawn stared down at her perfect face. Challenging the Destroyer was just more proof of his mental defect. He'd somehow survived defying the Savior and now he was antagonizing another god. What was wrong with him that he didn't stop? "I'll tell you about the flowers…"

"You'd better!"

"…if you make me." He finished, simply.

She blinked. "Make you?"

"Kick my ass." He invited. "Do something to prove that you're a god."

She didn't move.

Rhawn arched a brow at her worried expression and knew he'd been right. She wasn't powerful, at all. He wasn't sure whether he was relieved or not. He stepped closer to her, just because he couldn't stop himself. The woman drew him like a magnetized stone. He always wanted to be near her. "Did you lose your powers or did you never have any?"

Her gaze went wide. "I have no idea what you're talking about. I'm very, very powerful."

"Are you?"

"*Yes.* And you aren't going to like all the horrible ways I can prove it, so don't push me." She nervously licked the corner of her mouth and he felt a surge of lust that the loincloth did nothing to hide. Green eyes took in his reaction and she inhaled a deep breath, her breasts rising so they brushed his bare chest.

Rhawn groaned, heat and emotions swamping his mind.

Lucy's expression switched from concern to confusion, like she felt it too. "How are you doing this to me?" She whispered. "Around you, I feel… and I don't…" She broke off with a baffled shake of her head.

But he understood her perfectly. He felt the same way.

"It's our fate, Lucy." Rhawn stepped even closer to her, so she was pressed against him. "We were meant to be together." Dropping his head to the side of her neck, he breathed in her scent. She gave a small whimper of a sound at the animalistic move, but she didn't retreat. That just enflamed him more. "I cannot get images from the last dream out of my mind. Your body opening to mine and the feel of your skin and the taste of your lips…"

Lucy swallowed hard and he could see her mind racing. "I'm not going to sleep with you." She desperately shook her head. "I don't believe in fate and I don't care *how* good it was in that dream. We're *not* reliving it, live and in person. No way are we doing any 'Choosing.'"

Rhawn's mouth curved, amused by her frantic words. "But, I've *already* Chosen you. There is no sense in trying to undo what is done. You're already mine." Under every rule of god and man, her smooth, perfect body belonged to him and no other. *His*. The thought had his blood pounding.

"Bullshit. I never agreed to that and you know it."

"It doesn't matter. The law says you are my mate."

His certainty seemed to unnerve her. "Then I'll change the law." She said, but he could see she wasn't so sure.

Rhawn nuzzled her temple, trying a different tactic. "Do you desire another more than me?" He asked quietly.

Her eyes closed on a sigh. "No." It was a whisper.

"And I desire no one but you." He could smell her arousal and it nearly brought him to his knees. "I promise, I will do nothing you wouldn't enjoy, Lucy. You know that." If she would just give herself over, he could have them both naked and happy in a matter of seconds.

Sadly, she wasn't going to surrender so easily. No goddess would.

"I'm not having sex with you." She reiterated firmly, pushing away from him. "Probably not later and *definitely* not now." She ran a hand through her thick, dark, magical hair. "I need to think."

Rhawn had no idea what she needed to think about, when everything was so clear. Still, he saw the determined glint in her eye and he stepped back. "Alright." He agreed calmly.

Pushing Lucy would just make her more intractable. She was difficult. Stubborn. Rhawn wanted her to *welcome* him. But she wasn't ready for that and nothing else would be worth a damn thing, so he would have to wait.

She watched him, gauging his sincerity. "You're just going to stop?" She asked suspiciously.

"Of course." He frowned at the question. "*Vando*, Lucy. I would do anything you asked."

She stared up at him, looking astonished at the use of the word. He had no idea why. He'd been telling her for many cycles. "You really are my caveman." She finally murmured. "Only he would say that. You're really him."

Rhawn slowly smiled. She was starting to come around! "Of course." He repeated.

Lucy's eyes widened at his grin. "Damn it, that's not fair, Rhawn. Stop smiling like that when I'm being moral and strong. It's cheating to be so handsome."

He didn't know he *was* handsome. This was good news. "Women here rarely care about a man's looks." He assured her, reaching out to touch her hair so the strands slipped through his fingers. Even the dreams had not captured the exquisite richness of the dark tresses. "They care about survival. They want a mate who can best protect them." He met her gaze, wanting her to understand. "I will protect *you*."

"I know." She whispered. "And I know you think I'm screwing up your customs or whatever, but I'm still not just going along with this "Choosing" thing. Only *I* decide who I sleep with, Rhawn. Even if it really is you, I get a *choice*. I'm freaked out and I need to think and we're *not* having sex today."

Rhawn's mind went to Anniah's distressed face when Skoll announced he would claim her against her will. "The law of Choosing a reluctant woman is… primitive." He allowed, wincing a bit.

"No shit."

He tried to think of a way to deal with this new problem. Before Lucy arrived, everything had been so clear. "I will not pretend that I don't know what I know. You *are* my mate. I feel it with everything in me."

"That's very reassuring. I guess I'll just give in and start planning our wedding then."

Rhawn wasn't sure what a "wedding" was, but he could tell from her tone that she wasn't happy to be planning it. Shit. He did not like it when she was unhappy. Lucy meant everything to him. He just wanted her to smile.

He hesitated and saw only one way to go. "You will be in control, if that is what you need." That was close to heresy in the Clan. Going along with her odd ideas was a small price to pay if it won him her heart, though. "I want you to Choose me. I want you to want me back."

"And if I *never* want you back?" The woman enjoyed focusing on the negative.

He shrugged. "You will. It is fate."

She didn't appreciate his confident words. Green eyes narrowed in challenge. It turned him on. Everything she did turned him on. He could see her plotting her next move and he could hardly wait. She was so damn bright, he found himself eager to see what she'd do next. The woman was endlessly unpredictable.

"You know," she said after a moment, her voice going soft and sultry, "where I come from, there's another kind of kissing." Her eyes slipped down to his erection. "Lower."

Rhawn's jaw dropped as he realized what she was suggesting. This was some kind of test she was conducing. In his head, he knew that, but his body didn't care. "That would work?" He choked out in amazement.

"Oh yeah. With a big, strong guy like you, who's open to new and dirty things, it could be *amazing*. I could get on my knees and use my mouth to..." Lucy trailed off letting the words hanging there like succulent fruit.

"To do what?" He prompted, desperate to hear the rest.

"Well," she absently nibbled on her lower lip and Rhawn's eyes nearly crossed in lust, "you have to experience it firsthand to *fully* understand the mechanics of it all."

The idea had his body stiffening painfully and his mind boggling with possibilities. Gods, even in the dreams, he'd never imagined anything so amazing.

"Right now, there is an *infinitesimally* small chance

that I'll show you how it works." Lucy continued in a seductive voice, moving against him in a way that *had* to be evil. It felt too good to be anything else. "Probably, it'll never happen, but there's always a *tiny* ray of hope for an enterprising guy like yourself."

Rhawn was hanging on her every word.

"But, if you piss me off, your odds of exploring the mysteries of oral sex are gone forever." She summed up archly. "If you –for instance– refused to help me decide which way to go in our boats, I won't be happy. And when I'm not happy, all my clothes stay on. You'll be left wondering what my tongue would feel like, slowly licking at your…"

"West." Rhawn blurted out, reaching his breaking point. He pointed towards the sun. "From what I know of the currents, the flowers come from that direction."

"Then, we go west." She smirked at him, her tone going back to its normal clip. "See how easy it is to get along with a goddess?" She headed down the beach, pleased with her trickery.

Rhawn gaped after her.

Gods, but that woman had powers.

Chapter Seven

Lucy sits on the caveman's lap, admiring the perfect angles of his perfect face. He is so handsome and thoughtful and gentle. It's no wonder she has no interest in dating any of the idiots she meets in the real world. How could anyone ever measure up to her dream man?

"This must be a mental condition or something." She says, running her hands through his thick hair. "Reoccurring dreams of somebody who doesn't even exist? I mean, that's gotta be bad, right? There's probably some scary name for this condition and all kind of therapy involved to cure it."

"I do not wish to cure it."

She doesn't want to cure it, either, but it seems very strange. "Don't you think it's —well— kinda crazy to imagine the same person again and again?"

"Yes." He answers calmly, as if he's already thought all of this over himself. "But I would rather be crazy with you, than sane alone."

Rhawn and Lucy's Dream- Nine Years Ago

Stay away from the caveman.
Stay away from the caveman.
Stay away from the caveman.

For the next two days, Lucy silently repeated the mantra, but it didn't do much good. She wasn't listening to herself. Which was a shame, because she knew she was right. It was just that Rhawn was so damn awesome, it was easy to ignore all her own good advice about him. The more she was around him, the easier it was to get attached to the guy. He was generous and kind and protective and handsome.

And smart.

Rhawn was way, *way* too smart to keep lying to. That was the whole problem.

He was going to figure out she was a complete fraud in the goddess department. It was only a matter of time, if she kept hanging around with him. He put puzzles together too fast. Saw connections too clearly. Several times now she'd caught him watching her with a thoughtful expression on his face, like he was trying to see through her lies. He'd keep digging until he had every answer he needed to expose her. It was his nature to question. Within a very short amount of time, he'd figure everything out. It was inevitable.

Rhawn was a genius.

An *actual* genius, in the literal "Holy *shit*, is he smart!" sense of the word. The dawn of time probably didn't have any standardized tests to prove it, but Lucy didn't need them to know that this guy was something special. She could look into his eyes and practically see all the gleaming IQ points. It was a little intimidating to be face-to-face with that kind of raw brainpower. Back in reality, Rhawn would've been inventing lasers at Cal-Tech, or designing trillion dollar spaceships, or solving world hunger in a fancy think-tank.

He really would be changing the world.

Hell, even stuck on this damn rock he was changing the world. Rhawn's boats were their only hope of escaping the volcano. Lucy understood that, even if nobody else did. If this plan worked, he was going to save so many lives... And he wasn't even *trying*. That was the crazy part. He was casually, off-handedly, *apologetically* brilliant. God, if he was actually *focused*, he could do anything.

And given Lucy's *current* situation, that kind of intelligence was dangerous. How long could she really expect to get away with this whole "Destroyer" lie? He was already questioning her lack of powers. She *had* to stay away from him.

Which was why it was *such* a bad idea to be staying in his cave.

See? Where Rhawn was concerned, she was blind to logic. Shaking her head, she continued up the path to his home, taking a quick detour to check on Warren.

For reasons Lucy couldn't begin to understand, she was worried about the guy. It wasn't that she felt bad about hitting him with the rock, exactly. She just wished the big, dumb idiot would wake up. Lucy sighed in annoyed concern when she saw he was still out cold.

Why did Warren always have to make things more complicated?

Since he'd lost the glorious *Ardin*, most of the Clan seemed to have washed their hands of the "Savior." It must be quite a disappointment to discover your god is a doofus. Only the waif-y blonde, Anniah, was tending his splayed body. Lucy watched as she carefully dripped water into his mouth and petted his dark hair with more tenderness than Warren deserved.

Well that was interesting.

Lucy cleared her throat and the girl's head shot up in surprise. She quickly scampered to her feet, no doubt worried that Lucy was about to smite her. Her slim body moved between Warren and Lucy, like maybe she suspected Lucy was there to finish him off.

Lucy held up her palms in the universal sign of "I'm not a serial killer." "Hi."

Anniah's eyebrows slammed together, unappeased. She said something that was probably a warning to stay away from the Savior's comatose ass.

"Relax, okay? I'm not going to hurt you. Or him. Well, I guess I *did* hurt him, but..." Lucy trailed off with a sigh and sat down on a rock. "Shit. I'm really anti-social, so it's tough for me to make conversation. Just bear with me here, alright?"

Anniah blinked at her, losing some of her rigid posture.

Rhawn had said this girl was one of the few Clan's people who didn't hate Lucy, so it only made sense to try and be friendly. It didn't come naturally, but Lucy was all about trying new things, these days. If she was stuck leading this bunch of idiot cavemen, she might as well try to reach out to one of the few members of the Clan who didn't suck.

"I'm Lucy." She laid a palm on her chest. "*Lucy*."

Anniah's eyebrows compressed, but she was getting it. "Anniah." She said warily and pointed to herself.

"Right. Good." Lucy gestured to Warren, then her own head, and repeated the movement. "Does he need anything?" She gave an exaggerated frown to show her concern. "Is he okay?" Anniah was the island's leading medical professional. Hopefully, she would know how to treat him with roots and berries. If Warren needed a CAT scan, it might be a problem.

Anniah said something in her language, then smiled and bobbed her head. Okay. That seemed like a promising diagnoses. Probably. She also looked down at Warren like she might actually be Florence Nightingale-ing the big dummy, though, so it was entirely possible that the girl was high on herbs.

"Really?" Lucy arched a brow. "You seriously *like* this bonehead?"

Anniah seemed to be puzzling out those words.

"Warren." Lucy held up one index finger. "Anniah." Lucy held up the other and then drew them together, to make a couple. "Warren and Anniah sitting in a tree…" She arched a brow. "Am I close?"

Anniah beamed, piecing together the sing-song charades. "Warr-en *and* Anniah." She said excitedly and bobbed her head. Back in reality, the girl would already be booking reception venues.

Lucy felt honor-bound to warn her that was a *terrible* idea. "You know he's a used car salesman, with two bitter and vengeful ex-wives, right? Even *I* felt sorry for him after the divorces and I usually find his suffering funny. In his whole life, I don't think he's ever gotten anything right and he knows it. He's weak, whiny, annoying, can't hold his liquor… Face it," she swept a hand through the air, indicating Warren's football jersey-ed body, "he's a train wreck."

Anniah followed the gesture, her eyes traveling up and down Warren with obvious approval. She glanced back at Lucy with a small frown. She put her two index fingers together. "Warr-en and Anniah *oncho*?" She drew them apart again, looking crushed.

"No, I'm not saying you *can't* be with him. I'm saying that you can do *better*." Lucy gestured at Anniah and pantomimed approval. "See? You seem like a *nice* girl. Two thumbs up, for the little blonde." Then she looked at Warren and made a skeptical seesaw motion with her hand, her face creased into a "he's-kind-of-an-asshole" frown. "But, he's kind of an asshole. Trust me."

Anniah hesitated and then finally seemed to understand. She said something else in that incomprehensible dialect.

"Uh-huh…" Lucy squinted. Rhawn *really* needed to teach Lucy this language. The only word she kinda recognized was "*vando*." Rhawn said that sometimes. She wasn't sure what it meant exactly, but he always said it in a gentle tone, so it had to be good. "You're saying you want to keep him anyway?" She guessed, nodding towards Warren.

"*Vando*." Anniah repeated earnestly.

Lucy took that as a "yes." "Alright." She shrugged, seeing it was pointless to talk the girl out of her crush. "Well, if you want him, I'm sure you can have him. Believe me, once he sees you, he's not going to be real hard to seduce. Hell, I'm in charge now, so I can probably just give him to you." She paused. "And I guess he *is* a better choice than Skoll. Warren's a nitwit, but he's not a violent sociopath."

Anniah's expression darkened. "*Cantara un ta ber-na* Skoll." Lucy translated that as something like, "No way am I marrying that dickhead."

"Yeah, I don't blame you." Lucy agreed, kinda liking this girl. "The good news is, I changed the rules about "Choosing" around here. Now the women get a say. I've totally invented feminism. It's going to be awesome."

Anniah had no clue what that meant.

Lucy tried again. "Anniah." Up went the index finger again. "All the men in the world." She opened her other hand wide, counting off the possibilities. "Warren… Skoll… The guy with beard… Those big, ugly twins…" She paused meaningfully when she reached the thumb. "And Rhawn, of course, but Rhawn's *mine*." She tapped her own chest. "Rhawn and *Lucy*."

Anniah nodded earnestly, following this conversation with the intensity of an undergrad at their first college lecture.

"Good. So now *Anniah* Chooses." Lucy simulated deep

thought and then Anniah-the-index finger moved to tap on Warren-the-pinkie. "*Anniah* picks the guys she wants."

Anniah got the meaning and looked thrilled. "Anniah *touma-la-ho*." She pointed very deliberately at Warren. Lucy was gonna guess that meant, "Anniah's Choosing this dumbass."

Lucy shrugged. "Well, there's no accounting for taste, I guess. I mean, look what I'm wearing." She gestured to the plastic mardi gras beads around her neck.

Anniah gazed at the cheap green necklace like it was made of gold. "*Byanho*." She said longingly.

Lucy's eyebrows rose. "Wait... you *like* this? Okay. Here." She took it off and held it out to Anniah. "You can have it."

Anniah looked stunned. She sputtered out what sounded like a lot of caveman language-y reasons as to why she couldn't take something so valuable.

Lucy rolled her eyes and reached over to grab Anniah's wrist. "*Here*." She repeated firmly and pressed the necklace into her hand. "Take it. Please. It's the least I can do to repay you for looking after Warren."

Anniah clutched the beads to her chest, tears in her eyes. She *totally* would've sold Lucy the island of Manhattan for the damn thing. In fact, she looked so overwhelmed, that Lucy felt a little guilty. "*Yhannt*." She said in a heartfelt tone.

"You're welcome. Really. It was nothing."

Anniah unlooped the strands on shiny stones from her own neck. "*Hynart*." She held them out to Lucy, wanting to give them to her.

"No. Seriously, you don't have to..." Lucy began, but Anniah just grabbed her wrist and shoved the necklace into her hand. Apparently, she thought that was Lucy's custom for trading jewelry, because she looked pretty damn pleased with herself. Lucy certainly didn't want to insult the girl by refusing. "Um... *Yhannt*." She was taking a guess that that meant "thank you" and Anniah seemed thrilled with her efforts.

And really the necklace *was* pretty. There were three

strands of super-shiny white stones that caught the light every time Lucy moved. Rather than being drilled through the middle, they were tied together with a series of intricate knots. All in all, this necklace was a *way* better fashion statement than the souvenir beads from the ship's bar. The mix of rustic and glitzy looked like something from a hip boutique in the East Village.

Anniah was pretty sure Lucy had gotten the worst deal, though. She couldn't have been more pleased with her plastic treasure. The girl kept admiring her new beads, her expression turning downright friendly. All her reservations were quelled now that they'd found some common ground. Ah, the universal power of bling.

Anniah started talking a mile a minute and, even though Lucy didn't understand a word of it, she was soon enjoying herself. Anniah was good at making herself clear, even without a shared language. Her expansive hand gestures were hilarious. Lucy actually liked this girl and Lucy wasn't used to liking anyone except Rhawn. It was kind of awesome.

They were so busy talking that they nearly missed Warren waking up. He made a low groaning sound and his eyes half-opened. "What?" He croaked. "How fast was I going officer?"

"Warren?" Lucy blinked in surprise and moved to kneel down beside him, relief filling her. Thank God. She wasn't aware of how concerned she'd been that he wouldn't wake up until he finally woke up. "Warren, you scared me, you jackass. Can you hear me? How's your head?"

He tried to focus on her. "Moose-y?" He got out. "I think you killed me with a rock."

"I *hit* you with a rock, but you're still alive."

He blinked groggily and then switched his attention to Anniah. "I'm not dead? Then why's there an angel...?" He murmured and then he was out again.

"Warr-en? Warr-en?" Anniah gave him a shake, trying to bring him around.

"I think he's okay." Lucy assured her. "If he can use bad pickup lines, he's on the mend." Plus, Warren seemed to be snoring, now. That seemed like a good sign. It probably wasn't smart for a guy with a head injury to be sleeping, but how many brain cells did Warren really have to worry about losing? "Trust me, he's recovering." She added an impressed "oooh, he's doing *great*" facial expression to the assurance.

Anniah gave an encouraging nod.

"Alright. Good to know I'm not an accidental murderer." Lucy got to her feet. "I'm outta here, then." There was only so much socializing an anti-social person could do in one day, but that had gone pretty well. Lucy was proud of herself. "You keep watching over Warren and think about raising your standards." She gave a very deliberate wave, trying to get her point across. "Good-bye, Anniah." She said, spacing out the words

Anniah tentatively waved back. "Gud... Bide... Looo... ceeee." She pronounced one syllable at a time.

Lucy beamed. "Perfect!" Hell, the girl was already too articulate for Warren. "I'll see you later, alright? I gotta go home and find something vegetarian for lunch."

She continued up the path to Rhawn's cave. It didn't occur to her until she was halfway there that she'd called it "home." Shit. That probably meant something that she didn't want to consider, so she decided to ignore it. Instead, she headed inside and grabbed up the plate/shell full of flowers he'd left for her to eat. They seriously weren't that bad. They sort of tasted like fennel mixed with mango.

While she polished them off, her eyes went to all the drawings on the walls. Pieces of Earth mixed with Rhawn's own thoughts, like the bulletin board in some eccentric professor's office. Diagrams of a water wheel. Images of New York. The Golden Arches. A big, blue swirly thing. Plans for some kind of crop rotation on the island.

Lucy arched a brow at that one. Oh good. He'd discovered agriculture.

Jesus, underestimating Rhawn really would be a *huge* mistake. In a world where other people probably ate their own lice, he already had some kind of rudimentary table of elements sketched out on the rock. If he could correctly calculate the atomic weight of zinc in a *cave*, he could certainly see through her lies.

Of course if didn't help that Lucy kept forgetting to be wary of him. He was so frigging *handsome,* and he stood between Lucy and all the people wanting her dead, and he said things that made her smile and he looked at her like she was the most interesting calculus equation he'd ever come across. That was so incredibly arousing. Her whole life was a mess, but Rhawn made her feel wanted and safe. In the midst of chaos, he was the only thing that made sense to her.

She trusted him and Lucy wasn't a girl who trusted *anybody.* She'd always been a loner. Something about Rhawn just slipped past all her defenses. Like she knew him. Like she'd always known him.

Like he was *hers.*

Which was crazy. Lucy needed to forget the whole idea of keeping the guy, because it was totally impractical. Totally, *totally* not going to work.

...Which was why she wasn't *at all* thinking up ways to make it work.

And in the meantime, those damn dreams needed to *stop* rerunning in her head, reminding her of all the really nifty caveman-y things he could do to her body. His huge arms holding her still as he ripped off her clothes... The thick weight of his fingers inside of her, making her beg... That low, erotic growl in her ear, wanting submission from his mate...

Lucy swallowed. Yeah... It was *far* safer to steer clear of Rhawn. In fact, she needed to stop *thinking* about him, too. If he popped into her mind, she'd just imagine him doing boring, unsexy things. Like working on those dry and complicated boat plans.

Boats he'd *designed,* because he was brilliant.

God, that was hot.

And *now* she was thinking about him again. Damn it. Lucy turned away from the wall of pictures. This was ridiculous. She needed to...

Something moved outside the cave.

Lucy froze, her heart pounding. For half a second, she thought it was Skoll, come to kill her. The muscle-bound bastard was already looking for a chance to beat her to death with a rock. If he found out she was abolishing all the creepy, arranged marriages and encouraging Anniah to be with Warren, he'd *really* be pissed.

Instead of that criminal caveman, though, she saw a flash of neon orange fabric and a head full of professionally streaked hair.

Lucy blinked, realization dawning. "Taffi?" It couldn't be. Woodward High's prom queen couldn't *possibly* be on the island. The end of the world... everyone thinking she was a wicked goddess... no Cheetos for sale in this entire dimension... She could handle *all* of that. But not Taffi. Not even Lucy's luck was *that* bad, right?

Wrong.

"Lucy?" Taffi poked her head into the cave, her face wary and mascara stained. "Is it really you?" She was wearing the oversized orange t-shirt from the *Ardin's* gift shop, so her beloved dress must not have survived. The withered remnants of a corsage were still on her wrist, though. "Oh my God! I thought it might be you, but I couldn't be sure. I was sure my eyes were playing tricks on me when I saw you on the beach." She rushed forward to give Lucy a bone-crushing hug. "You have no idea what I've *been* through!"

"Oh, I have an idea." Lucy tried to squiggle free of her death grip. "Are you okay?"

Taffi ignored her efforts to escape. "Of course I'm not okay! The cruise ship sank!" She wailed as if only she'd been aboard.

"I know."

"And this island is full of Neanderthals!"

"I know."

"I think a big volcano is going to erupt."

"I know."

Taffi frowned, not pleased that Lucy had ruined her big reveals. Her crying switched off like a light switch, replaced with strident indignation. "Well, if you know all that, what do you plan to do about it? Why are you just standing here? It's your *job* to get me off this damn island."

Lucy's eyebrows climbed. Taffi had said plenty of stupid things over the years, but that one might just be the all-time champ. "*My* job?"

"*Yes.* You've always said you were Little Miss Special. Now's the time you prove it."

"I never said anything like that! I tried not to say anything *at all* to you, as a matter of fact."

Taffi scowled as best she could through the Botox. "As head of the Alumni Committee, I *need* to survive and you need to help me. It's your duty."

Jesus, it was a wonder Lucy hadn't dropped out freshman year, just to escape this kind of craziness. "Take a breath, okay? I'm going to try to get *everyone* out of here, but it might take some time. I'm not sure where we are or..."

"Well, find out!" Taffi started to cry again. "You're supposed to have the highest GPA –like– *ever*, but you don't even know how to get us home?!"

"No, I don't know. I'm not sure we can get back to New York." Lucy admitted quietly. She didn't like to say that out loud, but try a she might, she couldn't think of a way to return to Earth. It wasn't like she could whip up another shipwreck to recreate however it was they got here. "We could be permanently stranded in whatever reality this is."

"Oh, you're just like Tony. Full of excuses." Taffi rubbed at her eyes, refusing to accept the facts. "He's not even *on* the island, you know. Sickness and health obviously mean *nothing* to my loser husband. No wonder we're in couples' counseling."

She broke down in hysterical daddy-didn't-buy-me-a-pony-for-my-birthday sobs. Lucy recalled them from most of Taffi's childhood parties. ...Until her father finally bought her a horse when she was eleven, right before he got busted by the IRS. Taffi hadn't cried half as hard about him doing twenty years in the Federal pen.

Taffi kept wailing, oblivious to Lucy's immunity to her

drama. "Tony's probably forgotten all about me by now!"

Poor Tony was probably *trying*.

"Taffi, it's not going to do any good to…"

She cut Lucy off. "I never should have married him. His mother locked up all the family money in some stupid trust, anyway. It's for my *kids*, she says. I'm not having kids! Do you have any idea how fat I'd get?! Maybe *you're* okay with being huge, but I'm *not*."

Lucy rubbed her forehead. "Taffi, can we please focus on the real problems here?"

"I'm broke, my hair is a mess, and my husband thinks I'm sleeping with the dog groomer. Those *are* real problems." She sniffed, the tragic heroine of her own soap opera. "I *barely* got to second base with Carl. Tony blows everything out of proportion. He's the one who wanted that stupid Pekinese, in the first place. It's really *his* fault that I got so lonely during Taffi-Two's weekly blowouts and needed Carl's companionship."

"Let's not bring cute little dogs into this." Lucy warned. She was going to get a cute little dog one of these days, so she felt the need to defend Taffi-Two. "I mean, you've already done enough damage, just naming her something so stupid."

"It's a *boy*." Taffi snapped, barely paying attention. "Why doesn't anything ever work out like it's supposed to, huh? Why does everything *always* go wrong for me?"

"Probably karma."

Taffi missed that insult. "I was going to be a movie star, you know. Everyone said so. I was too beautiful to me anything else. It was going to be me up there on screen. I knew it. I just don't understand what happened to ruin my dreams."

Lucy considered the idea that Taffi was in some kind of shock, but quickly dismissed it. The girl had always been like this. "Do you *really* want me to stand here and tell you you're pretty, Taffi? Is that what you need?"

Taffi ignored that, too. She was a champ at ignoring

things she didn't want to hear. "And I had so much *talent*." She gave a small smile, lost in her own maudlin thoughts. "I was really good in *My Fair Lady*, wasn't I?"

"You were." Lucy said in a humoring tone, going along with Taffi's sad reminiscing. And it wasn't a lie. The senior play hadn't sucked nearly so much as Lucy had anticipated. Taffi's Liza Doolittle was no Audrey Hepburn, but even Lucy had been impressed. On some level, she'd always expected Taffi to make it big.

So had everyone else.

...Especially Taffi.

"And I never doubted it would happen, you know?" Taffi mused. "Never doubted I'd be an A-lister. I *knew* I was born to do something great." She stared at nothing for a long moment. "High school was the best time of my life. I had everything in front of me. So many possibilities." She sniffed again, shooting Lucy a frown. "I guess that sounds silly to you."

"No, it doesn't." High school had sucked for Lucy, but she understood the confusion and disappointment of looking back and not being able to see where you even started.

In a way, the regrets were much quieter on the island, though. Being stuck here made Lucy reevaluate everything else in her life. It burned away the bullshit that cluttered her days. Lucy had never really fit in, back on Earth. She'd always been out of step. The island had a way of clarifying her thoughts and linking her to other people. Sometimes, she almost liked it better here.

Also, there was Rhawn. It was hard to think your life had turned out *too* bad when you were kind of dating the hottest, smartest, kindest guy in whatever-the-hell universe this was.

Damn it, she was thinking about him again.

"I just want a do-over." Taffi complained. "A chance to start fresh and be the me who I was *supposed* to be, before I screwed it all up." She shook her head. "The shipwreck was a wake-up call. I've got nothing to look forward to now except expanding thighs. This is the prettiest and youngest I'll ever be again. I blew my whole life."

"You're only thirty-three. You have plenty of life left." Assuming they didn't get swallowed up by lava, anyway. "Listen, even if we're marooned here for good, you'll be okay. We just have to use our heads."

Sadly, logical thought had never been Taffi's forte. "I just wish..." She swallowed hard. "I just wish we got to grow up to be who we *planned* to be when we were eighteen, you know? I was so *great* back then."

"You were a raging bitch at eighteen, Taffi."

That undeniable fact startled a laugh out of her. "I really was, wasn't I?" She wiped at her cheeks, chuckling with pleasure. "I made *soooo* many girls cry. Janna Simmons switched schools, because I emailed everyone copies of her stupid fan-fic about sleeping with the whole cast of *Friends*."

"A prime example of why my karma-biting-you-in-the-ass-now theory is a good one."

"Oh please. Like it's my fault she couldn't take a joke?" Taffi tossed her hair back. "And you *deserved* me snarking at you all the time. I was afraid to raise my hand in class, because I knew you'd have some wiseass remark about my answer and make me feel dumb."

Lucy blinked. She hadn't known that. "I'm sorry." She said automatically. "I shouldn't have..."

Taffi cut her off. "Of *course* you should have." She straightened her shoulders, regaining her normal self-assurance. "We've been enemies since kindergarten, Lucy. No sense in pretending otherwise. Beautiful girls and fat girls will always be at war."

So much for bonding.

Lucy pinched the bridge of her nose. There really didn't seem to be a way to exclude Taffi from the rescue efforts, but it was damn tempting. "Look, all that matters is finding our way off this island. We're building boats and we're leaving. All of us. Even you."

"Good." Taffi nodded, adopting a brave face. "I can't stay a prisoner of Fraggle Rock for much longer. I'm missing *Project Runway,* and I've wrecked my nails, and had to eat bugs for dinner. Besides, I have a strict rule against sleeping with longhaired men, so my dating options are —like— zero around here."

That was so stupid on so many different levels, it boggled the mind. Lucy went with the simplest objection. "You're hardly a prisoner, Taffi. No one even knows you're here."

"That's because I've had to hide in the woods, afraid some T-Rex would eat me!"

"Trust me, that's the least of your worries. Everything here seems to be following pretty close to our Ice Age and dinosaurs were extinct millions of years before that."

Taffi snorted that incontrovertible paleontological fact. "Not all scientists agree with you."

"Yes, they do. Unless they're really dumb scientists."

"You're always so disagreeable! Would it kill you to be nice to me, for once? Why does *no one* understand what I'm going through? I can't believe I'm all alone here and nobody even cares that I've..." She stopped mid-word, her eyes going wide. "Whoa." She breathed in something like awe.

Without even turning around, Lucy knew Rhawn had followed her back to the cave.

Chapter Eight

Rhawn strokes the small nub of flesh hidden in the soft folds of the woman's body. He uses circles first, then he tugs it gently experimenting to see what she likes best. Tugging. He barely starts and her body is already arching into his touch.

"Oh God... Please." She begs.

Rhawn smiles, pleased with the reaction. He wonders what would happen if he tugs and then slips his other fingers inside her so she...

The woman cries out in pleasure, her channel constricting. She is panting for breath, completely opened to him. Rhawn analyzes the facts and realizes that she is close to release. Can women reach orgasm? He isn't sure, but –gods– how he wants to find out.

Rhawn and Lucy's Dream- Eight Years Ago

Lucy turned and immediately spotted a certain shirtless caveman standing in the mouth of the cave, looking like an ad for the Pleistocene Olympics. For once Taffi seemed to be speechless and Lucy didn't blame her. It was hard to think with all that golden skin shining at you.

Lucy sighed. For real, there was no way she was going to be able to avoid this guy. It would be like Charlie trying to stay away from the chocolate factory.

"This is Taffi." She told Rhawn by way of introduction. "Before you ask, *no*. She's not a god."

Fathomless brown eyes surveyed Taffi with math-geek concentration. "But she has come with you and Warr-en? She is from Newyork?"

"Sort of."

"I live in Queens." Taffi told him, rallying quickly. She beamed like the head cheerleader she'd once been and hurried towards him, her aversion to long-haired men forgotten. "I'm super happy to meet someone who speaks English. I was beginning to think we were stranded in some icky foreign place."

Rhawn clearly had no idea what she was talking about. Lucy could see him sorting through her words, trying to make sense of them. "You are a queen?"

"Why yes! Yes, I am."

"You're not a queen, Taffi." Lucy snapped.

"I was prom queen, wasn't I?" Taffi hissed back. "Shut up. I think he likes me."

"He doesn't even know you!"

"Men don't *have* to know me to like me. It's just a gift I have."

"I'm sure they like you *better* when they don't know you, but this particular man is spoken for." The words were out before Lucy even thought about them.

Rhawn glanced at her sharply.

"Spoken for by whom?" Taffi sneered. "*You*? Right. I'm so sure *you're* the dream girl of a guy who looks like a superhero. When's the last time you even wore lipstick? I mean, yeah you're *finally* accessorizing properly," she gestured to the shiny necklace Anniah had given Lucy, "but, it's too little, too late. You can't really believe..."

"Lucy is the woman of my dreams." Rhawn said simply, cutting her off. His attention stayed on Lucy. "She is... perfect."

Lucy stared back at him, hypnotized and a little afraid. That gaze was so intense. So penetrating. Like he could see straight through her. But, if he could, why didn't he already know the truth? "I'm not perfect." She whispered.

He shrugged. "You are perfect for me."

"She's *so* not perfect." Taffi agreed, not even hearing Rhawn's quiet assurance. "You should have seen her hair back in tenth grade. She dyed it this god-awful blue." She rolled her eyes. "Lucy always has to be *special*."

"I'm not special."

They ignored her denial.

"Lucy cannot help being special. Even in my dreams, I knew she was born to change the world." Rhawn looked at Lucy. "But I have not dreamed of this queen." He waved a hand at Taffi. "I only dream of *you*, goddess."

"You better *not* have dreamed of Taffi." Lucy scowled at him, outraged at the thought. Maybe she wasn't completely sure what was going on between them, but she knew damn well it was only between *them*. "You'd better not be dreaming of anybody else, at all! I mean it, Rhawn."

He liked that demand. "You have no need to worry. I've Chosen *you*. No others fill my thoughts."

"Good."

"Really?" Taffi exclaimed, throwing up her hands in frustration. "I mean *really?*" She turned back to Lucy. "You're dating *him*, now? While I've been eating shriveled up worms and gross, green berries, you've been shacking up with the Wild Man of Borneo?! I swear, you don't care about anyone but yourself! You're selfish and I'm *glad* I tripped you going across the stage during graduation!"

Lucy dragged her attention away from Rhawn and stabbed a finger at her. "I'm not in the mood for your bullshit, Taffi. The fat girls have won the war, so just accept it and *shut up*, before I throw you out on your liposuctioned ass."

"You don't own this cave! I can be here if I want! Why are you always so mean to me, huh? If you knew what I'd been through you'd be a lot more..."

Rhawn cut her off. "You ate the green berries?"

"Yes." Taffi muttered distractedly, her eye still on Lucy. "You know, it's all *your* fault that..." She suddenly seemed to process Rhawn's concerned tone and stopped mid-word. "Wait what?" Her head swung around to look at him in growing panic. "Yes! The green ones. I ate the green ones. Was I not supposed to eat the green ones?"

Rhawn didn't respond to that, but he backed away from Taffi with a worried frown. His eyes cut over to Lucy. "She ate the green ones." He said in a grave voice.

"Is that bad?"

Rhawn gave a shrug. "Perhaps."

"Oh God." Taffi whispered, looking a little green herself.

Lucy's eyebrows compressed. "Will she die?"

Rhawn gave another shrug. "Perhaps."

"Oh God." Taffi gasped again. "I *can't* die! I'm supposed to go to Italy in October!"

Even Lucy was concerned about her prognosis. "Can we do anything for her?"

A third shrug. "Pray to the Savior?" Rhawn suggested in a suspiciously dire tone.

Lucy paused, taking in his oh-so-grave expression. "Pray to the Savior?" She repeated skeptically and amusement began to take the place of worry. "The Savior who's passed out in the other cave? You really think that's going to cure her, huh?"

His mouth curved slightly. "As well as anything else will, I imagine."

"Oh *God!*" Taffi slapped a hand over her mouth, missing the joke. "I totally feel the like— poison poisoning me. It's seriously happening!" She went rushing from the cave. "I'm going to be sick."

"That is always a good remedy." Rhawn called after her.

Lucy didn't bother to follow her out. She crossed her arms over her chest and arched a brow at Rhawn. "The green berries are fine, aren't they?"

He shrugged, but his eyes were glinting with laughter. "Perhaps."

Lucy couldn't quite contain her snickering. "You lied to that poor girl about toxic berries? I thought I was supposed to be the evil one around here? High-five!" She held up a palm and he frowned at it in confusion. "Never mind." She dropped her hand again. Clearly, those weren't a caveman custom, yet. "What's important is that you were mean to Taffi in an awesome, *awesome* way. I *knew* I liked you, caveman."

"She will be fine." Rhawn was epically unrepentant. "The woman deserved far worse than she got. I do not like the way she speaks to you. Who is she and why is she here?"

"She's Taffi Dawson, the prettiest girl in Woodward High. And she's here because I'm having a real bad week."

Except for meeting Rhawn, anyhow, that didn't seem so bad, at all.

Rhawn blinked in total incomprehension. "Someone believes *that* woman is prettiest? Did no one in this Wood-Ward-High place see *you?*"

Lucy slowly smiled. "You just won yourself soooo many points."

He brightened. "Points are good." He reminded her.

"Yeah, points are *real* good, especially considering you want to see me naked sometime this epoch."

His eyes narrowed in deep thought, taking her literally. "How many points do I need before you will mate with me?"

"A *lot* of points."

"What is the specific number, though?"

"Sixty-one and a half." She randomly decided, because he wasn't going to be satisfied until he had a target. God, he really was the straight-A kid who asked about extra credit.

"How many points do I presently have?"

"Three."

He frowned at that news.

"Anyway," Lucy continued cheerily, "Taffi's a vapid twit. Always has been. I don't want to see her dead, though, so we're going to take her with us when we leave this island."

"You are still committed to this insane plan with the *ragan*, then?" Rhawn asked her that about nine times a day, like he just kept hoping that she'd change her mind. He was such an optimist. "Have I mentioned that *jigon* live in those waters?"

"A couple hundred times. But unless you have a better way to avoid being melted by the big ass volcano, we're still going with my plan."

"Believe me, I'm trying to think of one." He sighed. "In the meantime, we need to focus on more practical concerns. Like food. It's why I came to find you." He stepped closer to her, apparently just because he wanted to be closer to her. He did that a lot and it always made her heart race.

"Food?" She repeated dumbly, staring up at his

incredible face.

"Yes. We used the last of our stores for the Savior's feast. If you really plan to put us into *ragan*, we will need supplies. The rest of the Clan will not eat from the sea."

"I guess green berries and those vegetarian flower things are a no go?"

"We need to hunt a mammoth."

God, he said that so casually. "Hunt a mammoth?" Lucy repeated, pretending that those words weren't fucking crazy. "Like the huge hairy elephants, who could crush us with their huge hairy feet?"

"I am unfamiliar with this word 'ely-fanz.'"

She waved that aside. "I thought you said all the mammoths were gone."

"*Most* are gone. There is a small herd in the valley. Some females had to be spared, so they might breed and raise the young. Others are too large or bad-tempered to bring down safely. We saved them for last."

"So *now* you want to hunt the big, mean ones and the babies?"

"How else will we get food?" He retorted. "You might not enjoy meat, but there are few other options available. We will need weeks of provisions, if we're going on the *ragan*. Strips of meat will last longest and take up the least amount of space."

"Damn it." She tilted her head back, because he was right. What *was* the Clan going to eat for however long it took them to find land? She hadn't really considered the logistics of her plan, just the "getting the hell outta there" part. Of course Rhawn had thought about the nuts and bolts of it, though. He was a nuts and bolts kinda guy.

"What about –like– smaller, unextinct animals? Could we kill them, instead of a mammoth? Maybe mice. I don't like mice."

It hurt her to even ask that, though. Corny and tree-huggy as it sounded, Lucy really did love animals. One day, she fully planned to get a cute, little dog. Slaughtering fuzzy creatures was the last thing she'd ever want to do. Especially mammoths, for crying out loud. Every paleontology-student bone in her body wanted to study them, not eat them.

"Small creatures are scarce now. It would take too much time to gather enough to feed us all. And wolves, *tandar*, and long-tooths are very dangerous to hunt."

"*Tandar?*"

"Monstrous beasts with *septar*."

"Right." That really cleared it right up.

"So you see, mammoths are the best choice." He sounded positive and she had no reason to doubt him. Rhawn could probably show her some complicated graph proving exactly how much meat each person needed per day. The caveman was kind of a nerd.

Lucy sighed. "Alright." Jesus, twenty years of vegetarianism and now she was going on a goddamn safari. Her only consolation was that the volcano was poised to wipe out the mammoths anyway. They'd just be speeding up the inevitable. It still sucked, though. "Just promise me you'll pick an old and sick one. And that you'll be super, *super* careful during the whole spearing part, because I don't want you crushed to death."

His eyes softened. "I promise."

"I mean it, Rhawn. You don't want to piss off an evil goddess by dying. We can get testy."

Rhawn's gaze traced over her face. "I do not see evil in you, Lucy."

"Maybe you're not looking hard enough."

That seemed to amuse him. He smiled and Lucy's insides flipped. "Believe me, no one could look at you more closely than I do. I am unsure of what you truly are, goddess, but I know it is something bright and good."

Lucy stared up at him and knew she was never going to be free of this man. She didn't' even *want* to be. "Okay, you can have a couple of points for that one." She decided softly.

"I have five now?"

"Yeah. Fine. Five." She agreed with a shrug. "Just so you follow orders and stay alive."

"Do not worry. All will be well." One massive hand came over to caress her hair, his fingers tangling in the dark strands like they amazed him. "It is our fate to be together."

"I don't believe in fate."

"You did not believe in anything we have on this island, before you experienced it firsthand."

She sighed, leaning into his touch. "When you say things, they just seem to make sense. ...Even when they don't make any sense. I don't know how you manage that."

His mouth curved. "Because what I say *does* make sense." His free hand came up to absently finger her shiny necklace. "What happened to your green beads?" He asked after a beat.

"I gave them to Anniah."

"That was kind of you."

"Not really. Trust me. These are way prettier."

Rhawn paused. "That necklace is meant to be worn alone, on bare skin." He pointed out hopefully. "You should remove your fabric chest coverings and it would be even *way-er* more prettier."

Lucy laughed at that. "Nice try." She shook her head. "You're not supposed to be flirting with me, remember? You said you'd wait until *I* seduced *you*."

"Those were not my words. I said I'd wait to *mate* with you, until you were ready." He smiled and it was adorable. "But, there is *much* we can do to keep busy until then."

"You're sort of a smartass, you know that?"

"I am not smart." But, his denial wasn't quite so forceful this time. Maybe he'd been listening to her on the beach and was starting to consider that endless questions might be a good thing. "You do not see me as others do."

"The way I see you is the only way that matters. If we're in any kind of relationship," and she had the strange feeling they *were*, "then *my* vote is the one that counts, right?"

His nod was immediate and certain. "You are my mate." He moved forward, edging all the way into her personal space bubble. Lucy found it comforting. Years of being a loner evaporated around Rhawn. He pushed his way in until she couldn't remember him not being there. "Your feelings are always paramount with me, Lucy."

Lucy wasn't so sure about the "mate" thing, but the rest sounded right. "Okay, then listen to me. I don't think I've ever met anyone as smart as you, Rhawn. I look at what you've done on these walls and it's... amazing. *You* are amazing. I mean look at these drawings!"

"I am not sure what some of them even are. I just paint what I see in my dreams."

"Well, this one," she gestured to a small painting on the wall, "this is an airplane. They fly through the air, carrying humans as passengers. And if we had one of them, we'd be off this island in no time."

He moved behind her, resting his cheek on the top of her hair. "Where would we go?"

"Someplace else. Someplace better."

"Newyork?"

Lucy cuddled into his embrace, feeling secure. "New York isn't better. I mean, there aren't any volcanoes, but it's so... lonely."

He arched a brow. "You said this before."

"Because it's true. The city is filled with people, but you're by yourself in the crowd." In fact, the person she'd always felt closest to was the caveman in her dreams. Sometimes she'd talked to Rhawn in her head, even when she thought he was just a figment of her imagination.

As if she was missing someone she'd never met.

"It wasn't Newyork that made you feel alone." Rhawn murmured like he was reading her thoughts. "You were lonely because you weren't with me. Just as I was lonely because I wasn't with you. Separation isn't natural between mates. We were meant to be together."

Lucy tilted her head back to look at him. "Even when we were separated, I think we've always been together." She whispered.

Rhawn smiled at that.

"And I think these pictures are genius." She continued.

"I think *you* are a genius. This is more than just stuff you saw in dreams. Your own thoughts are on these walls, too."

He self-consciously glanced away and cleared his throat. "This one is the oldest." He gestured to the picture of the blue whirlpool. "I dream of it often."

Lucy frowned slightly, her eyes tracing over the interconnected swirls. There was something eerie about the image. Something familiar. A glow and a depth that shouldn't be possible from basic pigments on stone. "What is it?

"I'm not sure. I thought you might recognize it from your world."

She shook her head. "It looks familiar, but I can't place it. Sorry."

Rhawn studied the drawing for a beat. "Well, we start your journey across the water, soon. Maybe it's what awaits us on the other side of the sea." He paused meaningfully. "Or, more likely, what we'll find at the bottom of it."

Before Lucy could respond to that prime example of his smartass-ery, the whole world began to move. A terrible rumble sounded from deep within the mountain, shaking the ground and the walls and the air itself. It felt as if a giant had lifted the cave up and was violently tossing it around. Unable to keep her balance, Lucy stumbled and nearly fell.

Rhawn grabbed her before she hit the floor, holding her upright. "Lucy, we must go!" He shouted over the horrific noise and pulled her towards the cave entrance. "This shaking is too big!"

She certainly wasn't going to argue. Small stones were raining down from the ceiling. For all she knew, the whole damn thing could collapse. Cracks appeared in the cave walls, splintering through Rhawn's artwork. Dirt and pebbles bounced off the floor like popcorn.

Lucy staggered for the exit, still clinging to Rhawn for balance. He was half-carrying her, shielding her from falling rocks as they made it outside. Things weren't much better out in the open. Smoke poured from the top of the volcano, billowing up and clouding the sky. Way, way, *way* too much steam.

"Oh God." Lucy whispered.

The volcano seemed to swell for a split second and then it exploded with a terrifying "crack." Uooloa wasn't even erupting. She could tell, because they were still alive. The volcano was just letting off some steam and it *still* sounded like a thousand cannons going off all at once.

"Holy *shit!*" Lucy instinctively reached up to cover her ears, cringing at the noise.

When Krakatoa erupted, back in 1883, it was the loudest sound in recorded history. In fact, it was so loud that science didn't even *classify* it as a sound. Technically, it had been a shockwave. The noise generated was so massive that it ripped the air apart, pushing through it with so much pressure that human eardrums burst nearly fifty miles away. At the time, Lucy first read that, she'd thought those reports were probably exaggerated.

Now, she totally, *totally* believed every word.

If this was even a fraction of what a full eruption was like, no one could possibly survive it for long. The island would be blown apart.

"This is worse than it's ever been!" Rhawn pushed Lucy back so she was against the side of the mountain in case the path beneath them gave way. His arms came up to protect her head from the small landslide of debris pouring down the side of the mountain. "Something is changing below us!"

He was right. The whole forest seemed to be rolling like the waves in the ocean. It was impossible to see one fixed point, no matter where she looked. Trees fell and people ran. Giant voids were opening up like special effects in a movie. As millions of gallons of water were spewed out of the volcano as vapor, the ground beneath lost its support. Sinkholes appeared out of nowhere, swallowing massive clumps of trees.

The island itself seemed to slip further into the sea, another six feet of beachfront vanishing beneath the waves. Jesus, whatever was going on down there, it was indeed sinking the island. Lucy still wasn't sure how plate tectonics worked in this world, but she knew that wasn't normal.

"I told you the ocean is swallowing us." Rhawn called, because he loved to be proven right.

"I don't know what's going on with the beach, but magma is moving closer to the surface and creating the sinkholes." Lucy shouted back, recalling that PBS special. Maybe the island was built on unstable ground and that was why it was in danger of collapse. "The heat is evaporating the water and changing the structure of the bedrock. It's one of the warning signs that a major eruption is imminent."

"This is not *major?*"

"I think it's just the warm up." Lucy let out a long breath as the island stilled again and the horrendous venting finally slowed. "Okay, for real," she got out hoarsely, surveying the damage and shaking her head, "we need to build those boats faster."

Chapter Nine

The woman is back!

Rhawn's heart leaps in his chest. It is always like that when she finally returns. She is all that he wants to dream about and it's been a full cycle since he last saw her.

She turns to smile at him like she's happy to see him, too. "Hi, caveman." She holds out a hand to him and he grabs it, yanking her against his chest. "Missed me, huh?"

He has been desolate without her. If he had a choice, he would be by her side every minute of his life. His mouth curves into a smile and his hands slide over her body, hugging her close. He has so little time with her and he doesn't want to miss a moment of it.

Rhawn and Lucy's Dream- Seven Years Ago

For the next three days, Lucy insisted they work on the *ragan* night and day, even ordering torches and bonfires lit so they could see in the darkness.

Oddly enough, most of the Clan accepted her orders with little grumbling and set about their work with diligent concentration. Leaving the island might've seemed like a huge risk, but staying was guaranteed death. No one could deny that Uooloa would soon blow. That massive earthquake had been enough to convince everybody and the smoke pouring from the mountaintop grew thicker each hour.

In many minds, escape truly was their only alternative. Thoughts became whispers and whispers became actions. Even Notan had stopped pushing for Lucy's assassination and was helping to prepare clay water vessels for the journey. His excuse was that they'd prayed for a sign, maybe the *ragan* were the gods' answer.

One by one, most of the Clan began to follow the Destroyer. One by one, they convinced themselves that her crazed plan was their only chance. For a woman who insisted she was "anti-social," she'd taken over the job of leader with remarkable ease. Everyone looked to her for decisions and followed her instructions. Lucy just seemed to know what she was doing. She was confident. Determined.

Special.

Lucy wanted *ragan*, so they built *ragan*. Skoll might hate Lucy, but most people were just happy to have a constructive outlet for their frustration. A task that was doing *something* to help their future.

Ironically, the Destroyer was the first one to offer them hope.

Rhawn was still pretty sure this plan was doomed, but at least he had a committed work force. He'd been overseeing the *ragan's* construction, making sure the others stuck to the plans he'd sketched for them on the rocks. When he'd built his *ragan* it had taken him two weeks of trial and error. Repeating the process and having dozens of extra hands meant they'd be finished all ten of them in less than half that time. Already they'd completed most of the work.

Since that just meant Lucy was ten *ragan* closer to drowning them all, he felt conflicted about the progress. He still didn't like all the uncertainties of this plan. Rhawn preferred to test and retest his ideas with controlled variables. There was no way to predict what might happen if they sailed off the island.

That worried him.

Deeply.

Lucy seemed happy with their progress, though. Or as happy as the Destroyer *ever* seemed. Since she wasn't nagging him about speeding up the process, he could only imagine she was satisfied with his efforts. She hadn't destroyed the world or killed anyone, yet. Those were good signs.

His mate was a difficult woman. Beautiful and special and perfect, but difficult. She still insisted that he sleep on the opposite side of the cave and she hadn't kissed him since the beach. He *had* won sixteen more points, here and there, though. That was always a joyous thing. Rhawn was keeping closer track of them than Lucy was, so she might not have noticed the way they were adding up. Or maybe she preferred to just ignore it. Clearly, the woman had it in her mind to resist sex for as long as possible.

Hell if he knew why.

In the meantime, Rhawn was content with what he had. More than content. His woman was finally with him. He could look at her. Talk to her. Touch her. She *smiled* at him. She met his eyes without fear. Welcomed him into her confidence. Relied on him for help. Rhawn was the one she looked to when she was unsure or moved towards when she was scared. Lucy's instincts understood the truth, even if her mind wasn't willing to admit it yet.

Deep down, she knew they were mates.

He may have been lonely on the island and she might have been lonely in Newyork, but now they were finally together and it was like coming home. When they were done working, they would go back to his cave and sit by the fire together. They discussed things great and small. Stories from her world and stories from his. What they dreamed of when they weren't dreaming of each other. Hopes and plans and ridiculous things that mattered not at all. Rhawn talked to Lucy more than he'd ever talked to anyone. And she *listened*. Everything he said, she paid attention to. Like he mattered to her. Like they were truly connected.

It was more than Rhawn ever imagined having. The reality of Lucy was far, *far* better than any of his most outlandish fantasies. He hadn't slept with her yet, but if the world ended tomorrow, he would still die happy just because he'd known her.

...But he *really* wanted to sleep with her, so he was doing his damnedest to make sure the world stayed put.

Needing a break, Rhawn sat down by one of the fires on the beach and rubbed the back of his neck. He'd barely slept since he'd woken up from his dream of Lucy in the cave. With Skoll around, he didn't like to let his guard down.

Skoll refused to build the *ragan* and he belittled everyone who did. His scorn didn't stop the rest of the Clan from pressing on, though. The man's hatred of Lucy grew, as he lost his influence over the others. Before she arrived, he had been second only to Notan, next in line to be leader.

Now Lucy was in charge.

Since the woman liked to be in control, the situation suited her perfectly. Granted, it meant that she couldn't be "a loner." Whatever the hell that meant, it seemed to be how she saw herself. At times, Lucy would complain about all the people surrounding her or demand Rhawn translate blistering insults to someone who'd pissed her off. But mostly Rhawn saw her blossoming under the new responsibility.

And when she smiled, his whole life made sense.

Skoll wasn't nearly so pleased. Skoll would kill Lucy if he could. Not only was she taking his place, but she'd been spending time with Anniah convincing the other woman that she did not have to accept Skoll's Choosing. That was not a popular decision, at least among the males. The females of the Clan seemed very receptive to her ideas, though, and they were far louder than the grumbling from the men. There was no stopping what Lucy started and they all knew it. Even Skoll. Anniah seemed positively smug over his fuming.

Rhawn made sure he was either watching Skoll or by Lucy's side every minute. When she slept, he watched over her. During the day, he made sure Skoll was always within his eyesight. It was the only way to keep Lucy safe.

The night before, she'd woken up and spotted him standing by the cave entrance. "Why aren't you in bed?" She'd asked in a drowsy voice.

Rhawn had looked over his shoulder, smiling slightly. "Because, you instructed me to sleep on the floor."

"You know what I mean. You've been working all day. Go lay down on your pile of murdered fur and *sleep*. I don't want you killing yourself."

"I'm fine."

She'd propped herself up on her elbows and frowned when he didn't move. "Is something wrong?"

"No. I am just... watching."

"Watching what?"

He hadn't answered that.

"Hang on, are you *protecting* me? Do you really think that's necessary?"

"There are some people who do not care for you as much as I do." He'd explained as diplomatically as he could.

Lucy had studied him for a beat. "I don't think there's *anybody* who cares for me as much as you do." She'd said quietly. "Maybe you wouldn't care so much, if you knew me better."

"I do know you, Lucy."

She'd sighed and moved to stand beside him. "No, you really don't. You think I'm a goddess."

"You *are* a goddess."

"See?" She'd said, as if that response proved her point.

Rhawn was not about to argue with nonsense. "You are a very difficult woman." He'd told her instead.

"So they tell me." One of the pelts was wrapped around her shivering body. Lucy might complain about the animals he'd skinned to get the blankets, but she appreciated their warmth. Lucy winced as the night air blew through the cave's entrance. "God, is it always so cold here?"

"No. This is our summer season."

"Smartass."

It amused him that Lucy thought he'd been joking. The island's climate didn't suit her. What Rhawn considered a slight chill had Lucy bundling up under a pile of furs. It was why he kept the fire lit, night and day. A sweltering cave was a small price to keep Lucy comfortable.

Rhawn had glanced down at her, knowing she could probably see every tender feeling inside of him. It wasn't like he was trying to hide them. "No one could *possibly* care for you as I do." He'd agreed quietly. There wasn't enough space inside a person to feel any more love than he experienced whenever he looked at her. There wasn't even a word for 'love' in his language and he knew that.

Lucy had stared up at him. "You scare me sometimes." She'd finally whispered.

His eyebrows had compressed in concern. "I won't harm you, Lucy. Not ever."

"I know. It's not that." She'd leaned into his body, her head resting on his shoulder. For a being with the personality of a small tornado, Lucy's body was so delicate. "It's just really, really easy to get used to being with you. It's the one place I've never felt lonely."

"That's because it's where you belong. With me."

She'd snorted at that. "Well, that's lucky, since I have no clue how to get back to New York."

Rhawn had closed his eyes in relief at the news that she was not able to leave him. He'd been afraid to ask, but it was a nagging concern. Without Lucy, he might as well sink with the rest of the island. He would have nothing left to care about, anyway. "You cannot return to Newyork?"

"I'm thinking maybe this was a one way trip."

"Can't you use your vast powers to escape?" He'd asked and was proud of how serious he made his tone.

She'd winced a bit, looking adorably guilty. "No." She'd muttered.

Rhawn had nearly chuckled. He had no idea why Lucy didn't just admit that she was powerless. Rhawn could see for himself that she wasn't capable of magic. Whatever divinity the woman possessed, it wasn't going to help her escape this island.

He'd kissed the top of her head, charmed by her. "I would not want you to go. My world would be desolate and cold without you."

"It's already pretty frigging cold." She'd snuggled closer. "Seriously, deep down, I'm afraid that coming here was just a freak accident. Just a random door that I stumbled through. I'm not even sure how to *attempt* to recreate it."

"I do not believe it was an accident that brought you here. I believe you were always meant to come. It's why I dreamed of you for so long." He'd brushed the hair back from her face, his body aching for her. "Will you mate with me tonight?" He asked that often, but so far her answer was always the same.

"No."

"Why not?"

"I'm still thinking."

Rhawn had rolled his eyes. "I do not see what you are considering. I have Chosen you as my mate. You desire me and I desire you. There seems little reason to wait any longer, Lucy."

"Except, I have to Choose you back, remember?"

He'd expelled a frustrated breath. "I am unlikely to forget. I cannot believe I ever agreed to such a crazed notion."

"Oh don't be such a sore loser."

"I have not lost anything. You merely postpone what is *going to happen*. Even you know that."

She hadn't refuted that statement. "Well, if it makes you feel any better, you're the reason I'm not actively diving to the ocean floor and looking for the cruise ship, trying to jumpstart a quirk of quantum mechanics." Lucy had shrugged. "So *maybe* I like you a little bit. *Maybe* there are way worse places to be than on a desert island with you."

"Maybe." He'd agreed sarcastically.

She'd laughed, enjoying his irritated tone. "If I believed in fate, I'd even say *maybe* I was even supposed to wind up right here, right now, with you."

Rhawn adored this difficult woman. "I *do* believe in fate, so I know that idea is a *certainty*."

"Well, accident or design, it doesn't much matter. We're partners in this mess, now."

"We have always been partners, Lucy. From the minute I saw you. You know that."

"Maybe I do." She'd smiled and looked out into the darkness. "It's you and me, Rhawn the Accursed, sitting at the edge of the world. ...And getting ready to sail right off the edge."

In a day's time, the *ragan* would be ready, so her whimsical words might prove true. Rhawn consulted the building schedule that he'd painted on a flat rock. At this point, they were nearly ready to hunt the mammoths and stock up on supplies so...

"We're out of wine." Warren announced sourly.

Rhawn blinked, surprised out of his thoughts. It seemed the Savior had finally left his cave and found his way down to the beach. Wonderful. He scowled as the god flopped down beside him. "You've had enough of wine." Warren's odor made that abundantly clear.

"Hey, Lucy hit me with a rock!" The Savior complained, a hungover expression on his face. "I need liquor to medicate myself. It's not like I can go to Walgreens and buy some aspirin." He settled on the log beside Rhawn like he planned to stay for a while. "Damn man, I think I give off –like– a pheromone or something that attracts all the violent, psycho, broads to me. My first ex-wife broke my arm with a putter. True story."

Ever since Warren had woken up from the *Ardin*, he'd been drinking and sulking and staying away from everyone. Rhawn had been pleased with that arrangement, but now Warren seemed ready to talk. That was the *last* thing Rhawn wanted to do.

Just seeing the man pissed him off.

"You deserved to be hit with a rock. I would have done worse to you, if Lucy had given me a chance." Rhawn snapped. "Do you remember what you said?"

"Kinda." Warren admitted sulkily. "She can't hold any of that against me, though. I was shitfaced, ya know?"

"You said you wished to Choose Lucy." Rhawn shot Warren a sideways look. "You will not Choose Lucy."

Should Warren have any crazed ideas to the contrary, the challenge would resume and the island would be down by one drunken god. No great loss. Rhawn sincerely doubted anyone would even notice. ...Except Anniah and Lucy, who seemed inexplicably attached to the idiot. Since their opinions meant the most to him, he was trying to refrain from ripping out Warren's throat.

It took a *colossal* amount of effort.

"Yeah. I mean *no*. I'm not hitting on the girl, okay? Christ." Warren scrubbed a palm over his eyes, trying to clear out the grit. "I feel like I got chewed up and spit out by one of her Wooly Rhinos, too. Isn't that punishment enough?"

Rhawn still didn't recognize that animal's name, but he wasn't about to admit it. "Probably not enough for Lucy."

"She's pretty peeved at me, huh?"

"Kinda." Rhawn mocked. He slanted the man another glare, disliking him for countless reasons. "You have lost the *Ardin*." He reported, in case Warren hadn't figured it out on his own.

"Whatever that means."

"It means Lucy is in charge of the Clan now."

Warren snorted. "Typical. She's always been the special one."

Taffi had said the same thing and Rhawn had to agree. Lucy was *very* special. Destroyer or not, there was no one else like her in all the universe.

Warren brooded for a beat. "Lucy always knows what she's doing. Always figures out the right moves. I used to crib off all her tests when she wasn't looking. Only way I passed half of my classes." He made a face. "And even *then* she somehow screwed up the curve for me."

Rhawn saw nothing wrong with Lucy's curves.

"I wanted to ask her to the junior prom." Warren continued. "She can sometimes be pretty hot, when she's not hitting me with stuff."

Rhawn really, *really* should have killed this asshole when he had the chance. "Lucy would never, *ever* Choose you. She is so far above you, it's a wonder you can see her, at all."

"Yeah, that's what my dad said." Warren lamented.

Rhawn nodded. The Savior's father was clearly a wise man.

"I went to him for advice about her and ya know what he did? He *laughed*. Said, 'That Meadowcroft girl is the brightest thing ever to come outta this town, idiot. She's gonna leave here and change the world. You think *you* really have a chance with her?'" Warren turned to frown at Rhawn. "A *real* dad would've helped me score with her, ya know?" He pouted for a beat. "He wouldn't get me a Camaro, either. My parents sucked."

Rhawn was without sympathy. "My parents were sacrificed in your name when I was a boy." He had no memory of them, except that they'd liked to pray. They'd volunteered for the death ritual, secure in the knowledge that the Savior would welcome them into his realm.

If they'd met the Savior first, they might have reconsidered.

"Oh." Warren muttered and then shrugged. "Sorry about that."

Rhawn grunted.

Anniah came bounding over, beaming to see Warren out of the cave. She was still wearing the beads that Lucy had given her. In Rhawn's opinion they had looked much better on the Destroyer, but the girl at least appreciated the generous gift. There was nothing else like the green necklace in the world, so Anniah's treasure was the envy of the Clan.

"The Savior has awakened?" She asked in the Clan's tongue. Her blue eyes flicked to Rhawn and then went back to staring at Warren with something like awe. "He looks better, yes? Is he feeling alright?"

It was perfectly obvious that god was conscious and not dying, so Rhawn didn't bother to reply to her questions. Anniah herself was a sweet little thing. Unlike others in the Clan, she never ostracized Rhawn or treated him badly. The least he could do in return was warn her away from the mess of a man beside him.

"The Savior is weak, selfish, and stupid." He told her in their language. "Do not set your sights on him, Anniah. He has nothing to offer you."

She held out some *yhannee* fruit for Warren, tenderly brushing back his hair to check his head wound. "I see greatness in him."

Rhawn scoffed at that lunacy.

"What's going on?" Warren asked with his usual degree of understanding. "Who's this chick...?" He glanced at Anniah and froze. "*Wow.*" He gaped up at her, like he was seeing her for the first time. Actually, he *was* seeing her *face* for the first time. Usually, his eyes were fixed on Anniah's uncovered breasts, so it was no wonder he didn't remember meeting her. He blinked rapidly as he suddenly noticed she was gorgeous. "Holy shitburgers." He sat up straighter on the log. "Hey, who *is* this?"

"Anniah, daughter of our chief."

Anniah smiled, recognizing her name, and inclined her head.

"Wow." Warren repeated. He swallowed and blindly took the fruit she offered him. "She's like *really* pretty, ya know?"

"Yes." Rhawn arched a brow. "It is why Skoll wishes her to be his mate." The words were a warning, but he doubted the other man even heard them. Warren was mesmerized.

"Right." Warren cleared his throat, his gaze staying above Anniah's neck. That was undoubtedly a bad sign. The man had so far regarded all women as interchangeable, but something about Anniah had captured his attention. "I remember her from when I was sleeping. She was —like— taking care of me or something. I thought I dreamed her up. No one's ever taken care of me, ya know?"

Rhawn was not surprised by that revelation, given the man's dismal personality. "Anniah is the Clan's healer. It is her *job* to care for the sick."

Warren disregarded that. "What was she saying about me just now?"

Rhawn hesitated. "Anniah believes she sees greatness in you." He explained, even though he knew he was doing the woman no favors.

"Really?" Warren seemed puzzled by that idea. "In *me?*"

Rhawn shrugged, still at a loss to explain it himself.

"Well…" Warren floundered for a beat. "Tell her thanks. I guess. I mean, do you people say 'thanks'?" He waved a dismissive hand. "No, never mind. Say something cool. Maybe compliment her or… No. Wait. All guys probably compliment her. Shit. Say…" he racked his brain, "*thanks*. Yeah. Say thanks."

Rhawn rolled his eyes and glanced at Anniah. "He thanks you for your kindness. He is also a total fool. I believe you might just be better off with Skoll as a mate."

"But I have Chosen *this* man." She retorted calmly, her eyes staying on Warren. "Fool or not, he is the one. I knew it from the first. Lucy said he could be mine."

"Lucy says you may Choose, but Notan and Skoll will not agree."

"They do not have a say in the matter. Lucy is the goddess and she has given Warr-en to me."

Warren smiled up at her, smitten. "What is she saying now? I think she said my name. Is it something good?"

Rhawn ignored him. "Anniah, if you wish to forsake the Choosing laws, I will help you stand against Skoll and find a true mate. But, you can do far better than *this* idiot." He gestured to Warren. "He is not worth the struggle he will cause you. …And cause *me*, since Lucy will insist I help you win him."

"I have already won him." Anniah said smugly. "He just doesn't know it yet." She headed off again, sending Warren a flirty smile over her shoulder. "Goodbye Warr-en." She sang out in passible English. She must have been practicing with Lucy, trying to learn how to communicate with the Savior.

See? Another really bad sign.

"Bye." Warren called back dumbly. "Jesus, that is the prettiest girl I ever saw." He whispered.

That was a terrible, *terrible* sign.

"And I *do* remember her." Warren continued in a reverent tone. "When I was lying on the floor of that cave, my head cracked open like a melon, she was *definitely* the one who took care of me. She's like an angel. My own pretty, topless angel."

Rhawn dropped his head into his hands. It was hopeless, just as he knew it would be. Fate and/or Lucy were joining Warren and Anniah together, no matter the bloodshed that would result. Damn it.

Why did these things always happen to Rhawn?

Warren spared Rhawn a quick glance, not even noticing his gloomy posture. "Do you think she likes me? She touched my hair. That's some kind of girl-code for liking a guy, right?" He seemed thrilled over the possibility, his words coming out too fast. "Do you think I should ask her to dinner?"

"I think she is too good for you." Rhawn told him flatly.

Warren deflated. His excitement vanished so quickly, it was like it had never been there, at all. His eyes flicked to Anniah's back and then away. "Yeah." He said after a beat. "I think she is, too." He tossed aside the piece of fruit and gave a sad chuckle. "She'd figure it out, too, if we went on a date or something. I mean, I sure don't have any greatness in me. We all know that."

"This is true." For some reason, Rhawn liked the man a tiny bit better for seeing the obvious. He raised his head and hesitated, searching for the right words. "Anniah is a compassionate girl. Very generous. Very smart. She is very drawn to you, for reasons that are beyond my understanding."

"Totally don't understand it, either." Warren readily agreed.

"But, if someone like Anniah sees greatness in you, then *perhaps* there is a small amount hidden somewhere." Rhawn paused. "Somewhere very, *very* deep.

"I doubt it." Warren said with a sigh.

So did Rhawn, but he was simply trying to bolster the man's spirits. The gods only knew why. "Lucy says Anniah can have you, if she wants."

Warren squinted. "Lucy *gave* me to that girl? Can she do that?"

"She is the Destroyer. She can do whatever she wishes."

"Oh." Warren puzzled that over and began to look touched. "Wow. So... I have to do whatever the pretty blonde says? That is *awesome*. It's like a *Penthouse* letter, ya know? Lucy's a *really* good friend."

"Understand, if you pursue Anniah, Skoll will challenge you." Rhawn warned. "He wishes to mate with her. Since you lost the *Ardin*, no one is intimidated by your powers." Rhawn doubted he even had any. If Lucy didn't possess magic, surely this moron didn't either. "Skoll will fight you for her and he will win."

Warren frowned. "Ya think?"

"I know it. He is a great warrior and you are not a great anything."

"I know. I blew my chance at greatness senior year." Warren reported in a melancholy tone. "All the scouts came to the Homecoming game and I was *ready* for them. I needed that fucking scholarship so bad I could taste it. Then, I'd be outta Clovis for good. Away from all the people who know what an asshole I am and what a *bigger* asshole my father is. Just a total clean slate, ya know?" He made a face. "Of course, I fucked it all up."

Rhawn tried to piece that story together, but it made no sense. "You failed at a *game?* This has ruined your whole life?" He couldn't imagine such a thing. "Why? Just play another."

"It wasn't just *a* game. It was *the* game and I blew it." Warren ran a hand through his hair. "I thought I was going to break records, ya know? ... And I did. I'm the high school quarterback who threw the most interceptions in a single quarter. *That* was my big football legacy."

Rhawn wasn't sure what that meant exactly, but he heard the defeat in the other man's voice. Obviously, this game had been some kind of manhood ritual and the Savior had fallen short. Having met Warren, Rhawn was not surprised.

"Football was over for me, after that." Warren continued. "And without football, I was nothing. Just a fucking car salesman, with two greedy ex-wives and a bankruptcy filing on my credit report." He went back to staring after Anniah. "Too bad you don't get any do-overs in life, huh? Once you miss your shot at greatness, it doesn't ever come back." He reluctantly looked away from Anniah. "She can do better than me. She's gonna see that pretty quick."

"Yes." Rhawn concurred. "For both your sakes, stay away from her until then."

"I guess." Warren cleared his throat, not at all convinced. "Hey is that Taffi over there?" He asked after a long moment.

"Of course." How could he *just* be noticing that? "She's been here for several days."

Warren looked insulted. "And what? She didn't fucking say 'hi' to me?"

"She's been busy." Rhawn intoned, switching his attention down the beach.

The-Queen-of-Whatever-She-Was-Queen-Of had recovered from the berry scare and had taken her place as another goddess. Notan seemed at a loss as to how she fit into the Clan's pantheon, but it didn't much matter. Everyone treated Taffi with frightened deference and she clearly enjoyed it.

Lucy said it probably reminded her of "her glory days as an eighteen year old bitch."

"Whatever." Warren rolled his eyes. "I'm over that skank. Taffi always did think she was too good for me, ya know? And her breasts are *totally* store bought. I know. I was there when she picked 'em out."

Rhawn ignored that, watching Taffi flirt with Skoll. The other man might be planning to Choose Anniah, but he was giving most of his attention to Taffi. It didn't seem to occur to him that she was manipulating him for her own benefit. He was too enthralled by the kisses Taffi doled out when he did her bidding.

Rhawn understood her motives, though. It was why Taffi was the person on the island who worried him most. She was cold and calculating in a way that made her unpredictable.

It made her dangerous.

Taffi understood social cliques on a highly advanced level. The Queen was savvy enough to see the divisions in the Clan, even without understanding the language. In response, she'd sidled up next to Skoll and wasn't letting go. It was a wise move. Taffi was envious of Lucy, and Skoll was obviously the one who hated the Destroyer most. Their interests aligned.

More importantly, if conflict erupted, Taffi would be safe from Skoll *and* Lucy. Skoll believed Taffi to be a benevolent goddess, trying to undermine the Destroyer's cause. And no matter what she might mutter to the contrary, Lucy had no intention of harming the girl. Taffi was therefore the only "god" on the island who no one was plotting against. On some level, Rhawn nearly admired the girl's maneuvering.

Mostly it just worried him, though.

Skoll still wanted to overthrow Lucy. Rhawn didn't want Taffi helping him succeed. He was fairly certain he'd have to kill Skoll, but his plan was to wait until after the mammoth hunt. They would need the extra hunters to bring down a large creature. After that, Rhawn would simply ensure that Skoll didn't get on a *ragan*. It was cold and effective. That son of a bitch wouldn't be a threat to his mate for much longer. Rhawn would make sure of it.

"I used to date Taffi." Warren put it. "She was my girlfriend back in high school."

"The two of you do seem well-suited." It wasn't a compliment.

"She's a real bitch. Set my stereo on fire when I got her *white* roses instead of *pink* roses for her birthday. Then she went and slept with Craig Turkana at the party. Eighty bucks worth of flowers, totally wasted." Warren went back to watching the fire. "She wasn't worth all the attention she got from the guys. Lucy was always the special one."

"Yes." Rhawn agreed.

"Lucy was just so fucking *smart*. Doing geometry problems in her head smart, but also like *clever* smart. She could figure shit out and she didn't even have to *think* about it. That's why Taffi hates her. Can't keep up. It can intimidate a person, ya know?"

"Lucy is brilliant." And she wouldn't settle for a man who wasn't *also* brilliant. That fact preyed on his deepest fears. Rhawn may have Chosen her, but Lucy would never fully accept him if he was as stupid as everyone believed.

He sighed wearily.

"Yep. She's brilliant." Warren lamented with a shake of his head. "Way too brilliant to ever let me see her naked, I guess."

"Way too brilliant for that." Rhawn intoned and wondered if it was too late to strangle the god.

"Probably for the best. I'm more like her brother, now." Warren surmised in a nonchalant tone. Clearly, he wasn't pining for the Destroyer. "We're almost too close to ever get it on, because it would fuck up our really deep bond, ya know?" He glanced at Rhawn, again. "She's digging on you, though. Sort of threw me, at first. You don't seem like her type. She likes the puny geek-squaders, ya know?" He tapped his temple. "Brainiacs."

Rhawn didn't understand all of that, but he got enough. "She wants an intelligent mate." It wasn't a question. He already knew the answer.

"Oh *yeah*. She and Teddy O'Connell were *totally* almost an item in high school and he ended up in MIT."

"Ted-eeo-connell." Rhawn repeated. "This is the male she desires?" Then, Rhawn would hunt this unknown rival down and challenge him, too. When you wanted to keep a woman like Lucy, you fought everyone who threatened to steal her away.

"Nah." Warren said, ruining the burgeoning plan. "Teddy and Lucy never got together. She never really got together with *anyone* that I know of. Which is why I'm surprised she seems to like you. Sorry I got a little touchy about that, by the way. Go ahead and nail her. Might loosen her up. Really, you have my permission, as the guy who's almost her brother."

"I don't *need* your permission. I challenged you for her and won. She is *mine*." Rhawn frowned, close to pouting himself. "I now seek *her* permission."

"Good luck with that." Warren scoffed. He seemed to notice the *ragan* building for the first time. The man's observation skills truly were abysmal. "Hey, what's with all the boats?"

"Lucy wishes us to leave the island."

"Great." Warren muttered. "We're all going to die."

The fact that he agreed with the Savior made Rhawn seriously reconsider his stance. "Do you know the way to our new land?" He asked without much hope. For a god, the other man seemed fairly uninformed about... everything.

"*New* land?" Warren echoed. "Dude, I don't even know where *this* land is."

Rhawn wasn't surprised to hear that. It occurred to him that Lucy would have been a much better Savior than Warren. *She* was the one who'd won the *Ardin*. *She* was the one with a plan. *She* was the one who wished to save everyone from Uooloa. *She* was the kind of deity his parents had hoped to see on the other side. Lucy should have been the one sent to save the Clan.

Lucy should have been the one sent to save the Clan.

His eyes went wide, his mind repeating the words like an echo.

"Where *is* Lucy?" Warren asked, looking around.

"She is supervising the tar gathering." Rhawn reported, his mind racing.

How *had* his ancestors determined which god would be the Destroyer? They'd predicted the arrival of a man and a woman, which had come true. But, had they just *assumed* that the male would be the stronger and more virtuous? That he would be the one to lead them? That *he* would be the Savior?

What if they'd been wrong?

Or, what if they'd gotten the legend *right*, except for the most important part? What if they'd mixed up the roles of the gods? What if Warren *wasn't* the Savior, destined to guide them to a new home?

What if *Lucy* was?

"She's at those pits?" Warren snorted. "Probably trying to save that damn lion, then."

"What?" Rhawn barely heard the other man, still considering possibilities.

"This big cat attacked me earlier and got stuck in the

tar. That Skoll guy wanted to kill it, but Lucy pitched a fit and wouldn't let him. She's got some kind of obsession with it being all 'extinct.'" His fingers made air quotes around the word. "She keeps saying we're stuck on Planet Ice Age or something." He snorted. "No way, right? I still think this is Aruba."

Rhawn wished he would just be quiet. He couldn't think with the man's constant chatter.

Warren didn't let the lack of response slow him down. "Anyway, I'll betcha she wants to get the cat out. Lucy's always been a friggin' animal lover." He made a face. "I *know* she's the one who took Chipper the Woodward High woodpecker back to the forest and let him out of his cage. That bird was our *mascot*, man. Totally jinxed our winning streak, sophomore year."

Rhawn slowly turned to look at Warren. "*What?*" Even in his distracted state, he processed enough of that gibberish to understand that his woman –the most special being in the world and the possible Savior of his people– wanted to free a man-eating predator from a lake of tar. "No. She would not go near a trapped long-tooth." He said, because he wanted to believe it. "Even she would accept that that it's too reckless to attempt such a thing."

"Too reckless?" Warren arched a brow. "Dude, have you *met* Lucy?"

Yes. Yes, he had.

Shit.

Rhawn took off towards the pits at a dead run.

Chapter Ten

Her hand tangles in his hair, as his mouth slides down the column of her throat. She tilts her head to give him better access to her neck. It's a sign of feminine surrender. Not the kind a male needs to force, but a deeper, more primitive instinct. An unconscious signal that her body is yielding to his, recognizing his claim.

His mate.

Rhawn scrapes his teeth against her throat like an animal. He feels like an animal. Wild, Raw. A low sound escapes him, almost a snarl. She answers with a small whimper, accepting his dominance, and he barely holds onto reason. If he cannot have her soon, he will explode.

"Vando." He can barely get the word out.

"I don't know what that means," she pants, "but right now it sounds fucking amazing."

Rhawn and Lucy's Dream- Six Years Ago

Since the island was about to be blown to tiny charred bits, it seemed pretty pointless to worry about the sabretooth. Unless they wanted to try some kind of *Life of Pi* thing, it would stay stuck on this rock even if they got it *un*stuck from the tar. When the volcano erupted, the poor cat would be incinerated along with the rest of this tropical hellhole, so why not just leave him be?

Because, Lucianne Meadowcroft *never* just let things be.

Being unreasonable didn't exactly win her any popularity contests, but it did get things done. However long the cat had left, she didn't want him suffering a slow death by starvation. He was such an amazing, majestic creature. He deserved to run free. And she was *going* to make it happen. It had taken her a few days to find a rope, but now she was ready to act. She might be losing a mammoth tomorrow, but she was damn well saving the cat.

…Even though Rhawn was going to be *pissed* when he

found out.

Which was why Lucy hadn't told him, in the first place. Rhawn was smart enough to know this plan was stupid and she didn't want him talking her out of it. He was way too logical, sometimes.

Lucy felt a little bit guilty about excluding him, though. Rhawn was her partner. She'd never had a partner before and she liked the sensation of having someone by her side. The two of them complimented each other. Understood each other. Lucy could look over at Rhawn, and he'd arch a brow, and they'd both know *just* what the other one was thinking.

All their strengths and weaknesses found a balance when they were together. Lucy was pushy and he was calm. She saw the big picture and Rhawn focused on the details. She was an antisocial control freak and he was... kinda perfect.

Lucy felt a deeper connection to him than to anyone else she'd ever met.

That worried her. A lot.

Lucy had pretty much come to the conclusion that she wasn't getting back to New York. She had no idea how she'd arrived on the island, so backtracking her steps was impossible. She couldn't very well recreate whatever worm-holey, string-theory-ish, *Interception*-esque quirk of physics that had brought her here. For better or worse, she was stuck in this place for the foreseeable future.

Obviously, that wasn't great news. She was going to miss electric blankets and sesame bagels and *The New York Times Book Review*. Lucy wasn't about to kill herself over losing them, though. Not even the bagels. She didn't even have a cute little dog that she needed to get home to, so she could survive here. Thanks to her master's degree, she mostly knew what to expect from this faux Ice Age, so she was even enjoying herself sometimes. When the volcano wasn't trying to kill her, anyway.

She would be okay.

The much bigger problem was Rhawn. The gorgeous guy who she was sort of almost living with. ...And who just happened to think she was a goddess. Deep down, she knew Rhawn was the reason she was so okay with maybe staying marooned in this world. Just so she was marooned with the caveman, Lucy could deal with anything. Did she even *want* to go back to a world where she only dreamed of him once a year?

Hell no.

But, when he finally figured out the truth, Rhawn was going to hate her. He wouldn't want to stay with someone who'd lied to him. Lucy did *not* want to lose Rhawn. She'd spent years imagining him and now he was real and right in front of her. She wasn't going to let anything screw that up. Especially not her own lies. Before they went any farther, she needed to figure out how to tell him the truth. It was the only way he'd ever be able to trust her, again.

But it was seriously, *seriously* going to suck.

All her life, people had assumed that Lucy was going to do something special. All her life, she'd failed to meet expectations. Sure, she'd done well in school. And as an adult, she paid her taxes and could rattle off the names of all the presidents. But, she'd never quite lived up to the hype and changed the world. In her heart, she knew she never would.

Lucy could live with disappointing her teachers, her hometown, and even herself.

Disappointing Rhawn would gut her, though.

He really thought she was special. A goddess. It was going to kill him when she explained she was just Lucy Meadowcroft, from Clovis. He was never going to look at her the same way again. That was the main reason why she wouldn't sleep with him. It wouldn't be fair to him, unless he knew who she really was.

And he was a damn hard guy not to sleep with, so she totally deserved some credit for her thoughtfulness,

Lucy managed to loop one end of the sinew rope around the sabretooth's neck through sheer effort of will. The four other Clan members standing around watched her like she was out of her mind, but they didn't try to run when she pantomimed for them to start heaving. Inspiring fearful obedience was one of the perks of being an evil goddess.

At first, the cat thrashed and fought. Afraid that he was going to snap the ropes, Lucy started talking to him. Actually, she started *singing*. Her musical virtuosity could clear a karaoke bar in ten seconds flat, but the cat seemed bizarrely fascinated with the off-key serenade. Who knew sabretooths were such Nirvana fans?

Midway through the second chorus of *Smells Like Teen Spirit*, Lucy realized that the cat had stopped fighting and that they were making some progress in freeing it. He edged closer to solid ground, inch by painful inch. This was going to work!

Lucy met the creature's yellow eyes, still wondering over his existence. If she was being *really* honest, most of the reason she'd majored in paleontology was the dreams. When your head was filled with a certain gorgeous caveman, it kind of sparked your interest in the past. But, above and beyond her obsession with Rhawn, she'd fallen in love with sabretooth cats. They were her unicorns. Magical, perfect beings that she'd spent all of grad school fantasizing about. They fascinated her.

To see one alive... it was more than she'd ever imagined.

The cat stared at her, like he understood that she was trying to help. Maybe he did. They were social animals. She was sure of that. In fact, it had been the entire premise of her thesis.

Fossils showed some cats had survived with crushed bones and crippling injuries. It would have required months to heal many of their wounds, months where they couldn't have hunted on their own. But somehow the cats recovered and lived for many more years. Lucy believed that it would only have been possible if other cats nursed them back to health. Like modern lions, they probably lived in prides.

This sabretooth was used to having someone care if he was in trouble. Used to giving and receiving assistance. It was so clear to her. If only she had more time, she could've proven her thesis was right.

Hopefully if any of his feline buddies *were* watching from the forest, though, they would also understand that she was just lending a hand, because those teeth weren't just for decoration. They were for ripping out the insides of anyone who got in their way.

Lucy jolted at the sound of leaves rustling. She looked around, her heart pounding.

Other kinds of man-eaters were probably out there, too. Animals stuck in the tar always drew the attention of carnivores. Then the predators often got stuck themselves, trying to devour some incapacitated creature. The La Brea tar pits back in LA had hundreds and hundreds of fossils, almost all of them from carnivores looking for an easy meal. If she recalled correctly, dire wolves were the most plentiful specimens on display. They hunted around the edges of the pits, looking to strike. Lucy had a soft spot for sabretooths, but studying those gigantic wolves freaked her out.

Crap, it was freaking her out just *thinking* about them.

The cat's golden gaze locked on hers like he knew she was worried. Like he wanted to reassure her. Lucy found herself relaxing, hypnotized by the intelligence and beauty of this animal. For an endless moment, they stared straight into each other's souls. It was magical.

The gunshot sounded like an explosion.

Lucy jumped a foot in the air, a horrified cry leaving her throat as the sabretooth collapsed sideways in a lifeless heap. He had been shot in the head! Fucking *shot*! Blood poured from the wound, his magnificent body sinking deeper into the tar. Someone had just killed her unicorn.

Her head slowly turned to gape at the murderer.

Craig Turkana, Woodward High's resident drug dealing scumbag, stood there with rubber flip-flops on his feet and a scary looking gun in his hand. The ominous black weapon stayed trained on the dead sabretooth.

"Where the hell have you been, Meadowcroft?" Craig demanded at a roar. "You think you could just leave me for fucking dead!?"

"You son of a *bitch*." Lucy advanced on him, even as the helper-cavemen went dashing off into the jungle. "How could you do that?!" She gave him a shove, too furious to even care about the gun. "Are you out of your *mind?* You just *slaughtered* that poor animal!"

"So what?" He bellowed back. He was still wearing cargo shorts and that classy "Fuck the World" t-shirt, but he didn't seem to notice the cold. Opiates must've kept him warm. "I've been lost in the goddamn rainforest for days. I'm hungry and tired and all my cigarettes were drowned at sea!" He pushed her back and Lucy nearly fell. "And instead of coming to rescue *me*, you're wasting your time on some mangy lion?!"

"It was a sabretooth cat, you asshole!"

"I don't give a rat's ass if it was Tony the Tiger! I want off this rock and you're the only one here smart enough to make it happen. So concentrate on Swiss Family Robinson-ing our way back to civilization *or I will shoot you in the fucking brain!*" He waved the gun in her direction, his eyes glazed with anger and fear and some kind of drug.

Wait a minute...

"You brought a revolver to the class reunion?" Lucy shouted, realization dawning on her. "Why? How did you even get it on the ship, you psycho?"

"It's a *Glock*, not a revolver." He mocked. "And I bought it for protection, which I *obviously* needed since you've stuck me in that fucking Tom Hanks movie with the volley ball!"

"You are seriously deranged. What did *I* do except warn your worthless ass to get up on deck?" She glowered up at him. "But –hey!– with 20/20 hindsight, I'd definitely leave you to sink, now."

"You snotty little bitch. You think I won't kill you? *Huh?*"

"I think you've sucked at everything you've tried, so the odds are certainly in my favor. You haven't accomplished one damn thing in your whole damn life!"

That just made him angrier. "Bullshit! I'm the only person in the whole class who ended up a success! I'm the biggest fucking dealer in Fort Wayne, Indiana! I'm Walter frigging White, meets Gordon goddamn Gekko! I'm a *business man*, bitch!" He smirked. "Not too bad for someone who got expelled two weeks before graduation, thanks to you."

"Thanks to *me?*"

"Yeah, it's *your* fault I got kicked out! *You* were the one who ratted me out for the library fire, senior year. Then you called me a loser, as the principal dragged me away."

"You *are* a loser!"

"*Shut up!*" He jabbed the gun at her. "You tried to wreck my life. You think any colleges were going to let me in with *arson* on my permanent record? I wanted to be a photographer, but you screwed up everything for me!"

"If you want to be a photographer, you'd buy a camera not meth."

He ignored that inconvenient use of logic. "Do you have any idea what it's like to get turned down by fifty-six different art schools? *Fifty-six!* I was supposed to be nailing models, and taking pictures on the covers of magazines, and saying something that people would *listen to!*"

"Maybe they would listen better if you weren't pointing guns at them."

He shook his head. "*You* are the reason my life ran off the rails. Sure, I've fucked up since then. Got stupid and got arrested and, that one time, I sold my kidney to that rich guy in Toledo."

"Eww."

He kept ranting, ignoring her appalled face. "But, I don't deserve to get eaten by velociraptors. No *way!* I don't deserve that!"

"Dinosaurs didn't live in the Ice Age, genius." Why was she the only one who knew that? Did everyone else sleep through science class?

"In the end, I *made* something out of myself." Craig continued. "I got into fencing gems. Got into selling dope. Got into the *bigtime*. That's why I showed up at this dumbfuck reunion. To tell you you were *wrong* about me, Meadowcroft." He spread his arm out "ta-da" style. "I'm *not* a loser, after all."

For a girl who spent four years being the weird loner in the back of the cafeteria, she sure was the epicenter of a lot of idiots' high school memories. Why did everyone always think she was so damn special? Lucy totally didn't understand it, but it pissed her off. "Of *course* you're a loser!" She bellowed. "You sell your kidneys for drug money! How is that being a successful human being?"

That was *not* what Craig wanted to hear. "I had two of them, didn't I?!" He took a menacing step forward. "Besides, it's *your* fault that…"

"Lucy!" Rhawn raced into the clearing. "Are you alright?" He didn't wait for her to answer that. Brown eyes went from the dead cat, to Lucy's enraged face, to Craig's gun, quickly piecing events together. The caveman wasn't Mary Ann or Ginger. He was the damn Professor. She saw him calculating odds and angles.

Amazingly, that made her feel better. With Rhawn there, she knew she was safe. *Nobody* was as smart as Rhawn. He was going to get them out of this mess. Lucy took an unconscious step towards him. Rhawn reached over, grabbing hold of her arm and tugging her closer.

"Who the hell is this?" Craig demanded.

Rhawn must have recognized the Glock as a weapon, because he very deliberately placed himself between the muzzle and Lucy. His gaze stayed on Craig. "I am Rhawn, Lucy's mate. Who are you?"

"He's Craig Turkana." She told him, ignoring the "mate" part. Over the last couple of days she'd stopped correcting him on that. Not that she was *accepting* it exactly, but it didn't sound quite so weird anymore. "He's from my world and he's a murdering dickhead."

"Eat me." Craig told her. He looked Rhawn up and down. "What does this guy mean, he's your mate? You fucking these cavemen guys? Getting on their good side?" He snorted. "Shit, I didn't think you had it in you, Meadowcroft. I should've known the smartest kid in school would do what she needed to do in order to survive."

Rhawn's jaw ticked.

"You know she's a bitch, right?" Craig glanced over at

Rhawn. "I mean, you must have noticed that she thinks she's better than everybody else."

"She *is* better." Rhawn said softly.

Lucy winced a bit. That "goddess" lie weighed heavier all the time. "Rhawn, I'm really not..."

Craig talked right over her. "I *know* she's better. But she doesn't have to act so stuck up about it. And she didn't have to call me a loser, man! That fucking *hurt*. And she got me kicked out of school and..."

"Nobody *cares*, Craig!" Lucy interrupted. "Jesus, I'm sorry I called you a loser fifteen years ago, okay? Get over it. I'm sick of hearing how high school is still ruling everyone's life. We have bigger problems. If any of us are going to survive, we need to get *off* this island."

"How? I saw the end of fucking *Lost*, man. I didn't understand it, but I saw it. I think we're all –like– dead or some shit."

"We have boats. Put the gun down and we'll let you on one of them."

He squinted. "You've got the Neanderthals building *boats?*"

"We don't have much of a choice. This is an island and that volcano is going to explode. I don't want to be here when that happens. Do you?"

"I don't want to be here, at all. I want to get back to fucking *America.*"

"Well that's obviously not going to happen if we stay put. Movement is life." She either heard that in a self-defense seminar or a Brad Pitt movie. She couldn't remember which. "We're building boats for everyone to evacuate and we'll make sure you have a seat, if you give me the gun. Do we have a deal?"

Rhawn didn't look happy about that idea. "This man will not come with us, Lucy. We clearly cannot trust him."

"Do you have a better idea?"

"*Yes.*" His tone left her in no doubt that his idea involved Craig's body disappearing into the tar pits.

"We can't kill Craig!" She hissed back.

"Why not?"

"It's illegal for one thing."

He snorted at that. "No, it isn't. Our laws do not allow for dangerous men to threaten our mates without repercussions. I am well within my rights."

Craig seized onto the one part of Rhawn's complains that he'd overheard. "That's right. I *am* dangerous." He sucked on his teeth, his eyes going crafty. "Now, you're bright about most things, Meadowcroft. But you know shit-all about people. You think I'm going to just fall in line with your plans, like you're the Mother of fucking Dragons?" He waggled the revolver at her. "With the gun, I can just take *your* boats."

"And go where?" Lucy arched a brow. "Any idea which direction to sail?"

"I'll figure it out, with –like– astrology."

"Astrology? How is it going to help you to know if you're a Capricorn or a Libra?"

"I'm a fucking Taurus." Craig snapped, looking annoyed. His eyes flicked down to the sparkly necklace for a beat and it seemed to distract him. He frowned and shook his head, like he was trying to focus, again. "Fine. Whatever the hell you call it to drive around using the stars, then. As*tron*omy. *That's* what I'm gonna do."

"Sure." Lucy pointed upward. "Remind me again: Which of the moons should you navigate by, Magellan?"

Craig looked up, apparently noticing for the first time that there were two bright orbs in the nighttime sky. When you were high, you didn't pick up on a lot of details. "Holy *shit*." His jaw dropped. "What happened to the moon? *What did you do to the moon?!*"

"It wasn't me, you idiot. The sky looks different because we're not on Earth anymore."

Rhawn's hand came up, keeping her behind him. His eyes stayed on Craig.

Craig was lost in his chemical-induced mania, convinced that Lucy was to blame for everything that had ever happened to him. "You did something to send us here, then!

The last thing I remember before we sank was *you*, somehow knowing it was going to happen!" He pointed the gun at her. "If I get rid of you, maybe all this goes away!"

Lucy felt her heart racing. "You can't be serious. Not even you are paranoid enough to shoot me for..."

Craig started firing.

Chapter Eleven

"I'm thinking of getting a dog." Lucy says conversationally, brushing a hand through the caveman's thick, tawny hair. "Like a cute little one."

"A little dog?" He seems puzzled. "No. You should get a large one. Then there is more meat on it for cooking."

Lucy stares at him for a beat. "...So I take it you're more of a cat person, then."

Rhawn and Lucy's Dream- Five Years Ago.

Lucy instinctively ducked to the side, narrowly avoiding getting shot in the brain. The bullet impacted one of the mutant trees, the sound like a thunderclap. How the hell was that damn thing even working, after it had been dunked in the sea? Craig must have kept it and his precious dope sealed up in plastic or something. Before she had time to figure it out, Rhawn was shoving her to the ground.

"Stay down!"

Lucy landed on her backside, cringing as more gunshots exploded. "Rhawn!" She shouted in panic. The lunatic was headed *towards* Craig, rather than away. "Don't go near him! He's going to..."

Her frantic warning was cut off mid-word, as it became clear Rhawn didn't need it. One huge palm locked around Craig's hand, forcing the gun into the air through brute strength. Craig futilely struggled for control, but it was like fighting against the Terminator. Rhawn was bigger, stronger and he wasn't going to stop.

Lucy's eyebrows climbed in amazement.

"*Shit!*" Craig shrieked. "You're gonna break my wrist!"

Rhawn ignored that. His other fist hammered out, slamming into Craig's jaw. Lucy flinched, pretty sure she'd just heard some teeth being pulverized. Clearly, the caveman wasn't going to solve this using his superior brainpower. Craig ended up flat on his back, crying. He was literally *crying*. The whole fight took about three seconds and Rhawn made it look so damn simple that Lucy could only blink. She couldn't believe it had been that easy.

Neither could Rhawn.

Three seconds wasn't enough time for him to adequately work out his frustrations. Cursing in caveman-ese, Rhawn tossed the gun aside and hauled Craig back up to hit him again. "You threaten *my* woman?!" He roared. "You try to take her from me?! *I should throw you in the pits to die!*"

"It wasn't my fault!" Craig screeched. "She started it!"

By this point, other members of the Clan had shown up, drawn by the unfamiliar sound of gunshots. They stood around in a loose circle, not one of them doing a damn thing to stop the show. Nobody knew exactly what was going on, but they were ready to be entertained by the bloodshed.

God, Lucy didn't care what Rhawn said about their wonderfulness. Most of the time, her "followers" were completely unhelpful.

In fact, *all* of the time.

"Awesome! Someone should have beat the piss outta Craig years ago." Warren said cheerfully, coming up beside her. He looked pretty good, considering he'd been on a bender for days. His hair wasn't oiled down and his face looked younger, like he was happy about something. This place was actually good for him. "Hell, maybe I like your boyfriend, after all, Moose-y."

Lucy flashed him a distracted glare, staggering to her feet. "Aren't you supposed to be out cold someplace?" She hurried over to grab the gun off the ground before somebody else got it. Aside from Rhawn, there was no one around here she trusted with a weapon.

"Hey, you're just lucky I didn't use my green belt on you earlier." Warren retorted with a snort. "I *do* know karate, ya know?"

She barely resisted the urge to shoot him.

"Warren?" Taffi came strolling over, like they were all

meeting up for cocktails. She even had her hair fixed in a jaunty braid high on her head. "Don't tell me you're finally out of that cave."

"No, I'm still in there. I'm just a fucking mirage, right now." Warren snapped back, in possibly his wittiest remark ever.

Taffi sniffed, unimpressed. "Well, as you can see, Lucy and her missing link boy-toy have been screwing things up royally, while you were plastered. As usual, it's up to *me* to lead the way. No wonder I was vice-president of the class and not you." She gave Skoll a careless wave from across the clearing. "Luckily, I'm totally winning over the savages. They believe I'm a god or something."

"Yeah, that's kinda common around here." Warren agreed sourly. "It's a way worse job then it seems at first, though. Trust me. People throw rocks at you."

"Oh, don't be such a whiner. I know what I'm doing."

Lucy seriously doubted that. "Skoll is a psycho, Taffi." She warned, distractedly. Damn it, Rhawn had better not hurt himself fighting. "You should stay away from him."

Taffi's eyes took on an angry glow. "Why? So *you* can be the one to save the day? So *you* can get the credit?" She shook her head. "Oh no... You're not taking *this* from me, too, Lucy! First it was my prom dress and now it's the spotlight. Well, *you* might have given up on getting us home, but I haven't! I'm going to figure out a way to save us all and then I'll finally be the star!"

Warren blinked over at Lucy. "You've given up on getting us home? Hang on... we're stuck here *forever?*" For some reason, he didn't look too broken up about that idea. In fact, he started to grin. "That's fucking *tremendous!* My ex-wives are going to be *so pissed* about losing their alimony checks." He chortled with glee.

"No!" Taffi raged. "*I'm* getting us home! Aren't you listening?"

"Oh be real, Taff." Warren rolled his eyes. "If Lucy can't do it, then *you* sure as hell can't. Face it, we're stuck in

Jurassic Park."

"Dinosaurs didn't live during the Ice Age." Lucy interjected automatically. She got *so* sick of telling people that.

Taffi's collagen plumped lips flattened into a thin line, ignoring her. "This place is *my* second chance. *My* do-over. This time, Lucy's not the special snowflake. *I* am."

"I was *never* the special snowflake, Taffi. I never did *anything*, except score high on a couple of standardized tests. And really? I think that fucked up my whole life, because of the unrealistic expectations that got heaped on me. In real life, I haven't done anything extraordinary."

"No kidding!" Taffi shouted. "But you're *still* the one everyone asked about, when I sent them invitations to the reunion. 'How's Lucy doing?' 'What kind of amazing job does Lucy have?,' 'Is Lucy off changing the world someplace?' Teddy O'Connell even wanted your phone number and *I* was the one who gave him a hand-job at graduation!"

Lucy rolled her eyes. "Just stay out of my way, while I go help Rhawn, okay? I'll listen to your oversharing later."

"Since Craig is the one crying, I don't think Rhawn needs any help." Warren said casually. "I think he'd want you to stay outta it."

He was probably right, but that didn't do a lot to make her feel better. To his credit, Craig *was* trying to fight back, even through his tears. Somehow he broke free of Rhawn's hold and slithered forward, heading for a rock to use as a weapon. He didn't get far. Rhawn grabbed him by the back of the neck and lifted him right off the ground. The rest of the Clan cheered enthusiastically.

Lucy flinched. "Rhawn, please be careful!" She spared Warren a quick glance. "You see? He's going to strain his back doing that." She held up a palm to shield her eyes, as the caveman tossed Craig into a prickly-looking purple bush. "God, I can't watch this." Rhawn was following her wishes and not killing Craig, but there was still way too much violence for her liking.

"Just give Rhawn a second to work through some stuff." Warren soothed. "It's a perfectly natural guy thing. I

wail on people all the time at karate. Relieves stress, ya know?"
Meanwhile, his attention kept flicking over to Skoll. "Hey, do
you think that dude is better looking than me?" He asked
suddenly.

"Yes." Taffi said without even checking to see who he
was pointing at.

Warren made a face. "Well, I think Skoll's a dickhead."
He grumbled. "He wants to date Anniah or something."

"Who's Anniah?" Taffi asked without much interest.
"That girl who looks like Twiggy?" She clearly wasn't worried
about competition for Skoll's fair hand. In her own mind, Taffi
would always be the head cheerleader who all the boys wanted
to ask to prom.

Lucy ignored her narcissism. "Warren, this isn't high
school." She reported although no one else seemed to have
noticed that. Lecturing him provided a welcomed distraction
from the bloodshed, so she gave it a shot. "If you encourage
Anniah's crush on you, there will be *real* repercussions. You get
that, right?"

"Well *you're* the one who gave me to her."

"I didn't 'give' you to her. I just said she could have
you, if she wanted."

"How is that not giving me to her?"

Lucy had no idea, but she wasn't going to admit that.
"Just shut up and listen, okay? I want you to think about what
you want. Skoll could smash you into little pieces without even
trying and he's totally *going* to, if you date that girl." For
whatever reason, Lucy didn't want this idiot dead. Warren was
an annoying pest, but he was *her* annoying pest. "I like Anniah,
but use your head! You couldn't even beat *me* in a fight."

He brightened, missing the point. "Hey wait... Did you
say Anniah has a crush on me? Why? What did she say? Tell
me *exactly*."

Apparently, she was wrong. It *was* high school. Lucy
sighed. "She keeps saying you're her 'vando.' I think that
means she likes you. That's really not the point, though..."

"It *clearly* means, 'I love him' or 'I love you' or 'I love *whoever.*'" Taffi interjected importantly. "They don't really use verb conjugations around here, so you have to use context to get an exact translation."

Lucy and Warren glanced at her in surprise.

"What? I double-majored in French and Mandarin. Languages are –like– my thing. I can figure out what these brutes are grunting about, if I pay attention." Taffi was happy to have the attention back on her and she wasn't letting it go. "So, is that *Craig* your orangutan of a lover is pounding?" She asked Lucy, even though she already knew who it was. It wasn't like there were a lot of people running around the jungle in "Fuck the World" t-shirts. "God, they will just let *anyone* onto this island, won't they?" She shot Lucy a pointed look, making sure to include her in the insult.

Lucy didn't give a damn. Her mind was whirling.

Holy *shit*. All the times he'd said *vando*, had Rhawn been telling her he *loved* her? He must have been saying it all along! Her mouth curved. Wow, that was...

Craig gave a sudden bellow of pain, drawing her attention back to the fight. Lucy winced as Rhawn broke Craig's nose and kept going. Craig was back to crying. Clearly, this wasn't going to wind down on its own.

Crap.

"You know what? Forget it. Both of you do what you want." Lucy waved aside Warren and Taffi's problems. Right now, all that mattered was Rhawn. "I've had it. Warren, help me break this up, will you?"

"Don't worry, Moose-y. Your boyfriend's got Craig on the ropes, for sure."

"I want him to *stop*, though!"

"Why? Craig's always been a dick."

Craig gave a choked sound of terror and lifted his arms to cover his face, trying to hide from Rhawn's wrath. It didn't work. Since no one else was going to be the adult here, Lucy would have to do it herself.

"Don't, caveman." She headed over, intent on saving Craig's life for Rhawn's sake.

"He *threatened* you, Lucy! He could have killed you

with that weapon!"

"I know, but I'm fine." She assured him, even as her eyes went down to the gun in her hand. Just looking at it had fear coursing through her system. She could've been killed. *Rhawn* could've been killed. Really, that possibility frightened her even more. Either way, she was fine with Craig getting beat up, as payback. She wasn't about to let Rhawn do something he'd regret, though. "Come on, you won. Now let him go. This isn't who you are. We'll just…"

Lucy stopped mid-word, cut off by a bloodcurdling, horror-movie-sound-effect howl. The eerie notes of it played over her spinal cord and stopping her heart. She instantly realized what animal had made the sound.

Damn it, she'd *known* the tar pits would attract the dire wolves.

"What the hell was *that?*" Warren demanded.

Rhawn was already moving. He dropped Craig in a heap, focused on the new threat. "Lucy, do not move." He caught hold of her arm, dragging her behind him. "Understand? *Stay still.*"

Easier said than done.

She looked around desperately trying to spot the damn things. It wasn't hard. Dire wolves were bigger than modern wolves and modern wolves were already scary big, so it was terrifyingly simple to see the monstrous beasts coming towards her. There were four of them, their gray fur matted and their teeth bared.

"Oh *shit.*" She whispered and then they attacked.

Taffi let out an ear-piercing shriek as the pack charged into the clearing. "*Help!*" She grabbed onto Warren, violently shaking him like it might rattle loose some heretofore unknown heroism. "Werewolves! There are *werewolves* here! Do something! *Do something!*"

Warren rallied himself and quickly did something.

…He grabbed onto Lucy and shook her arm. "Do something!" He shouted.

Lucy was too busy *not moving* to respond to that

idiocy. All around her, it was pure pandemonium.

The pack was half-starved. They weren't backing away from an opportunity to eat, even if it meant attacking humans. Skoll, Tammoh, and some of the other men clambered up into the closest palmy-pine tree, pulling others up behind them. Craig dragged himself into a sitting position, trying to figure out what was going on. Then he saw the wolves and started crying, again. A few Clan members tried to race back to camp, but that just drew the animals' attention.

Lucy cringed as the wolves gave chase. One of them wrestled a Clan member to the ground, its teeth flashing. "Oh *God*."

Rhawn's arms swept back, making sure she stayed behind him. "They follow the movement." He reiterated. "It's how they hunt. Just like the long-tooths. Do not run and do *not* watch."

She nodded, burying her face in Rhawn's back so she wouldn't have to see the blood. Too bad she couldn't block out the screams as easily.

"I'm not running." Warren sounded like he was hyperventilating. "You see how I'm not running? I learned from that tiger chasing me, ya know? I'm just going to do whatever you say and you're going to get us out of this, right Rhawn?"

"Correct." Rhawn turned his head, gauging the distance to the tree line. "Now, we must *very slowly* move towards the forest. Whatever you do, don't run or..."

Taffi took off running.

"*Shit!*" Warren and Lucy chorused.

Rhawn rolled his eyes in disgust.

The prom queen tore off towards Skoll's tree, waving her arms. "Help, help, help, *help!*" She barreled right past Notan, inadvertently kicking his walking stick. The old man fell, his bad leg twisting under him. The Clan let out a collective gasp of horror as the biggest wolf moved in on him.

Anniah screamed and tried to reach her father.

"Fuck!" Warren let go of Lucy and chased after her. For once, he was the one to make an interception on the field.

He grabbed Anniah as she rushed by. "Stop!" He pulled her against him, trying to keep her still. "You can't do anything, damn it! Do you think he wants you dead, too?"

She tried to push him away, sobbing out frantic words in the Clan's language.

Lucy had no clue what she was saying, but it didn't much matter. Warren was actually right and Warren was *never* right. But there was nothing the girl could do except get herself eaten, too. "Anniah listen to him!" She shouted.

Warren held Anniah tightly, making soothing sounds to quiet her. It was undoubtedly the first time Warren had ever tried to help anyone. And it worked. Anniah collapsed against him, sobbing.

Warren look surprised for a beat, like he hadn't expected her to need his comfort. No one had ever leaned on Warren for anything, because he was always so damn useless. This island had a way of giving you second chances, though. Turning you into who you were always supposed to be. It was a place for do-overs.

Warren lifted Anniah right off the ground, cradling her against his chest. Amazingly, she let him. He looked overwhelmed and a little scared, but also pleased with himself. Like he'd done something he was proud of and he wasn't used to the feeling. Anniah's arms wrapped around his neck and – weirdly– it actually seemed like they... fit.

In the tree, Skoll's eyebrows slammed together in fury.

Rhawn ignored the brewing love triangle. "Lucy, stay here." He started forward, like he might be about to somehow get Notan to safety.

Oh *hell* no.

Rhawn was *not* going to die to protect that preachy octogenarian. She was going to have to stop this before he got himself killed being a hero.

Lucy grabbed onto Rhawn's arm, keeping him still. With the other hand, she raised Craig's gun and fired it up in the air. The report echoed across the island. Cavemen and wolves all jolted in unison turning towards her. It was the closest any of them had ever been to such a loud sound and it caught them all off guard.

The wolf stopped his attack on Notan, his eyes fixing on Lucy. Leaving the old man, he edged towards the new threat.

Okay... this had maybe not been her best idea.

"Can you kill the beast with that weapon?" Rhawn whispered fiercely.

Lucy swallowed hard. "I told you, I'm a *vegetarian*. I'm not going to shoot an animal, unless I have no other choice."

He flashed her an incredulous look over his shoulder. "You have no other choice, Lucy!" He roared.

"Just let me think!"

"Give the weapon to me and *I* will do it!"

"Give him the gun!" Warren bellowed, shifting so his body was between the wolf and Anniah. "Give him the fucking gun!"

Lucy disregarded that, her attention focused on the wolf. Clearly, he was the pack leader and he still wasn't fully convinced he couldn't take her in a fight. She needed to find a way to scare him off. If she did, the others would leave, too.

The wolf's ears went back and he snarled low in his throat, testing her.

Lucy fired again, this time much closer to him. She'd never fired a handgun before, but she had played a hell of a lot of video games. She knew how to aim. The bullet whizzed past his head and he stopped his advance. His icy blue gaze locked on Lucy.

She stared back. For a long beat of time, neither of them moved. No one in the glen even breathed, for fear of triggering another attack

...And then the wolf backed away.

One step. Then two. With a final snarl, he turned and finally loped off. Frightened by the gun, all the wolves followed their leader and disappeared back into the forest.

Lucy released a breath that she wasn't even aware she'd been holding. "Jesus." Her knees couldn't support her, so she steadied herself on Rhawn's shoulder. "Paleontology is so much more stressful outside of books."

The Clan was gaping at her with something like awe. Even Warren looked impressed. The only ones not amazed at her awesomeness were Skoll and Taffi and who really cared about them? For once, Lucy felt pretty damn cool. As soon as she stopped being sick with panic, she might even exchange some high-fives. Well, first she'd have to teach cavemen *how* to high-five, but whatever.

Anniah scrambled free of Warren and rushed over to hug Lucy in gratitude. ...Which was awkward, considering she was topless and all. See? The exact sort of situation where a high-five would work better. Lucy gave her back a "you're welcome" sort of pat and nudged her back towards Warren. Let him be useful for once.

Notan got to his feet and began sputtering something to Rhawn, gesturing to Lucy with an astonished expression on his face. Lucy figured the rough translation was probably something like, "Why did that evil bitch just save me?"

Rhawn snapped something back at him and everyone gasped. All eyes went to Lucy and she could see their surprise. Notan fell to his knees, praying up at the sky again. So did several others. The big, ugly twin guys, Ugghot and Uyhot, hugged each other, crying with something like gratitude.

Lucy's eyebrows soared. Whatever the hell was going on, it was clearly a big deal. She would've asked Rhawn about it, but he didn't seem like he wanted to share. In fact, he didn't even pay attention to the Clan's newest weirdness. All his focus was centered on her.

"Do *not* do that again." He commanded, spinning around to face her.

"Do what? *You* were the one being a maniac and trying to get yourself torn apart by wolves! If anyone should be pissed off, it should be me." What would she do if anything happened to Rhawn? This guy was her whole world.

Unfortunately, Lucy's "whole world" wasn't listening to her perfectly logical complaints. "You should *not* have come back here to free the long-tooth. You should *not* have antagonized a large, angry male. You should *not* have left the beach without telling me. You should *not* have challenged a pack of hungry animals." He seized hold of her arm, dragging her against his chest. "You should *not* put yourself in danger. I cannot bear it, Lucy. I cannot bear it." Then his mouth was slamming down onto hers.

Lucy's toes curled inside her high-tops, her lips opening under his plundering kiss. *Wow.* She might have showed this guy the basics, but he'd taken kissing to another whole level of awesome. Nobody could kiss like Rhawn. It was like being blasted with heat and urgency and desire. Lucy couldn't even think. All she could do was want him.

Rhawn suddenly lifted his head, ignoring her sound of protest. "And you will no longer be a vegetarian." He decided. "It is too fraught with risk."

She smiled at how damn cute he was. "Thank you for protecting me from Craig and the wolves." She said instead of telling him he was adorable. He probably wouldn't appreciate it. She reached up to touch his face. "Ten points for you, caveman."

For once, winning points didn't distract him. Rhawn tilted his face to kiss the inside of her palm. "I will *always* protect you. You are my mate. It's my right and duty." He arched a brow. "But I do not think you *needed* much assistance. You are *so* powerful, Lucy."

She winced, still feeling guilty over the whole "goddess" lie. "That wasn't me being powerful. It was me having the only machine in the garden." She gestured to the gun.

Rhawn shook his head. "The weapon was just a tool. The bravery came from *you*. The heart and honor that you have. *That* is the power."

Lucy stared up at him for a long moment, overwhelmed. That was the nicest thing anyone had ever said to her. "I'm still thinking about Choosing you." She blurted out a little frantically. Examining her feelings would be a disaster. If she discovered what she *thought* she was going to discover, her whole life was going to change. Maybe it *had* already changed.

     Shit.

     What the hell was she going to do?

     Rhawn arched a brow. "Think faster." He said simply.

     Notan came limping over, his palm outstretched to Lucy. He was talking a mile a minute and making praying motions with his hands. It immediately made her nervous. Now what was he up to?

     "This is new and unsettling." She looked up at Rhawn with a frown. "Why's Mr. Burns being so friendly, all of a sudden?"

     "Notan is thanking you."

     "Why? I'm the Destroyer. He probably thinks I commanded the wolves to attack in the first place, using my evil Jedi mind tricks."

     Rhawn's mouth curved. "He no longer believes you are the Destroyer. I have told him the truth."

     "The truth?" That didn't sound good, considering how many lies she'd told lately. "What truth?

     "That you are the Savior, of course."

Chapter Twelve

She makes a soft noise that has his teeth grinding together. He has her pinned beneath him, her hands stretched over her head and his mouth on her breasts. The woman tries to move wanting him to go faster, but he's not releasing her wrists.

Rhawn lifts his head, as she tugs against his grip. As usual, he doesn't want her to see his eyes and be repelled, but he can't give her a chance to get away. "Not yet."

She doesn't want to wait. "Just hurry. Please."

He slowly shakes his head. "Again." He says and switches to the other breast.

Her pupils dilate at the rough word and the feel of his lips on her skin. The pulse in her neck speeds up. "Again." She agrees with a languid sigh.

Rhawn and Lucy's Dream- Four Years Ago

"She's not the Savior!" Skoll shouted.

The Clan was gathered back in the main cave, waiting to hear what Notan had to say about the revelation of who Lucy truly was. Most people accepted the idea with visible relief. If Lucy was the Savior, it meant that their belief system was still intact. It helped everyone to rationalize their actions in building the *ragan* and look to the future with ever-growing hope.

The Savior had a plan to save them.

It was just as the legends predicted. Really, news that the Savior had actually won the *Ardin* was a time for rejoicing. Even Notan was jubilant. In fact, the only two people appalled by the idea were Skoll and Taffi.

Well... and Lucy herself.

"He's right. I'm not the Savior." She whispered fiercely. "Rhawn, you need to tell them I'm not the Savior, before this goes too far."

He shot her a confused look. "But you *are* the Savior." It was astonishing that he hadn't known it from the first. This woman wasn't evil. Wasn't trying to end the world. Just the opposite. She'd been sent to save them. He saw it all so clearly now. "Lucy, you are the one we've been waiting for."

"This is ridiculous!" Taffi threw up her hands. "Shouldn't we –like– vote on who gets to be Savior? Because, I sure don't vote for Lucy. I vote for *me*."

Rhawn ignored that. So did everyone else.

"Just think about this for a second." Lucy persisted, her gaze on Rhawn. "If I'm the Savior, then that would make Warren the Destroyer, right? Does that dumbass seem like an evil genius to you?" She waved a hand at the boy, who was presently staring at Anniah with limpid eyes.

Rhawn shrugged. "No, he does not seem like a Destroyer... but he seems even *less* like a Savior." He hesitated. "Besides, he is not the only one who could be the Destroyer." His eyes went over to Craig and he switched back to the Clan's language. "This god is dangerous. He killed a long-tooth without cause and tried to harm Lucy. I believe the legends of the *Ardin* became confused as the cycles past. Lucy is the Savior, which means the Destroyer could be a male."

"It is not Warr-en." Anniah put in swiftly.

Skoll glowered over at her. He was nearly as furious at Warren as he was with Lucy. "That spineless creature you are so taken with is not man enough to be the Destroyer." He scoffed. "We all know that, Anniah."

"Warr-en has greatness in him." Anniah shot back. "I see it, because I am not as blind as you."

Warren looked between them with a concerned frown, understanding his name and not much else. "What's going on?" He glanced over at Rhawn. "Is that asshole threatening her?"

"No. He's telling her you are a weakling." Rhawn assured him distractedly and then switched back to the Clan's language. "I do not think Warr-en is the Destroyer, either." He said, returning to the point of this meeting. He gestured at Craig. "*This one* is the true Destroyer. He must be."

Not knowing what else to do with him, the Clan was

holding Craig prisoner while they debated his fate. He scowled at Rhawn, bamboo sticks on either side of his broken nose, keeping it straight. "I don't got a clue what you're saying, but I know it's all bullshit. Once I get out of here, I'll make you sorry for this, ya cave-douche. I know people at home who will kick your ass if I front them a couple grams of product."

Rhawn met his eyes. "You will *never* leave this island." He told him quietly. "So that will be a very difficult deal to strike."

Craig glowered at him with pure hatred.

"The Craig god must be the *Savior*." Skoll decided, pacing around in agitation. "That is why he tried to kill the Destroyer. He was attempting to strike Lucy down and win the *true Ardin*."

Rhawn rolled his eyes. "You believe *that* man is the Savior of our people?" He waved a disparaging hand in Craig's direction. "I would not trust him to lead us out of a cave, let alone across the Infinite Sea."

There was some chuckling throughout the Clan. Even Notan smiled.

"Besides, even if he *was* the Savior, the Craig god still lost the fight." Anniah pointed out smugly. "Rhawn made him cry. We all saw it. So Lucy would *still* have triumphed in the *Ardin* and she would *still* be in charge."

Skoll wasn't giving up. "*Rhawn* would have triumphed, not Lucy." He insisted.

"We are the same." Rhawn said flatly. "She is my mate. Her battles are mine to fight. Even if they are against small men and their magical weapons."

"Are they talking about me?" Craig demanded. "It seems like they're talking about me."

"They're not very impressed with your fighting skills." Taffi told him, her face intent as she tried to piece together the Clan's language. "But they still think you might be a god."

"A god?" Craig sat up straighter. "Really?"

"Oh, they think everyone's a god." Warren scoffed. "Don't let it go to your head."

Taffi laughed and it wasn't a pleasant sound. "What

would Craig even be the god of? Jewelry thieves and dope fiends?" She arched a brow. "I'm pretty sure he stole my high school ring and hocked it for weed. Did I ever tell you guys that?"

"Shut up, Lucy!" Craig snapped as if she was the one to accuse him.

Everyone else ignored Taffi's sniping.

Lucy kept her attention on Rhawn, looking concerned and a little guilty. "Rhawn, sweetie, I really need to talk to you about this whole 'goddess' thing. There's some stuff you need to know."

He nodded distractedly. "Whatever you wish to say, I wish to hear. *Later,* though. When Skoll is not trying to undermine your position as Savior."

"But he's right. I'm *not* the Savior."

"I have *no doubt* that Lucy is the Savior." Anniah continued, passionately. "At first, we were mistaken as to her identity as a test of our faith, just as my father said." That was indeed Notan's new theory and the majority of the Clan was convinced he was right. "But when she saved my father's life, I knew we had proven ourselves to her."

There was much nodding and congratulatory smiles among the Clan.

"And Lucy has made many positive changes, since she's been here." Anniah was always eager to talk about her idol's accomplishments. "She's allowed women to Choose, so we will not be stuck with cruel mates. She gives us hope for a world beyond this island and leads us in building the *ragan.* She's invented the wonderful game of *Pictionary.* She's protected us from..."

Skoll cut her off, in a rage that Anniah would stand against him. *"She's an evil bitch!"* He jabbed a finger at Lucy. "And she has no power to change the rules of the Choosing. I have Chosen you as my mate and you *will* submit."

Rhawn's eyes narrowed.

"I will never be with you, Skoll!" Anniah shouted back. "Lucy has given me Warr-en and her word is the law now. *He* is the one I Choose."

They both turned to look at Notan, like he might be the deciding factor.

The elderly man hesitated. His attachment to the old ways warred with his eagerness to please Lucy. In the end, it was most likely his desire to see his daughter mated to a god that swayed his final decision, though. What parent wouldn't want a deity for a son-in-law? "It would be most unwise not to heed the words of the Savior." He declared. "If she believes Warr-en and Anniah should be mated, who are we to question it?"

Anniah smiled smugly.

Skoll looked apoplectic.

"Wait." Taffi held up her hands. "Skoll, are you seriously trying to pick that skinny little teenager over *me?*" She glowered at Warren. "Would you do something about this please?"

"Do something?" He repeated blankly.

Unfortunately, the two words were all it took to catch Skoll's attention. A new idea seemed to pop into his head. "I contest the mating of Anniah and Warr-en!" He thundered, raising a hand over his head. "I will challenge him for her!"

Cheers erupted. The Clan was always eager to watch a fight. Skoll strode to the center of the cave ready for battle, while his friends pounded on his shoulders in encouragement.

Warren looked baffled as equally excited members of the Clan seized hold of him. "Hang on. What's happening?" He squawked in alarm, trying to resist the waves of arms pushing him forward.

"Oh shit." Lucy whispered and glanced up at Rhawn. "This is bad, isn't it?"

"It is bad."

Anniah bounded to her feet looking panicked. "Stop!"

"Skoll has challenged you for Anniah." Rhawn told Warren, unsure how to prevent the unfolding disaster.

"He's *what?*"

"He wishes her for his mate. I *told* you this."

"Well, he can't do that!" Warren protested. "Lucy

gave me to her."

Lucy pinched the bridge of her nose like she was developing a headache.

Rhawn hesitated, debating their best course of action. "It might be safest for you to renounce your claim on her." He reluctantly suggested.

Since Anniah didn't want Skoll, they would have to come up with a way to stop him from Choosing her, obviously. But, there was no sense in allowing Warren to die in the process. Lucy had grudging affection for the boy. Not to mention Anniah's inexplicable attachment to him. It would upset both of them to watch Warren get pounded into the cave floor and there was no *way* he'd ever defeat Skoll in combat.

Warren pointed at Skoll. "This asshole thinks he's going to –like– *marry* her or something! You want me to be okay with that?"

"I want you to live." In theory anyway. "Tell Skoll you will not seek to mate with Anniah and maybe you will survive this."

Anniah grabbed hold of Warren's arm, turning him to face her. "You must not fight Skoll." She cried, shaking her head. "I could not bear to see you hurt, Warr-en. I will go with him. Please."

Warren didn't need a translation of that. "No!" He thundered. "I'm not just handing you over to that 'roided up barbarian. I've never belonged to anybody before and I'm not giving that up! Besides, you don't even *like* him! What the fuck kind of man would I be if I let this happen?"

Rhawn nodded, because the boy had a point.

Anniah dissolved into sobs, seeing that he wouldn't back down from the challenge.

"Warren, that guy is twice your size and kills things on a daily basis." Lucy interjected, visibly distressed. "He's going to peel your skin off and eat it!"

"Rhawn," Anniah put in desperately, "do not let him do this!"

"Enough with the mewling of women!" Skoll cracked

his neck, preparing for battle. "The challenge begins now!"

"You back off!" Lucy warned him and moved forward, trying to shield Warren.

Rhawn sighed and moved in front of *her*. This would end in blood and he was going to ensure it wasn't his mate's. "Skoll, think about what you plan to do." He instructed in the Clan's language. "Warr-en is a god. He will use his powers against you and strike you down." Rhawn gave himself credit for delivering that warning with a straight face. He doubted it would work, though.

Skoll certainly wasn't buying it. "A *woman* beat him in combat!" He scoffed, waving at hand at Lucy. "You think I fear a god that pathetic?"

"Let's all just take a breath here, okay?" Lucy glanced back at Warren. "Just sit down." She hissed. "You know you can't possibly win this fight, so stop acting crazy."

"Lucy's right." Taffi called in a bored tone. "You've been a loser your whole life. It's like your fate or something."

"*I'm not a loser. Lucy!*" Craig screamed. The man did not seem to be working with all his facilities, blaming Lucy for Taffi's comments and somehow assuming they were about him. "Take it back. *Take it back!*" He lunged at Lucy, coming in from the side. His fingers clawed out, trying to catch hold of her throat.

Lucy jerked back in surprise.

Craig's grasping hands missed her neck and tangled in her necklace. One of the strands snapped, sending several shiny beads falling to the floor. Taffi absently scooped one up and examined it between her fingers, unconcerned about all the animosity swirling around her.

"Damn it, *now* look what you did, Craig!" Lucy started to shove him back, but Rhawn was already turning to grab him.

He lifted Craig right off the ground and threw him backwards into the cave wall. Craig impacted the rock with a sickening "crack" and crumpled to the floor in an unconscious heap. Rhawn made a frustrated face. The man passed out *a lot*. No doubt that was one of the reasons he was such a piss-poor fighter.

Lucy gave an exaggerated wince. "I think you just fractured his skull, sweetie."

"We can hope." Intent on finishing the bastard off once and for all, Rhawn stalked over to drag Craig to his feet again. At least, that was his *intention*. He'd only gotten to the "stalking" part when Skoll interrupted the plan by punching Warren.

Lucy and Anniah gave panicked cries.

The Clan cheered.

Why did these things always happen to Rhawn? He let out an irritated sigh. He should just kill all of the idiots in his life and be done with it.

Warren staggered and nearly fell, his hand on his bleeding nose. "*Shit*, man! Doesn't anybody around here give some warning before the fighting starts?"

"I will crush you like a *byggo* bug!" Skoll slapped his hands to illustrate his point, rubbing and twisting his palms together as if he was squashing Warren between them. "No one will take Anniah from me! Especially not a flaccid god like you."

Warren didn't need to know all those words to understand the universal message of "fuck you." His blue eyes narrowed. "Anniah, is *not* yours." He said in a more serious voice than Rhawn had ever heard him use. "She will *never* be yours. You want to challenge me for her? *Fine*. Bring it on, asshole." He spread his arms wide. "I will kick your blond ass right into the ocean."

"Warren..." Lucy began in a worried voice.

"No." He shot her a quick frown. "I'm fucking *doing this*." He looked over at Rhawn. "Just let me do it, alright? I don't think they'll let me keep her, if I can't do this. And I *know* I can do this, ya know?"

Rhawn nodded, understanding the need to defend your woman. "I know." Warren would lose, but he would fight anyway. It made him respect the scrawny man. "The first one to fall forfeits the challenge. That is how you must win. Do everything you can to knock Skoll down." He stepped back to give the combatants room.

Anniah and Lucy gaped at Rhawn like he was crazy for encouraging this. "Are you crazy?" They demanded in two different languages.

Rhawn gave an expansive shrug. "He wishes to prove himself to you." He told Anniah and then glanced at Lucy. "Do not worry. I will stop the fight before he gets hurt. Just allow him an opportunity to save face and to show Anniah that he is not completely useless..."

Rhawn didn't get a chance to finish that thought.

Warren swung his leg up in some kind of complicated kick. The blow caught Skoll right in the midsection and he stumbled backwards. His face wore an expression of pure astonishment as Warren delivered a strangely graceful punch to his jaw and then followed up with an impossible flipping maneuver that had Skoll landing on his back.

It was the fastest challenge win in the history of the Clan.

Warren stood over the Clan's greatest warrior, not even winded from his victory. For a long moment, the spectators were too amazed to even cheer. They just stood there, trying to process what they'd seen. Even Rhawn found himself blinking in confusion.

Maybe Warren actually *did* have supernatural powers. There just didn't seem to be another explanation.

"Oh for God's sake..." Taffi sounded disgusted. "That's it? That's the big showdown?"

Anniah's lips parted in wonder, her eyes going from Warren to Skoll and back again. A huge smile spread across her face. "Warr-en wins!" She cried in delight. "Warr-en wins the challenge!"

"How in the hell did he do that?" Rhawn demanded, still trying to process the impossible.

"Karate." Lucy gave a delighted laugh. "Warren has a green belt. Damn, that was *awesome*. High-five." She held up a palm and Warren turned to slap it in an odd celebration ritual. "Forget all those times I said I hated your guts. You just became my favorite classmate *ever*."

Warren grinned at her, looking proud of himself. "Yeah, I'm much better at martial arts than I was a football." His attention was already shifting to Anniah. Moving away from Lucy, he held a hand out to her. "And the cheerleaders are *way* hotter."

Anniah grabbed hold of his wrist and tugged him forward. "I knew there was greatness in you, Warr-en." She breathed and then her lips found his, trying her best to kiss him the way she'd seen Lucy kiss Rhawn.

Clearly, she was doing a good job. Warren lifted her off the ground, his mouth sealed over hers. The Clan started cheering again and chanting Warren's name. Rhawn found himself smiling.

"This is unfair!" Skoll finally regained his wits and scrambled to his feet. "Warr-en cheated! He used magic to defeat me! It was not a true victory!"

"Warr-en followed the rules of a challenge." Notan shook his head. "We all saw. Accept your defeat as the will of the gods."

"I will *never* accept this!" Skoll spat. "The rest of you might have been fooled by these outsiders, but I know better. They are not gods. They are not special. They are *nothing*. I will *never* follow them!"

"You will damn yourself with such blasphemy, Skoll." Tammoh warned and the rest of the Clan nodded in agreement.

"I am next in line for leader!" Skoll insisted, not relenting. "I have waited long enough for my turn as head of our Clan. I demand Notan stand down and allow me to rule, before his blind ways lead us all to ruin. Before *she* ruins us all!" He jabbed another finger at Lucy.

Dead silence filled the cave. No one seconded the idea of a change in leadership. No one moved to support Skoll. No one would side against Lucy. It was a crushing defeat for the old ways.

Rhawn felt his mouth curve.

Maybe he wouldn't need to kill Skoll, after all. It seemed as if the man no longer held any sway over the Clan.

They had switched their allegiance to Lucy and all her new ideas.

"You have made your choice!" Skoll shouted, seeing he was alone. "None of you are worthy of my leadership, anyway! I *abandon* this Clan. I make my own path in this world and it does not lead across the sea!" He went striding out of the cave and into the night.

Taffi hesitated for a beat and then moved to sit next to Craig's unconscious body, switching to a new team.

Warren snorted at Skoll's retreating back. "Dude, that guy is *such* a sore loser."

Chapter Thirteen

The woman sits astride him, fumbling to remove her strange garments.

Rhawn watches her struggle, amused when she gets tangled in the stretchy chest covering she wears. She curses in frustration and he laughs. Only she can create such feelings inside of him. It is a gift. She is *a gift.*

"Do not leave me." The stark demand comes straight from Rhawn's heart. If he can just remain here with her –keep her with him– everything will be alright. For the first time in his life, he would be welcomed. He knows that.

She is where he belongs.

She finally frees herself from her bizarre clothing and arches a brow. "Believe me, caveman, I hate waking up way *more than you do."*

How can she wake up? He is *the one dreaming. It makes no sense, but he doesn't have time to figure it out. He knows that she will slip away in a matter of seconds. Maybe one day, he'll just stay asleep forever and he can finally stay with her. Rhawn hopes so. Oh gods, please, let him just stay here with her...*

Rhawn and Lucy's Dream- Three Years Ago.

"I'm *not* the Savior."

Rhawn glanced up from his lobster to arch a brow at her. The two of them were back in his cave, eating dinner and arguing. Or rather *she'd* been arguing, while he sat there in calm and quiet certainty. The jackass was so sure he was right he wasn't even bothering to debate it.

It drove her crazy.

"I mean, do I look like a Savior to you?" For over an hour, they'd been going back and forth and he refused to see reason. Once Rhawn decided something, he wouldn't change his mind. Lucy wasn't sure how to get through to him. "Think about it! You're a genius, for God's sake!"

"I am smart enough to know the truth when I see it."

Rhawn said simply. "Can we be done with this soon? I still need to go kill Craig."

Lucy made an aggravated sound, plowing both hands through her hair. "I told you, we're *not* killing Craig. He's locked up in that bamboo cell and I've hidden the gun under a really big rock, so he's no longer a threat."

"The man is still alive, Lucy. He therefore remains a threat."

"Can you just concentrate on what's important, please? I'm trying to tell you something here and you just won't listen. I'm. Not. The. Savior." She spaced out each word for maximum effect. "Got it?"

Lucy had rarely been so on edge. The real problem wasn't even her new role as the Good Witch in the Clan's little *Wizard of Oz* fantasy. Now that she'd been cast as a White Hat, the others were all much happier. Even Notan was smiling. Getting the idiots on the boats would be a breeze. They couldn't *wait* to follow her to Shangri-La.

No, the problem was Rhawn.

The connection Lucy felt to the guy got deeper all the time and this "goddess" story was weighing on her conscience. She couldn't keep lying to him. Not if anything was ever going to be real between them.

She had to tell him the truth.

Lucy just hoped that he didn't hate her afterwards. God, what would she do without Rhawn? She woke up every day, wanting to talk to him and spend all day admiring his incredible body and genius-y way, and went to bed feeling safe, because he was watching over her. Even the thought of returning home depressed her. Without Rhawn, her life would be so *empty*. This couldn't be the end. Somehow, she had to come clean and make him forgive her.

Maybe it would be okay. Pretending to be a deity wasn't *so* big a lie, right?

Shit.

Lucy cleared her throat. "Look…. I've been wanting to talk to you about something," she began, searching for the right words, "and I don't think you're going to like it. Just hear me out before you freak, okay?"

Rhawn glanced at her through his lashes. "Okay." He said warily.

"Um... I haven't been completely honest with you." Lucy tried to find the right words, but there really *weren't* any. "I didn't really *start out* lying, it just sorta happened. When Skoll and the others found me, they made assumptions and I didn't correct them. It all just kinda snowballed, from there. I didn't..."

Rhawn cut her off. "Do you desire another?" He asked in a tense voice.

"What?" She frowned. "*No*. This has nothing to do with another man. Jesus, how can you even ask me that? There's nobody but you, Rhawn."

His big shoulders relaxed. "Then it does not matter to me what you've done." He decided with a relieved sigh. "Do not worry over it."

"Just remember you said that, because it's bad."

He gave a humoring nod. "I imagine it is. You are a difficult woman. But, I have accepted this. But, whatever troubles you, we can fix it."

"I don't think even you can fix this one." Lucy took a deep breath and finally said the words. "See... I'm not really a god."

Rhawn stared at her.

"I'm just an average person." Lucy insisted, when he didn't say anything. "Really, I don't know any magic spells or supernatural tricks. I'm not immortal or all-seeing. I have no idea what I'm even doing half the time. I'm not *anything* except Lucy Meadowcroft from New York."

Rhawn kept staring.

"And New York isn't divine, either." She pointed to the cave paintings. Some of them had been damaged in the quake, but most of the images were still visible. The blue whirlpool picture even seemed glowy-er somehow. "My homeland is just another island. We have more space and technology, but it's just like here. It's an average place and I'm an average girl and I am definitely –*definitely*– not the Savior of your people."

The words hung in the air for a beat.

Lucy braced herself for Rhawn's betrayed response. She deserved it. Not only had she lied to him, but she was screwing up his whole theology. He was going to be pissed. He might never forgive her or never want to see her again or…

"You *are* the Savior." He said quietly, interrupting her growing panic.

Lucy blinked. Hang on… *That* was his reply to her jaw-dropping, world-changing confession? Was he in some kind of denial? "Did you just hear what I said?" She sputtered.

"Of course."

"I'm just an average person." She reiterated, because he still wasn't getting it. "No Batmobile or utility belt or superpowers whatsoever."

"I knew you had no powers."

"And you're not fucking mad about it?!"

"It is probably for the best. If you could smite those who annoyed you, I suspect many of the Clan would've been subject to your terrible wrath by now. You have a temper, goddess, and many people here are irritating."

The man was unbelievable. "*I'm not a goddess, Rhawn.*"

He shrugged, colossally blasé in the truth. "You do not *think* you are. You are wrong. Who can say what a goddess is or is not?"

"*I* can! I'm telling you, I'm not the person you've been waiting for."

Finally, she had his attention. Fathomless brown eyes locked onto hers. They were so deep and beautiful that she couldn't have looked away, even if she'd wanted to. "You *are* the person I've been waiting for, Lucy." He corrected softly. "Even if you weren't the Savior, it would still be *you.*"

Lucy couldn't think of anything to say to that. Rhawn was the only one who'd ever been able to render her speechless. He said such beautiful things and she didn't deserve them. Didn't deserve him. "You're really not angry at me?" She finally got out.

"No."

"Why not? I lied to you."

"I think you lie to *yourself*."

Lucy swallowed hard, her mind racing. There was only one reason in the world why a brilliant man would be so blind to the truth. "Does 'vando' mean 'I love you'?" She blurted out.

Rhawn smiled at the question, like it amused him. "No."

"*No?*" Lucy scowled at Rhawn, hurt and annoyed. It had been stupid to get her hopes up based on stupid Taffi and her stupid translation skills. When had that girl ever been right about anything? "What the hell does it mean, then?"

"Lungs."

"*Lungs?* You've got to be fucking kidding me. All this time, you've been saying '*lungs*' to me and not 'I love you'?!"

"The words 'I love you' do not have a direct translation in the Clan's language. It is too... ephemeral for our culture. We are people of action."

Lucy stared at him for beat. "Fine." She muttered, even though it wasn't fine, at all. "You *shouldn't* love me, because I'm a mess! That was my whole point here. I'm not at all like you think I am, so..." She trailed off, growing more and more upset. "You really don't love me?" She demanded. "What the hell is wrong with you, huh? How can you not love me? We've been together for fifteen years!"

Rhawn arched a brow. "I said I did not have the *words* in my Clan's tongue, Lucy. That does not mean the emotion isn't in my heart. Of *course* I love you. I have loved you since the moment we met in the dreams. I loved you before I even knew you really existed. I loved you when I believed it would damn me. The love I feel for you is far deeper than any language could ever convey."

Lucy stared at him, speechless for a long moment. "Oh." She finally whispered.

"Why are you surprised at this? I have never hidden my feelings. I challenged a god for you, remember? Is that not a clear show of either insanity or love?" He smiled. "And I am not crazy."

"It's just… No one's ever said they loved me before." She finally whispered. "You're the only one I would ever *want* to say it to me, Rhawn."

Tenderness filled his gaze. "*Vando*, Lucy."

She was too agitated to ask why in the hell he was talking about lungs in such a gentle tone. Panic rushed in again, driving out the brief surge of euphoria she felt when he said the words. Rhawn loving her was wonderful. Perfect. Just what she'd always wanted. …Which just made everything scarier.

"People always think I'm going to do something amazing, but I never do." She got out. "I disappoint everyone. I'll disappoint you."

"You couldn't. I know you, Lucy. Inside and out."

"Then you know I'm not the Savior! I'm not special, at all!"

"The legends of the *Ardin* were passed down for generations. Some facts were switched or exaggerated, but the heart of the story is true. Whoever you are and wherever you come from, you were sent to save us. And you will." He reached over to touch her face. "I know that, even if you do not. You are the most special part of this world."

She swallowed, trying not to cry. "Are you still going to love me when you're proven wrong?"

"I'm not wrong."

This was the trouble with dating a genius. He always thought he knew best. "Just answer the question, Rhawn!"

He rolled his eyes like she was the crazy one. "*Yes.* I will always love you." He said in a humoring tone. "Why is this confusing to you? I've been showing you that I love you forever. Long before I thought you were the Destroyer *or* the Savior. You are my *heart*, Lucy."

Lucy found herself smiling, her eyes damp. All the specialness she didn't quite have in the rest of her life didn't matter. Not at all. Lucy had been given something much more extraordinary. Something that would change the world.

Rhawn the Accursed was her mate.

She looked at her caveman and wondered how anyone could be so handsome. "Taffi said something interesting the other day." She said after a moment.

Rhawn arched a brow at the non sequitur. "I very much doubt that."

Despite everything, Lucy snickered at that remark. "I know right? What are the odds?" She shook her head and wiped at her eyes. "But seriously, Taffi was talking about high school. About how her life hadn't turned out the way she planned. How she wishes she was the person she *thought* she'd grow up to be. And I was thinking, maybe she had a point. I'm not who I'd planned to be, either. Maybe no one is."

Rhawn opened his mouth to respond to that, but she wasn't done yet.

"Since I've been here, though, I'm the me I'm *supposed* to be. I'm so much happier than I was back in New York. So much more myself. It wasn't even working in the bookstore that was holding me back. *I* was the one who'd given up on doing anything that mattered. You can do great things working in a bookstore. But you have to remember that you *want* to. I thought being here made me see that. That this island clarified everything and gave second chances."

"The island doesn't determine who you are. It comes from a desire deep inside of you. I think that is all part of the gods' plan."

"I do, too." She leaned closer to him. "It isn't the island that makes everything clearer for me. *You* are what makes things clearer for me, Rhawn. *You* are the one who makes me a better person." She leaned forward to kiss him gently. "*You* are what's special about my life."

Rhawn whispered a torrent of foreign words, his mouth moving across hers. She had no idea exactly what he was saying. About half of it was her name and *vando*, though, so she could take a guess that it was something nice.

Lucy pulled back to grin up at him. "So listen. You don't have an internet hook up here and I don't think TVs getting invented, any time soon. Not even by you. Seems like we have to do something to pass the time." She hurried to get the words out before she lost her nerve. "Would you —maybe— want to try that *other* kind of kissing?"

His attention snapped up to Lucy's face. No one had ever looked at her with such intensity. "The lower kind?"

Lucy took a deep breath and went for it. "Yep."

Brown eyes narrowed into predatory slits. Rhawn leaned in even closer, taking up most of her personal space. Lucy had to fight the urge to look away from him. It was always like that with him. In this primitive world, Rhawn was undoubtedly the dominant animal. Hell, drop him into any time period and he would've dominated. It was just his nature. She swallowed and met his gaze.

"You really believe that idea will work?" He asked, like he was still suspecting a trap. But she could feel his growing arousal and it made her own insides melt.

"I'm willing to experiment if you are."

His mouth slowly curved. "I will try *anything* with you, Lucy. Especially that." He bounded to his feet. "Explain how we should begin."

Never let it be said the guy didn't love education. "It's really more of a 'learn by doing' thing." She maneuvered herself so she was kneeling in front of him. One of his hands came up to fist in her hair, holding her still, and she arched a brow. "Okay?"

He was breathing faster and she hadn't even touched him. "I just… like this already."

Oh, he liked this *a lot*. She could see that and it gave her confidence. "Good. Regular kissing wasn't invented until I got here. Wanna see what other sensual wonders I can dream up for you?"

That was all it took to convince him. He jerked the loincloth aside, already straining for release. "Show me."

Lucy stared up at him, once again struck by how damn *big* he was. For a second she wondered if this was going to work. In the dreams everything had been kinda fragmented and fuzzy, but this was *super* real and a little intimidating. She gathered her confidence and leaned forward to brush him with her lips. Rhawn jolted like she'd shocked him with a Taser.

She mentally grinned. Okay, never mind the nerves. This was going to work just fine. "Tell me if you want me to quit." She whispered, her tongue tracing along his skin

He *totally* didn't want to quit.

"Oh gods..." He shifted his stance, dragging her closer. "Again."

Her mouth sealed around the hard length of him and Rhawn's head went back with a choked sound of pleasure. He started chanting in the Clan's language, again. The big guy had found something he liked even more than kissing.

His giant hand clenched in her hair, like he was afraid the sensation would vanish if he let her go. Usually, the man tried his damnedest to be restrained with her, but his first foray into oral sex had broken the dam. He just wanted more. *Now.* Rhawn held onto her thick curls, thrusting against her. His whole body arched, urging her to take all of him.

Lucy pulled back. "Too much, caveman."

He looked dazed. "I'm sorry." He gentled his grip. "I just *need* and you are so perfect..." He broke off and shook his head, like he was trying to clear it. "Do you wish to stop? We can stop if you are scared."

She looked in his eyes and saw the soul deep honor of the man. "You could never scare me, Rhawn. I know you too well."

His mouth curved, understanding the walls she'd torn down to let him inside. "And I know you, Lucy." He whispered back.

Smiling, she resumed her work. This time she allowed him even deeper. Her tongue rubbing against the base of his shaft and she felt him shudder. This wasn't going to last long. She tried to drag it out for him, but when her teeth very gently scraped along the tip of him, he erupted with a roar that shook the jungle. When he was spent, he stood there panting for breath.

Lucy looked up at him, expecting him to say something rhapsodic.

Deep brown eyes burned into her. "Again."

The stark demand had her insides dipping. "You just finished." She whispered, simply to see what he'd do. She appreciated his restraint, but it turned out she flat out *loved* when she could break through it.

"I will never be finished with you." He nudged her back towards his rapidly hardening erection. His recovery time was amazing. Apparently, cavemen had supersonic sex drives. Or at least Rhawn did. "Again." He commanded and pushed into her mouth with a moan of pure bliss.

She did it, again.

His hips pistoned helplessly. "Lucy! *Gods*, yes." He loved the fiercer pace she set, his huge form shaking with need. "If anyone else saw you doing this, they would kill me to take you for themselves."

Teasing him seemed cruel, so she gave it a try. Lucy pulled back. "Well, I certainly wouldn't want to put your life in danger. It was hard enough watching you fight with Craig before." She gazed up at his glistening body and almost came herself at how stunning he was. "Want me to stop?" She pretended to stand up.

Just like she knew it would, his hand found her shoulder, keeping her down. "Again." He stared at her like she was the only thing keeping him alive.

Lucy took the hint. Her lips carefully went back to nursing him until he was even more taunt than before. He let out a hiss as she nipped him. "They would *have* to kill me. I would never willingly part from you." He slid even deeper into her mouth. "Slower now." This time, he guided her head, trying to find the speed he liked best. "Use your teeth." He whispered, his face thrown back in ecstasy. "Oh *yes*. Just a little more, Lucy. Please."

She had the feeling he'd keep experimenting as long as she was willing to let him. The man was insatiable. He wanted to do everything and then take it apart, piece by piece, until he understood how all the components worked.

"*Vando!*" He jerked under her ministrations and she knew he was thrilled with the results of his testing. Rhawn grinned, his expression triumphant. "I never imagined anything would feel this good. *Vando*, Lucy. *Vando, vando, vando.* Don't stop. Don't ever stop."

She wasn't going to stop. The more leisurely pace suited her fine. It gave her the opportunity to explore. She took her time and made him beg before, at long last, letting him come. Rhawn's fingers stayed tangled in her hair as he climaxed, making sure she suckled every drop of seed from him. He watched it all, memorizing everything for future reference.

As soon as his hoarse shout of completion faded, he beamed as if he'd discovered the meaning of life. "Again."

Lucy had anticipated the request, but her jaw was getting tired and not even he could keep up this pace. "If I keep doing this, are you going to reciprocate?"

His eyebrows tugged together like he had no idea what she meant.

She broke it down for him. "It feels just as good for women when men kiss them there."

Just like that she'd diverted his attention. His big head tilted in genius-y consideration. "It does?"

She nodded.

"You would allow me to do that?"

She nodded.

Rhawn slowly smiled.

Lucy gave a squeak of surprise as he yanked her to her feet and tossed her over his shoulder. She found herself upside down and facing his back, her hair brushing against the top of his thighs. He carried her like she weighed nothing at all, his arm braced against the back of her knees.

It was so easy to forget his size when he was being his usual soft-spoken self. But, when he picked her up, Lucy was reminded of just how massive he was. His strength didn't scare, though. Just the opposite. It seriously turned her on.

He dropped her onto the bed of animal skins and began stripping the clothes off the lower half of her body. Lucy's eyes widened at how fast he was moving things along. Suddenly, she felt self-conscious. The man was built like a professional athlete and she... wasn't. It was scary to have this gorgeous guy see her naked outside the protective cocoon of their shared dreams. What if he wasn't attracted to real live her?

"You know, we don't have to do this right now. I don't mind waiting..." Cold air hit her damp flesh and she knew a moment of nervous panic. "Really. Maybe this wasn't my best idea. We could just..." She trailed off with a whimper as his hand found the center of her body, parting the tender folds.

He shifted her legs so he could have an unobstructed view, his full concentration on her body. His fingers pressed deep, his other palm holding her still when she would've squiggled to less a vulnerable angle. He wanted everything and he was going to take it. That jacked her arousal up even higher.

Cavemen clearly didn't care about shyness.

Rhawn watched as her hands twisted on the thick pelts and his eyes gleamed. "You are perfect." He said simply and she relaxed.

"I'm super glad glasses don't exist here, because you need them."

"I am unfamiliar with this word." He didn't seem like he cared too much, though. He stretched her weeping depths, all his attention on her obvious arousal. "You're growing wet," he sounded awed, "just like in the dreams. I'd hoped you would."

Clearly that didn't happen much around here. It was amazing that the female members of the Clan hadn't revolted long ago. Thank God she was here to put some equality into the system. "When a woman wants a man, her body gets damp to welcome him in."

That was *just* what he wanted to hear. "You welcome me?"

"Always." She got out, trying to hold on. "And —Jesus— you get double points for being so damn good at this."

Rhawn smiled at that. "Double what I previously had?"

"What? Sure. Just keep going."

He looked smug. "I plan to. Tell me if I hurt you." He

moved to replace his fingers with his mouth. For a brief moment, she felt his breath against her swollen core and she wondered if she should provide some kind of instructions...

"*Oh!*" Lucy's eyes went wide as his tongue slid inside of her.

No tentative touches or false starts, he just started devouring. Once he was offered something, the man didn't hesitate to seize it. Within a matter of a few heartbeats she was on the verge of the biggest orgasm of her life. It was right *there*, if only he'd move just a tiny bit.

"Oh please, oh please, oh please." She tried to shift beneath the relentless onslaught, but now both his hands were on her hips, holding her down. All she could do was grip his golden hair and wail. "Rhawn, *please*. Just a little higher."

He let out a warning growl, keeping her just where he wanted her. "I like the taste of you." He murmured and continued tormenting her.

The bastard didn't want her to finish so fast. He wanted to take his time and discover *everything*. Lucy gave a sob as he methodically licked and nibbled and explored every inch of her. This was what she got for hooking up with a caveman who thought like a scientist. He was ruthless and wouldn't be happy until his curiosity was fully satisfied.

Just when she thought she was going to die if he didn't do something to end the torture, he drew back to gently blow on her aching flesh. Lucy came so hard it was a wonder she didn't black out. Her body bowed upward, her mouth opening in a scream of pleasure.

Rhawn watched with hot approval as she spasmed, drinking in her response. "I've just discovered that women can have orgasms." He deduced, looking smug. "I suspected as much, from the dreams. I could feel you get close so many nights, but I never had enough time to prove it. Now it is indisputable."

Lucy stared up at him, panting for breath. "You're a fucking genius."

"Yes, I think I might be." He agreed gravely and then

went back to work. "Again."

Again.

And again.

And when she couldn't do anything but weakly sigh, he used his fingers to stroke her to completion one last time. Brown eyes stayed locked on hers, even as he used his other hand to remove her top, baring her breasts to his view. All that she was wearing were the shiny white beads and he left those right where they were. They slid against her nipples as she moved against his thrusting hand and he couldn't seem to look away from the sight.

"Perfect." Rhawn lowered his head to lap at her breasts. "You are so perfect, Lucy."

Everything he'd learned about her in the dream he put to use now, finding the exact spots she was most sensitive. He filed it all away in his brain, noticing each detail and achieving maximum results.

Lucy gave a soft mewling sound as she came against his talented palm, too exhausted to even cry out.

Rhawn loomed over her, fully aroused. "Sixty-two." He reported.

"What?" She could barely form the words, her mind and body humming. Her eyes drifted shut.

"I have sixty-two points."

Her eyes popped open again, processing that smug statement. She suddenly remembered she'd told him that she'd sleep with him if he reached a certain number. Lucy swallowed. Math never had been her best subject. "Wait, how many did I say you needed?"

"Sixty-one and a half." He kissed the side of her throat. "I have kept very close count and I now have sixty-two." His erection settled between her legs and she gasped at the feel of him pressing against her.

Lucy's body automatically shifted, wanting to welcome him in. Had she been tired before? Now she was wide awake, again. "You've been stacking up the points and not telling me? You're kind of an *evil* genius. I never noticed that before."

"Oh, I have come to believe I am very, *very* smart."

Rhawn agreed, with a smirk. "I have never felt more intelligent than I do right now." He caught hold of her hands, dragging them above her head. "I will claim my prize now." But he hesitated, waiting for her consent. "Will you mate with me tonight?"

No harm in making him sweat for another couple seconds. "Well, let me think… You worked really hard and a deal *is* a deal, but I really should add up those points myself to be *completely* sure."

He wasn't in the mood to play around. "Say yes, Lucy." Rhawn ordered and his shaft brushed against her core. He was holding her still, letting her get a feel of what was to come and it was driving her crazy.

Lucy gasped, needing him to ease the building ache. "Yes." Her eyes met his. "I'm yours, caveman."

Rhawn's mouth curved. "I know you're mine." His fingers interlocked with hers, pinning her down with his strength. "When I take you, I want to look into your eyes, understand? Keep your eyes on mine."

Lucy was breathing hard. "Okay." She was totally at his mercy and she loved it.

Rhawn dipped his head to kiss the tip of her straining nipple. "Will you mate with me tonight?" He asked for the millionth time.

This time her answer was different. "Yes."

She didn't even finish getting the word out before he was inside of her.

Lucy let out a cry as he filled her body, fast and hard. Rhawn was clearly not going to take his time with this part. Fifteen years of sexual frustration went into every hard thrust. It was *amazing*. Her body arched into his, wanting more.

"Keep your eyes on me, Lucy." He ground out. His free hand lifted her hips so he could go as deep as possible, his palm lingering over the ink of her tattoo like it fascinated him. "Take it all, goddess. That's it. You can do it. Gods, you're so *tight*."

She could barely concentrate enough to breathe. He

was so *big*, stretching places that even she didn't know about. "*Rhawn!*" She bit her lower lip as he finally slid home. With her eyes locked on his and his body pressed into her, she felt vulnerable. Primitive. Claimed.

She *was* claimed.

But, Rhawn looked just as stunned as she felt, so she'd clearly claimed him right back.

Lucy grinned, out of breath and delighted. "This isn't going to last long, caveman. Not this time. We both want it too bad."

Rhawn's expression went slack. Then his free hand twisted around the beads at her neck, making sure she continued to look at him. "Tell me again you want me." It was an order, but she heard the need in it. The desperation. "Tell me you want me back."

"Oh *God*, do I want you back."

That just dumped fuel onto the fire. He was wild for her and it was *way* better than any dream. It was hot and wet and it was going to happen *right* now, if only he'd hurry.

"Rhawn, *please*." Lucy's legs wrapped around his hips and he somehow tunneled even deeper. "Faster. Harder. I'm so close. Just a little more…"

He tugged the necklace up and her head automatically followed. His mouth slammed against hers in a scorching kiss and Lucy climaxed again. Holy *shit*, she was never taking off those stupid beads again. She sobbed out her release, even as Rhawn found his own. His huge body shuddered, his fingers tightening on hers, as he roared in satisfaction.

Lucy went limp, not even moving when Rhawn collapsed on top of her. His elbows were braced beside her, so he didn't crush her with his weight. She wouldn't have noticed if he had. All she could do was struggle for oxygen. "Wow." She whispered. "Those dreams totally skipped all the *really* fun stuff."

He chuckled at that and lifted his head to meet her gaze. "You make me happy." He said, the words simple and profound. "There is nothing that makes me so happy as you, Lucy. Do not ever leave me. I could not survive it."

Lucy's heart melted. "You make me happy, too." She whispered back. "All my best memories are of you, Rhawn. Even the ones we haven't made yet." She touched the side of his face, so their eyes would stay locked. "If I do find a way back to New York, will you come with me?"

"Yes."

She arched a brow at how quickly he said the word. "Do you want to think about it before you agree? It would be a big, *big* change. I mean, I'm absolutely not sure I *can* get us back to Earth, but if I do, you'd have to deal with pollution and IRS forms and weirdoes on the subway..."

He interrupted her. "I will go anywhere you are, Lucy. Anywhere at all." That level brown stare stayed on hers and, just for a second, she felt the inevitability of their connection. The absolute knowledge that this man belonged to her.

That he was her mate, in every possible way.

"I will stay here with you, if you'd rather." Lucy said and she meant it. "If this is where you'd rather be, I can make it work. I even have a cushy job lined up as unquestioned dictator."

Rhawn kissed her lavishly. "Given a choice, I would journey to your world. It is where I have always wanted to be. I am touched by your offer, though, considering this is a land without bagels."

"It is a hardship. You'd agree if you'd ever had one."

"Undoubtedly."

"Alright, so we'll try to think of a way back to New York, then. And if we can't, then we'll just stay here and rule *The Island of the Blue Dolphin* together. Agreed?"

"Agreed."

"Good. ...But, I'm *not* the Savior." She needed him to know that, because he still didn't seem to get it. "Really, I'm not."

"You *are* the Savior." Rhawn insisted with total faith. "Powers or no powers, it's *you*, Lucy. No one else."

Lucy shook her head, exhausted again but trying to get him to see the truth. "That's crazy. You get that it's crazy, right? What am I supposed to do? Stop a volcano from erupting? Somehow convince Skoll *not* to be a psycho? Magically keep an island afloat? Because they didn't really cover that in grad school. There's no way..."

Rhawn cut her off before she could start listing all the reasons why she wasn't nearly as special as he thought she was. "You are here to change the world. I know it with everything in me." He brushed the curls back from her face. "Sleep, now. Even a goddess needs rest."

"Fine, be stubborn about it. But, you'll see in the end." She sighed, feeling drained. Wide awake, she couldn't change Rhawn's mind, so there didn't seem much of a chance of her doing it now. The man was like a brick wall. "Remember I told you you were wrong about this, though."

"Of course. In fact, I will remind you of it often, when I am proven right."

That almost made her smile. "You really are a smartass. It's very sexy." She laid her head against him and yawned, her eyes dipping closed.

Rhawn's arms curled around her, sheltering her with his massive body. No one and nothing was going to touch her while he was there. She believed that completely. "I have never been as pleased as you've made me." He nuzzled her hair. "Sleep, goddess. I will keep you safe."

She cuddled closer to him and he rested his cheek on the top of her hair. They fit together so seamlessly it was like they were made to sleep that way. Fate. She gave a drowsy smile at the thought.

"Lucy?" Rhawn whispered after a moment, absently stroking her nipple in various patterns so it beaded for him. He never got bored with her body, constantly trying new techniques to coax the best response. It turned out lazy circles got it into the tightest point. Not even Lucy had known that. Smart guys were just *awesome*.

"Ummm?" She was already nodding off. Despite everything, she was more relaxed than she'd ever been.

He kissed her temple in masculine contentment. "When you wake-up, we need to do all of that again."

Chapter Fourteen

"Damn, but I wish you were real, caveman." She whispers. *"I always have."*

"I am real." Rhawn's breathing so hard he can barely get the words out. She is beneath him, soft and willing, and everything is just as it should be. *"You are the dream. And I don't care, just so you're here with me."*

Dark brows tug together. *"I'm not a dream. If I was, I'd be way thinner. And wearing – like– a lot of expensive jewelry and something designed by Galliano."*

Rhawn is not the smartest of men. Sometimes his weak mind creates words without definitions. He has no idea what a "galliano" could be. He wants to ask her about it, and about so much more... but then she is gone.

His roar of frustration and loss jolts him awake.

Rhawn and Lucy's Dream- Two Years Ago.

It was a fine day for a mammoth hunt.

Granted Rhawn was in such a good mood that it would have seemed a fine day for anything. Uooloa's smoldering, Skoll's ominous absence and the prospect of sailing off into an unknown sea did nothing to dull his pleasure as he headed into the valley.

Lucy was his. Her small body had welcomed Rhawn's, her wondrous eyes meeting his without revulsion as they came together. She'd slept in his arms all night, safe and content. It had been better than he could've imagined.

Lucy was his mate.

Even she must see that, although she had not said the words. Soon she would Choose him and Rhawn would have everything he wished.

Grinning widely, he propped the spear on his shoulder and walked through the tall grass. The valley was closer to the base of Uooloa, but it was where the last of the mammoths gathered. Rhawn was in an optimistic mood. It would take no time at all to kill one. Then the Clan could carve off the meat, prepare it in strips, and they would set off on their voyage. The *ragan* were ready and fresh water had been gathered. He was even devising meat racks for the trip, so they could dry the mammoth's flesh in the sun. Everything was going as planned.

Rhawn loved it when things went as planned. It happened so rarely.

Warren came bounding over and not even he could spoil the mood. ...Though he seemed ready to try. "Dude, I gotta talk to you. Like, right now."

Rhawn spared him a quick glance. "Is this about Anniah?" The answer was obvious, so it wasn't even a guess.

"Yeah. I think I'm —like— in love with her, ya know?"

"I know." He supposed it was inevitable. Helpless creatures were always drawn to Anniah and she to them.

"Should I be —like— proposing or something before we... *ya know?*" Warren gave a meaningful nod. "'Cause I think she might be a proposing-before-doing-it kinda girl."

"Proposing?"

"Yeah. To marry her. So she'd be —like— mine."

Rhawn squinted. "You won the challenge, Warr-en. She Chose you and you Chose her." What other confirmation of Anniah's feelings did the man need? "She *is* yours."

Warren blinked. "You mean... I'm done? I did everything I had to do? She's *already* my wife?"

Rhawn was not sure what that meant. "She is your *mate.*"

"So... I can sleep with her, then?" Warren asked, as if he wanted to be absolutely clear.

Gods, did Rhawn really need to explain this to the boy? It was very awkward. Why did these things always happen to Rhawn? "Yes." He said uncomfortably.

"You sure?"

"*Yes.*" Was it really so hard for Warren to understand? Rhawn felt like he was speaking to a particularly dull-witted tree stump. "Men often sleep with their mates and *she is your mate.*"

"Awesome!" Warren grinned and held out his palm in the "high-five" gesture he'd used with Lucy the night before.

Rhawn hesitantly smacked his hand and was inordinately pleased when that seemed to be the correct response. It was important that Lucy know he could adapt to Newyork customs. ...Odd and pointless as they may be.

"God, I was *so* hoping you'd give me the 'all clear' on this." Warren continued happily. "I want to take care of her and do everything right this time. But, it is really, really hard to sleep next to the chick I love and not touch all the naked parts of *her* naked body with *my* naked..."

Rhawn cut him off with a shudder. "We do *not* have to discuss anything you touched while naked." He assured him, swiftly. "Truly."

"Can we talk about what naked things *you've* been up to with Lucy, then?" Warren asked, arching a brow. "Because I'm detecting a certain bounce in your step today. We've been talking for two whole minutes and you haven't even threatened to kill me yet. Something's put you in a good mood and I don't think it's the weather, ya know?" He waggled his eyebrows.

"Lucy is *my* mate." Rhawn said simply. He glanced over his shoulder, to watch her walking besides Anniah. They two women were often together, communicating with hand gestures and exaggerated faces. His mouth curved. When Lucy forgot she was antisocial, she made friends quickly. "Soon she will Choose me. I know it." He looked at Warren again, wanting to speed the process along. "How do women Choose their men in Newyork?"

"Like with dating sites and hook-ups in bars, mostly. I don't think that's gonna work for you." Warren thought for a beat. "Did Lucy tell you she loved you?"

Rhawn hesitated. "No." He admitted with a concerned frown. "Is this bad?"

"Welllllll." Warren drew out the word and scrunched up his face, like a healer delivering tragic news to a sick man. "It's sure not good. She isn't going to Choose you unless she loves you, ya know?"

Rhawn's eyebrows slammed together. The Clan did not even have a word for "love," but people from Newyork evidently required it between mates. Luckily, this problem was easily rectified. "Well, Lucy must come to love me, then." He decided. "I love her. Now she must love me back. It is the only way."

"Yeah... that's easier said than done. Those are powerful words, man. Until Anniah, I only ever said them to Mr. Buster Fluff."

"Who?"

"Mr. Buster Fluff. He was my pet hamster, when I was seven."

"I am unfamiliar with the word 'hamster.'"

"It's —like— an adorable little mouse thing."

Rhawn squinted, unsure if he was really hearing what he *thought* he was hearing. He couldn't possibly be hearing that right, right? "You loved a *boga?*" He clarified slowly, just to be sure.

Warren took exception at his incredulous tone. "Hey, Mr. Buster Fluff was my best friend!"

Rhawn stared at him, not knowing what to say to something so stupid. Did Warren not understand the dangers of these creatures? "I was bitten by a *boga* once. I barely survived it and still counted myself lucky. No one else has *ever* recovered. Most die screaming within a few moments. Trust me, no good comes from befriending vermin."

"That's what they said about my two ex-wives. But, I wasn't afraid to try again and now I have Anniah. Don't live in fear, man." Warren nodded as if he'd just said something profound. "Lucy's going to need a little bit of courting before she spits out the words. Don't worry, though. I'll be here to help you every step of the way. Offering support nonstop, ya know?" Warren jerked a thumb over his shoulder. "But right now I'm going to go have sex with my incredibly hot new bride."

"Yes. You go do that." Rhawn nodded encouragingly at that idea, relieved to be rid of the boy. The difficulties in communicating with Warren went far deeper than the language barrier. "Just go far away."

"Good talk, man." Warren beamed happily and went bounding through the tall grass.

Rhawn shook his head in exasperation, glad for the silence.

It didn't last long.

"Warr-en seems most pleased." Notan mused, coming up beside him.

In deference to the old man's limp, Rhawn slowed his own steps. "He is very happy with his mate." It was strange for the Clan's leader to talk to him without anger and accusations, so Rhawn wasn't quite sure what to say. "Warr-en says he will take good care of Anniah."

More likely, *she* would take care of *him*, but no matter.

"My daughter has Chosen well." Notan studied Rhawn's profile. "You have Chosen well, too. The Savior is a good woman, once you understand that she is not purely viciousness and tyrannical evil."

"I'm sure Lucy will appreciate your change of heart. It will be a tremendous relief for her."

Notan missed the sarcasm. "I have told the rest of the Clan that we must go with her, across the Infinite Sea." He agreed. "I do not know what awaits us there, but it is our only hope. The legends say that the Savior will see us rescued and your woman is the Savior. I know we must follow her."

"So do I." Rhawn still didn't completely believe in this plan to sail the *ragan* without clear directions, but he *did* believe in Lucy. She would save the Clan and change the world. It was her fate.

"The Savior has also helped me see that I treated you unfairly." Notan continued, meeting Rhawn's eyes. "I feared you for your differences, instead of seeing them as gifts from the gods. It was a failing I will always regret. You were born special. I should have nurtured that and not feared it. I hope that you will forgive me."

Rhawn looked at him in surprise. "I do forgive you." He said without hesitation. At one time, he might have been bitter, but no more. "The past has no meaning now." Whatever he'd endured in his life, he'd ended up right where he wanted to be. Well, not *geographically*. At the moment, the island was a terrible, *terrible* spot to be stranded. But, he'd ended up with Lucy and that was all that mattered. The *future* was all that mattered. He reached over to clamp a hand on Notan's shoulder. "Soon we will begin again in a new land and all of this will become legends of our own."

"These are great and terrible days." Notan agreed with a smile. "Your grandchildren will never believe all we have witnessed. When you tell the tales, they will think you an old fool."

"I hope they do. I hope they never have to believe all the things we have seen and done. I hope they have far better lives."

Notan slowly nodded and patted Rhawn's arm. "You have become the wisest man of this Clan." He murmured sincerely and limped off to join the others.

Rhawn stared after him, his mouth curving into a smile. Notan thought him wise. Rhawn wasn't sure he agreed, but he certainly no longer saw himself as stupid. Since meeting Lucy, he'd been slowly realizing that everyone had been wrong about his lack of intelligence. *He'd* been wrong. As usual, Lucy was right about everything.

He was *smart*, goddamn it.

It was hard to erase so many cycles of believing himself to be dumb, but he trusted Lucy's judgement. Lucy would never rely on a halfwit. Never look to him for guidance or ask his advice. Never see him as a partner and mate. Lucy believed Rhawn was smart. She said so. Why should he believe all the people who called him stupid, when the one person who mattered thought he was a genius?

And once Rhawn started looking at the situation logically, he began to recognize that his ideas were *good*. His inventions worked. His thinking was sound. Why had he believed otherwise? He would never again let someone tell him that he was stupid or slow. He should have had more confidence in himself.

Rhawn was *smart*.

He knew it and it was a good feeling.

Now if he could just get everyone on the island to safety and convince Lucy to Choose him, he would have everything he'd always wanted.

Rhawn reached the edge of the valley and looked down the gentle slope. Off to the left, the island's river raged down a series of waterfalls and fed into a large lake. The water kept the grasses lush. A dozen mammoths grazed in the green fields in front of him. These were the creatures the Clan had spared, up until now. The breeding mothers, the very young, and the most dangerous males. Killing any of them would be difficult. The adults would fight and the smaller mammoths would not have sufficient meat for the voyage, so many would need to die.

This was why Rhawn had postponed killing Skoll.

The Clan always hunted together. They would isolate a mammoth and sneak up on it, hidden in the grass. When they surrounded it, one man would give a yell and the Clan would charge at their prey. Spears would pierce the animal's thick hide, again and again. It had to be done quickly and with great precision.

When the mammoth reared in pain and panic, the Clan would retreat, hoping that some of their blows had been killing ones. The rest of the mammoth herd would thunder away from the scent of blood, leaving the dying animal alone. Vulnerable. If the wounds were deep enough it would bleed and thrash until it collapsed, exhausted. Then the Clan could move in and finish it off.

Rhawn already knew Lucy would not like seeing a hunt.

It was a brutal business, which was why Skoll excelled at it. His expertise would've come in handy today, except Skoll was still missing. No one had seen him since Warren defeated him in the challenge. Whatever Skoll was plotting, it was bound to be bad. Deep down, Rhawn hoped the man stayed hidden until the rest of them were safely off the island.

He doubted he would be so lucky, though.

Lucy came up beside him, her eyes filled with wonder as she stared at the mammoth herd. Rhawn had tried to convince her to stay behind, but she'd refused, eager to see the creatures for herself. "Oh my god." Her voice was reverent. "Look at them! They're so beautiful. Rhawn, they're so *beautiful*." Her voice actually cracked on the word, like she was trying not to cry. "I knew they'd be beautiful, but to see them in person… It's like seeing magic."

Rhawn glanced at her from the corner of his eye, the feeling of foreboding settling deeper into his stomach. She would *really* not like what was about to happen. "Lucy…"

She ignored the warning in his tone and started down the slope, unmindful of the fact she might spook the creatures. "Do you see how there are adult males with the herd?" Lucy headed towards the valley floor, so she could get a closer look. "They live with their mothers for the first decade or so, but this group might stay together longer, since they're so isolated." She couldn't take her eyes off the creatures, cataloging every piece of them in her phenomenal mind. "They're big, like the Columbian Mammoth in America. At least thirteen feet at the shoulder. Do you see? But, their hair is longer, more like the European Woolies. You think these guys are a hybrid?"

Rhawn sighed at her excitement, knowing this hunt would break her heart. "Lucy," he hurried down the slope after her. The rest of the Clan stayed back, waiting to see what Lucy would have them do next. "Lucy, wait!" He called to her.

"Huh?" She sent him a quick frown. "I just want to get some measurements. Look at their tusks! My God. Some of them must be a dozen feet long."

"*Lucy.*" He caught up with her, his voice insistent. "Do not become attached. We must *hunt* these animals. You know this. You *agreed* to this."

She shook her head emphatically, her gaze going back to the herd. "I've changed my mind. I mean, hunt something so beautiful? No. *No.* We'll have to think of something else. We're *not* killing these animals."

"Uooloa will sink this island, at any time. They will perish anyway."

"I'm not killing them, Rhawn! If I'm the Savior, I want to save *them*. At least, from us." They were within a hundred yards of the mammoths, now. Lucy didn't seem to care that it was dangerous to get any closer. She kept going, hypnotized by the beasts.

Rhawn grabbed her arm, pulling her to a stop. "There *isn't* another way." He said firmly. "We will just kill a few small ones, yes?"

"Babies?!" She gasped in horror. "You want to kill little baby miracles?" He might as well have turned the spear on her.

Rhawn winced. "An old one, then. I did promise you I would choose a very old and sick one, remember? I will choose one that is already dying, alright? Go back to the caves and wait for me. This will be over soon." Rhawn did not want her to witness what was to come. Didn't want her watching him as he killed something she so clearly cherished.

Lucy was refusing to retreat, though. Green eyes stared up at him, desperate and pleading. "There *must* be another way. You're a genius. Think of another plan. *Please*. You can't just kill a mammoth."

Actually, he *could*... but not like this.

Rhawn tilted his head back, seeking guidance from the gods. Lucy did not come from this world. There had not been a day in her life when she'd been hungry. There was so much food in Newyork, people could pick and choose what to eat. Forgo meat entirely. She couldn't understand the very real struggle for survival that the Clan endured. It was beyond her frame of reference.

Lucy did not see the mammoths as food. All she saw were miracles.

And if she watched one of her magical creatures bleeding to death and trumpeting out in pain, she might never forgive Rhawn. Might never love him. More importantly, it would crush her and he did not want to see Lucy hurt. Beneath her antisocial snarking, she was an innocent. He would do all he could to shield Lucy from the darker realities of the world.

Still, they must eat. What else could Rhawn hunt, instead of mammoths? All the other options were bad, but not as bad as seeing her cry.

"Would you allow me to kill long-tooths?" He asked after a beat. Perhaps he could lure a pack of them into the pits and kill them while they were trapped. That way they could not fight back. It had worked well enough for Craig.

Lucy winced. "Sabretooths, you mean? I love them even more than mammoths. Aren't there any –like– ugly, mean animals you can slaughter?"

"Long-tooths *are* mean." He assured her, but he could tell that she would cry over the hunting of those beasts too. Rhawn blew out a frustrated breath. "We have already had this discussion, Lucy. We *must* have some kind of meat. If it cannot be mammoth, it must be something else."

"I *know*. But, I'm just asking you to murder something less magical. Please."

Rhawn thought for a beat, not wanting to disappoint her. There *had* to be something… A creature moved in the distance and he brightened. It was more dangerous to hunt *tandar,* but not even Lucy could care about such a monster. They were hideous and aggressive. He pointed to it, feeling pleased with his intelligence. "We will hunt that beast, instead."

She followed his triumphant gesture, her eyebrows climbing. "You want to spear a *rhinoceros?*" She gasped, sounding horrified.

Rhawn scowled. "It's a *tandar!*

"It's a wooly rhinoceros! Look at the horns!" She jabbed a finger at the two *septar* growing from its face, one on the tip of its snout and one between its eyes. "Look at its long, wooly hair! Look at the fact that it's a *fucking rhinoceros!*"

That was a wooly rhinoceros?

Rhawn made a considering face. Oh. Well, that explained why the animal had been unfamiliar to him when she spoke of it. Lucy's people called so many simple things by complicated names. Not that it much mattered. The beast was still unpleasant. And, at twelve feet tall and weighing half a ton, it had plenty of meat on it. It was a suitable choice for the hunt.

"What are you? Hemingway, now?" Lucy continued hotly. "We're not killing rhinos, Rhawn. Even the regular ones back on Earth are endangered. Keeping thinking of new plans, because all your current ones suck."

The woman made him want to tear out his hair. "You are the one being unreasonable, Lucy. In Newyork, I am aware there are buildings full of food to pick from. But here we must…"

His words were interrupted by the earthquake. The ground moved in waves as Uooloa spewed smoke into the air. Lucy and Rhawn were both knocked off their feet, their eyes going up, up, up to the very top of the fiery mountain.

This was it. They both knew it.

Uooloa was beginning its final eruption.

The rock sides of the mountain were already changing shape. Rhawn could actually see them swell from the pressure within, as Uooloa prepared to blow. They were out of time.

"*Go!*" He roared and shoved Lucy to her feet. He was right behind her, half pushing her back up the slope. They had to get to the *ragan*.

Now.

The mammoths panicked at the noise and shaking ground. The herd stampeded away from Uooloa, charging at Rhawn and Lucy. Thousands of pounds of muscle and bone bore down on them. Their massive bodies hemmed in Lucy and Rhawn, so they couldn't break away from the herd. They could not outrun them, either, so they were surrounded. At any moment, they could be crushed by a terrified mammoth.

Rhawn cursed and looked around for somewhere to hide. Options were limited. The mammoths' feet were huge and flat, capable of killing a human without even noticing the bump. If they stepped on Lucy or Rhawn, it would be an instant and painful death. He quickly dragged Lucy into a small crevasse between two of the large rocks dotting the slope. It was the best he could do for shelter, but he still wasn't sure it would be enough.

Especially, not when she tried to *touch* the damn things.

Lucy's hand reached out to try and pet the mammoths' wiry fur. Rhawn yanked her wrist back down again, sending her an incredulous look.

She shrugged helplessly. "But they're so *pretty*."

A huge mammoth walked over top of them, his legs like tree trunks, his huge form casting a shadow. Lucy still wasn't afraid. She craned her head back to gape up at the creature, as Rhawn covered her body with his own. He wanted to protect her. She just wanted to admire the animals threatening to stomp them. The beasts thundered by, blaring out their cries of danger and she was looking awed again.

For a second, Rhawn saw the mammoths through her eyes.

The animals towered over them, powerful and beyond human scale. Their thick brown fur and long trunks looked like nothing else in the world. This close they were even more majestic. Even he could appreciate the wonder of them. The sounds of their breathing and the wild smell of them and the glints of intelligence in their eyes... Maybe they *were* magical, just as she said.

But he could still eat them.

Magical or not, they were an ideal food source. It was fortunate that Lucy *had* stalled the hunt, though. If they had been any closer to the herd when the earthquake began, there would have been no way to avoid the stampede. The whole Clan might have been killed. As usual, Lucy had protected them all just by being her perfect self.

How could she not see she was the Savior?

"Lucy! Rhawn!" Warren bellowed, dashing to the top of the hill and peering around for them, as the mammoths galloped towards the river. The ground was still shaking from Uooloa and he was having a hard time keeping his balance. "Hey, did you see those furry elephants? And –shit!– there's one of your wooly rhinos over there, too, Lucy! Wow, I think you were *right*. This isn't Aruba, at all!"

"Can I at least kill *him?*" Rhawn asked, breathing hard.

"Go ahead. But I'm not eating Warren, either."

Warren frowned as they got to their feet. "You guys okay down there?"

"We are fine." Rhawn quickly helped Lucy up the slope. "At least for now. Uooloa is going to explode very soon."

"I was coming to tell you guys that Anniah and I were just back at the caves. We were gonna... *ya know*... and wanted some privacy. But then I noticed that Craig's escaped! I think Taffi let him out of that bamboo cell thing, ya know?"

Rhawn bit off another oath and glowered down at Lucy. "If you had let me kill Craig last night, he would not be a problem now."

"Oh, you just want to kill everything lately." Lucy retorted. "Besides, Team Taffi can do whatever the hell they want here on Fireball Island and it won't matter. We're *leaving*, right?"

Rhawn supposed he could not argue with that. "We're leaving." He agreed and hustled Warren and Lucy towards the beach. He could see the rest of the Clan making their way towards them, running over the unsteady ground. "We must get to the ocean!" He bellowed over the mountain's roar. There was no time to gather more food. They would just have to make do with the fruits and water already loaded into the *ragan*. "We must leave now!"

They raced through the forest, dodging falling trees and terrified animals. All the inhabitants of the island were fleeing Uooloa's wrath. Glancing over his shoulder, Rhawn could see that the smoke was glowing red now. Sparks were beginning to shoot up into the soot-filled sky. The top of the mountain seemed as if it was about to ignite.

"Oh gods." Rhawn whispered.

"There are different kinds of eruptions." Lucy got out, following his gaze. "Hopefully, this one isn't like Pompeii. Those poor bastards were cooked alive by superheated ash called a pyroclastic flow. Vesuvius didn't even *need* lava to kill them. Their brains just boiled inside their skulls. If that shit starts coming out of your volcano, we aren't outrunning it."

Rattling off facts seemed to bring her some comfort.

Rhawn did not find it nearly so reassuring.

"And I can't believe I'm *hoping* to see lava." Lucy continued, holding Rhawn's hand as he led her across the river. "I swear this island is making me crazy." They were stepping from rock to rock and Lucy's eyes instinctively went upstream. "Hang on…" She stopped walking, an amazed expression on her face. "Rhawn, do you see that?

"Yes. There is a waterfall." He dragged her forward. "We must hurry, Lucy."

"Not the waterfall. The cave. There's a cave *behind* the waterfall."

"Does it matter?" He lifted her onto dry land and kept going.

"Well, it does if… *shit!*" Lucy tripped over a tree root and fell to the ground.

The forest floor was teeming with small creatures, some of which ran right over her in their panicked flight. A *boga* scampered across her hand and Rhawn's heart stopped. One bite could kill her and Lucy didn't even seem to comprehend the danger, as she shooed it off. Miraculously, the rodent scampered away without sinking its fangs into her, but that had been far too close.

"Do not touch that!" Rhawn bent to pick her up and slung her over his shoulder, barely slowing his stride. He fastened an arm around the back of her legs, holding her with one hand and his spear in the other as he ran. "Why must you always try to *touch* things?"

"I didn't touch that mouse. It touched *me!*" She shouted back.

People from Newyork clearly did not understand the dangers vermin presented. Like with the "wooly rhino," they did not even call *boga* by their proper name. Rhawn tried to put it into words she would understand.

"Lucy you must be more careful. Hamsters are very deadly."

For some reason, the woman found that hysterical. She was all but crying with semi-crazed laughter by the time they reached the beach. Rhawn didn't mind. They were almost safe! Never had he been so glad to feel sand beneath his feet.

He headed for the *ragan*, shouting out orders to Warren and the others. "Get all the *ragan* into the water and..."

And that's when he spotted Skoll.

The other man was standing right in the middle of the beach, a torch in his hand. He stood above the completed *ragan*, preparing to drop the flames and ignite their only means of escape. The vessels were made of thick tar and drying wood that would burn beyond repair in a matter of seconds.

If fire touched the *ragan*, they would all die.

Rhawn very slowly set Lucy on her feet, trying to figure out what to do next. "We've been looking for you, Skoll." He said in a soft and humoring voice. "Uooloa is erupting." He gestured to the mountain, in case the other man had somehow missed it. "We must go *now*."

"This is all *her* fault!" Skoll snarled and there was something not sane shining in his eyes. His face was bruised from the fight with Warren, giving him the look of a demon from myth. He jabbed a finger at Lucy. "*All of it* is her doing. *She* is the one who brought this upon us. The gods are punishing us now, because the rest of you followed her and believed her lies."

"The ground was shaking before Lucy even arrived." Rhawn argued in a reasonable tone. "She did not cause this. She is trying to save us."

"She will have us killed out in the sea! I would rather die here on land, than perish lost and at her mercy on the waves! I won't let that bitch win!"

Rhawn's grip shifted on his spear. If he threw it from this angle, he could hit Skoll, but the other man would drop the torch on the *ragan* as he fell. If he changed angles, Skoll would no doubt drop the torch anyway.

They were at a stalemate.

The rest of the Clan was filling up the beach, everyone terrified of what Skoll might do if they pushed him and even more terrified of what Uooloa would do if they waited much longer.

"Skoll!" Anniah made her way to the front of the crowd. "Put the torch down. Please." She held up her palms in a gesture of peace. "I will be your mate, if you just let the others go. I swear it."

Warren seized hold of her wrist as she started forward. "No freaking way." He dragged her back, away from Skoll. "You are not going *near* psychos with fire, Anniah. Are you out of your mind?"

She turned to give him a desperate look. "But it is the best chance to save you and my father, Warr-en. I *must* go to him."

"Forget it." He pulled her behind him. "I don't even *have* to understand your language to know that's fucking crazy talk!"

Skoll cut off the argument. "I would *never* have you now, Anniah!" He roared. "You have sullied yourself with that pretend god and I wash my hands of you. The rest of you will *beg* to have me back, though." He jabbed the torch at the Clan. "You will all see that I'm right! I was right all along. I will kill Lucy the Destroyer and then Uooloa will stop its rage. *I* will be Clan leader, as is my fate!"

"No one will harm my woman." Rhawn said quietly.

Skoll smirked. "Then we will all die. None of us want that. Hand her over to me and no one else will have to suffer. The Destroyer's death will put everything back in balance. The island will be spared." He held out a palm. "Give her to me. You know it is the only way."

Lucy's gaze was swinging back and forth between them, piecing the argument together. "Rhawn…" She began in a serious voice.

He cut her off, knowing what she was about to say. "*No.*"

"If I go over there, it will at least be a distraction." She insisted. "Maybe he'll put down the torch. I'm obviously not saying to let the son of a bitch kill me or whatever crazy, violent thing he's planning. But we have to try *something* here. This will give you an opening to beat him to death."

Rhawn shook his head, his attention on Skoll's smug face. "He will kill you the second he gets his hands on you."

"No, he won't. You won't let him." Lucy said with utter faith. "You'll keep me safe."

"Yes, I *will* keep you safe." Rhawn agreed harshly. "I love you." He spared her a quick scowl. "There are not words in my language to say it and I don't *need* them. What I feel for you is beyond words. Which is why I will *never* hand you over to that maniac. Not for any reason in this world or any other. There is no point in even discussing it."

Lucy stared up at him, matching him glare for glare. "Oh, we *are* discussing it. I love you, too, jackass. Which is why you *have* to get on one of those boats. I didn't just Choose your adorable little ass to watch it burn up in a volcano. So, I *am* going over there to distract him. Deal with it."

Rhawn's eyebrows climbed up his forehead.

She loved him?

She *Chose* him?

She thought his ass adorable?

Despite everything, Rhawn's heart filled with joy. Happiness rushed through him. Peace. Belonging. Gratitude. He felt all of it and more. In that second, he had everything he'd ever dreamed of. "*Vando*, Lucy." He whispered.

"Surprisingly enough, saying 'lungs' at me isn't going to change my mind, Romeo. We need to do something to distract Skoll and this is our best..."

Notan solved the problem by hitting Skoll with his cane.

The old man was crafty enough to sneak up behind Skoll and catch him by surprise. In his youth, he had been the Clan's best hunter, after all, and Skoll wasn't expecting anyone from the Clan to stand against him. The heavy wooden stick slammed into Skoll's head, knocking him sideways.

Skoll gave a furious roar. His body whirled around,

preparing to strike the Clan's leader down. As he moved, though, the torch shifted from overtop of the *ragan*. The second it was clear of the vessels, Rhawn threw his spear with all his weight behind it

The projectile slammed into Skoll's neck and came out the other side. The point on the end was designed to go through the tough hide of a mammoth. Skoll's flesh put up no resistance, at all. According to one of Lucy's lectures on the topic, obsidian spearheads from the Ice Age could be made sharper than medical instruments in her world. Rhawn wasn't *exactly* sure what that meant, but he believed it was true about his weapon. It pierced Skoll like he was made of water. He collapsed to his knees, his mouth opening and closing, but no sound coming out.

"You will *never* lead our Clan." Notan pronounced, his cold eyes. "You have been judged unworthy."

Skoll fell to the sand, already dead.

"Whoa." Lucy blinked over at Rhawn. "Nice throw! Forget Cal-Tech. If we ever get back to reality, I'm going to sign you up for the Yankees."

Anniah raced over to check on her father, beaming with pride. Tammoh and Ctindel were already congratulating him.

Notan shook his head, refusing their praise, his eyes locking on Rhawn. "Rhawn the Accursed!" He called. "You have never been accursed, at all. Your Clan thanks you."

Everyone present nodded, smiling at him.

Rhawn inclined his head.

Warren stepped forward to kick the torch into the sea. "Bad guy's dead. Yay, Rhawn. Now, we gotta *go!*" He shouted, gesturing to the *ragan*. The rest of the Clan was already racing forward to drag them towards the water.

Rhawn moved, so he could stare down at Skoll. He didn't regret the kill. Still, he had never taken a life before. It was disheartening to stare down at the other man, knowing that he had been alive just moments before. Knowing that he would never be alive, again.

Rhawn sighed and looked back at Lucy, worried that

she might view him differently now. She cared for mammoths and *tandar*, refusing to see them harmed. Now he had ended a human life, right in front of her.

Rhawn met her eyes, looking for signs of disgust. "I had no choice." He said softly.

Lucy nodded. "I know." Her perfect green gaze stayed on his, never wavering. "You saved me. You saved *everyone*. You have no reason to feel guilty."

Rhawn crossed the sand to stand in front of her, one of his hands coming up to cup her cheek. "Do you truly Choose me?" He asked, studying her face. "Truly, Lucy?"

"I Chose you when I was eighteen years old, Rhawn. You know that." She gave him a tender smile. "You are the only man in the universe I could ever love. And –trust me– I know for a *fact* that it's a big, damn universe."

His mouth curved into a smile. "It *is* big. And I am happy to be in any small part of it, so long as I am with you, goddess." He swept her up into his arms, holding her tight. "I would never be anywhere, than by your side. You are my heart and soul." He lowered his head to kiss her.

"Can you two idiots make out *later?*" Warren bellowed, ruining the moment. "Come on, already! There's a fucking volcano exploding, in case you fucking missed it!"

Lucy and Rhawn turned to glower at him in perfect unison.

He had a point, but neither of them appreciated his timing.

Most of the Clan were in the *ragan*, now. The men were pulling them into the waves and paddling out into the ocean as fast as they could. According to Lucy, they needed to get at least several miles out to be safe. Rhawn did some quick calculations and wasn't sure they'd make it far enough before Uooloa blew.

And even *then* it might all be for nothing, if there were no other islands out there.

Anniah helped Notan into one of the vessels and then turned back to check on Warren. "Warr-en!" She shouted and beckoned him to join her. "Come."

"Get in the boat! I'm right behind you!" Warren helped push the largest *ragan* into the water. It was loaded down with the fresh water and fruit they'd gathered earlier. His head swung around to look at Lucy. "You coming or what?" He demanded, apparently not willing to leave without her.

In that moment, Rhawn actually liked the man.

Lucy was not similarly moved. "*Yes*, we're coming!" She shouted back, exasperated by his nagging. "What the hell do you think we're going to do, Warren? Take fucking selfies with the lava? Stop asking stupid questions and go with Anniah."

Warren nodded and stepped backward towards the water. "Well, hurry up then, ya know?! You're the only one with a clue as to what direction we're sailing in."

"West." She pointed towards the horizon. "We paddle that way until we hit an island with purple flowers on it. Alright?"

"Hey, you two are the smart ones. If you say that's the way we go, that's the way we go." Warren waded out into the water to climb aboard Anniah's *ragan*. "Hey, Moose-y!" He cupped his hands around his mouth to shout back at her. "In case we die later, thanks for getting us this far! I always knew you were going to change the world!"

Lucy glanced up at Rhawn, with a long-suffering sigh. "Ya know, if I'm about to be marooned forever on an uncharted alien isle with one of my moronic classmates... Warren really is the best option." She shook her head. "What does *that* tell you about our graduating class?"

"We do not know for sure there *is* a land with purple flowers." Rhawn reminded her, still hesitant to get in the *ragan*. This plan was the only option they had, but he still didn't like the uncertainty of it. Risking Lucy's life on such an unpredictable venture worried him.

...But not as much as risking her life with the volcano.

Rhawn cast another quick look at Uooloa, wincing at the horrible red glow of the smoke. Perilous or not, there was no other choice. "Yes. We must go." He held out a palm to her. "Come. There is one *ragan* left and we are taking it."

"No shit. The class reunion is officially *over*. Let's go home. ...Wherever the hell home turns out to be."

"My home is where you are, Lucy.'

She smiled at that. "My home is with you, too. But, let's hope it also has bagels."

Lucy was reaching for his hand when the gunshot rang out.

Chapter **F**ifteen

"Is it an earthquake?" Lucy reaches over to steady herself on his arm, as the floor moves beneath them.
"It's the Ardin.*" He corrects, softly. "The sinking."*
She, of all beings, knows that.
"The what?"
"The end of the world."
"The WHAT?*"*

Rhawn **a**nd **L**ucy's **D**ream- **T**his **Y**ear.

For a second Lucy thought she was shot.

She actually looked down at her shirtfront, expecting to see her insides falling out of a bleeding hole. It took her a second to realize that the gunman had actually fired at the ground in front of her. The bullet had left a small crater in the sand, three inches from her shoes.

"Fucking hell!" Lucy turned to scowl at the prom queen who'd just opened fire on her. "You could have killed me, Taffi! Have you lost your mind? What the hell are you doing?!"

"I'm self-actualizing." Taffi arched a brow. "By the way, you're really terrible at hiding things. Craig and I found this gun under that rock in –like– twenty minutes. Didn't we, Craig?"

"Yep." Craig came out of the forest to stand beside her, looking smug. They must have been waiting until Rhawn and Lucy were alone on the beach, before revealing themselves. "I told you I used to rob people, Meadowcroft. I can find *alllll* the hidey-holes folks like you think up. It was part of my job and I'm damn good at my job."

"Tell them what *else* you learned about in your line of work, Craig." Taffi urged, as if they were filming this as an infomercial on crime.

Craig smiled and it wasn't pleasant. "Jewelry." He

pronounced. "I learned a shit-ton about *jewelry*."

"Jewelry?" Taffi held up the missing bead from Lucy's necklace. "Like, for instance, uncut, D color diamonds the size of superballs, Craig?"

"Yeah. *Exactly* like that, Taffi."

They both turned to look at Lucy with identical, greedy expressions.

Aw hell… Those shiny rocks were *diamonds?* Lucy looked down at the strands of beads Anniah had given her, her eyes going wide. Under the circumstances, that was seriously, *seriously* bad news.

"You can probably imagine what Craig and I have been chatting about, ever since I got my hands on this and realized what it was." Taffi continued, rubbing the bead between her fingers. "You might have Mensa begging to hang your portrait in their Hall of Fame, but *I* know expensive rocks when I see them." She shrugged. "Turns out, *that's* going to make me the special one. It isn't getting us home. It's owning *all* the big ass diamonds here in Dinotopia."

"For the last time, *dinosaurs did not live in the Ice Age.*"

"God, I am so sick of your know-it-all-ing, Lucy! I swear to God, I would be shooting you even *without* the piles of treasure."

Rhawn stepped forward, trying to get to Lucy, but Taffi swung the gun around to face him. "Actually, the treasure part is where you come in handsome." She smirked. "Lucy might like you dragging her around by her hair and all, but I have a much more *important* job for you." She glanced at Craig, her eyes cold. "Grab him and let's get out of here."

Rhawn tried to shove Craig away when he approached, but Taffi switched the gun to Lucy. "I wouldn't." She warned. "Not unless you want Lucy to join poor Skoll." She spared his body a quick glance. "FYI, that man was the worst kisser *ever*. One time he bit my nose. I mean what the fuck is *that* about?"

"You can't get both of us, before one of us gets Lucy." Craig told Rhawn, in case he still didn't understand the threat.

"Who's the loser now, huh?"

"Still you." Lucy assured him.

Craig's eyes blazed with hatred and illegal substances. "You haughty bitch! Just because we need you alive for another hour, doesn't mean I can't cut off your face in the meantime and eat it right in front of..."

Rhawn interrupted the Hannibal Lecter-ish rants. "Lucy is cooperating." He stepped between them and allowed Craig to seize his arm. Clearly, he was more worried about Taffi, because his eyes stayed on the gun. "There is no need to threaten Lucy with that weapon. We will do as you ask."

"Good boy!" Taffi praised, like he was a very stupid dog. It was a wonder Taffi-Two didn't bite her, if she used that condescending tone on her poor Pekinese. "*You're* going to show me where the diamonds come from. I know I'm not your type, but I need someone who speaks English and knows his way around this dump. Which means I need *you*, Piltdown Man."

"No, you're not my type." Rhawn agreed quietly. "You are the Destroyer."

Taffi scoffed at that. "Oh fine. Make *me* the bad guy."

"My ancestors were too blind to believe two women could fight the *Ardin* alone, but there was never a male god, at all. I see that now. It was always destined to be you and Lucy in this battle."

"I hate Lucy." Taffi bit off, her eyes bright. "We've been enemies since kindergarten. I don't deny that. But *I'm* the star of this show. If anyone's the Destroyer here, it's *her*. I mean look at her clothes!"

Lucy flicked her off.

Rhawn shook his head, looking supremely calm and way too confident for a guy being kidnapped. "Lucy is the Savior and she will best you." He said simply. "This is the *Ardin* and it is her fate."

"*No!* She's not stealing this from me, too!"

"She does not have to steal anything. It is already hers."

Taffi's eyes narrowed in rage. The girl was fanatical

about staying in the spotlight. Her French manicured finger tightened on the trigger, wanting to shut Rhawn up and prepared to open fire to make it happen.

"I know where the diamonds are." Lucy blurted out before her mate got himself shot.

Rhawn and Taffi both turned to give her incredulous looks.

"You do?" Taffi demanded.

"That is impossible." Rhawn began with his usual candor. "The cavern where Anniah found those stones has long since sunk into the…"

Lucy cut him off. "But, the volcano is about to erupt, Taffi." She continued. "Going to the mine is pointless. It's too late to get the diamonds, now. We have to escape this island while we can."

"You want us to swim away from millions of dollars?" Craig scoffed. "Maybe *you're* the one who's high. The stupid volcano isn't going to erupt for hours yet."

"Are you basing that on your vast experience in volcanology?" Lucy snapped sarcastically. "Because it looks a *little* bit hot over there." She gestured to Uooloa, with a desperate wave of her hand.

"Hey, I saw a Paul Newman movie about volcanos okay?" Craig retorted. "*I* know what I'm talking about, because *Paul Newman* knew what he was talking about. That man was a god."

Rhawn frowned. "There is another god present?" He looked around, like 60s movie stars might be hiding in the trees.

Taffi's attention stayed on Lucy. "I think a fortune in diamonds is worth sticking around for a few minutes, don't you?" She asked with an arch expression. "Really, you're just being selfish."

"I'll give you the necklace." Lucy tried, pointing to the beads she wore. "You can have *these* diamonds. Just give me back Rhawn and let us go."

Taffi looked insulted. "I don't wear *used* jewelry! Honestly, what do you take me for?" She prodded Lucy forward with the gun. "Let's go. You and He-Man aren't going anywhere until I have my diamonds."

Lucy reluctantly headed into the forest. "This is the stupidest thing you've ever done, Taffi. And I read your college essay, so I *know* the depths of stupidity you're capable of."

The ground was still vibrating and flames were now visible over the lip of Uooloa. Or maybe it was lava, already beginning to boil up. Not that it really mattered. Either way, the odds of survival weren't good. Their chances this close to a large eruption were about 50/50. So statistically speaking, only half of them were going to get out of this alive.

...And Lucy knew which two needed to go.

"The white stones you want were only found one place." Rhawn interjected. "They were very hard and difficult to shape, so we did not even gather them before the water filled the cavern. There is no way to reach them now."

"Bullshit." Craig snapped. "No one would leave *diamonds* behind. You just want to keep them all for yourself."

"I have no need for shiny pebbles. I do not know what possible good they will do you, either. Lucy will defeat you soon and you will be dead. This seems a senseless way to use your remaining time."

Lucy winced a bit, as Craig and Taffi both glowered at him. "Thanks for the vote of confidence, sweetie, but it's really not helping."

"I only speak the truth. You will win the *Ardin*. It is foretold." He arched a brow. "Now are you *sure* this is the way to the cavern, goddess?"

From his tone, it seemed pretty obvious that this *wasn't* the way to the cavern. The real diamond cave must have been flooded as the island sank. Lucy didn't care.

"Yes." She said firmly. "This is the way. It's by the river."

"As you wish." Rhawn stopped arguing and headed back towards the valley.

Craig shot Taffi a fuming look, still certain that Rhawn was after his new fortune. "As soon as we find the diamonds, shoot him in the head, will you? No. On second thought, *I* want to be the one to shoot him in the...*fuck!*" His words ended with a violent curse and he lifted his foot to frown down at his ankle. "A gerbil just bit me." He was dressed in cargo shorts and flip-flops, so it was easy to see the red bite mark on his skin. "You assholes have man-eating gerbils here, for Christ's sake? Are they rabid?"

Lucy's eyebrows climbed, automatically scanning the forest floor for the rodent culprit. Small creatures were still skittering about in a frenzy, including those incredible dangerous hamster things. That was probably bad. Lucy's eyes flicked to Rhawn for a prognosis, already knowing what he was going to say.

"You stepped on a *boga*." Rhawn told Craig, without much sympathy. "The venom is deadly, unless you are very lucky. ...You do not seem like a man with much luck."

Craig did not take that news well. "What the fuck do you mean it's *deadly?!*" He screeched, very close to crying again. "It was just a goddamn gerbil!"

"It was a hamster." Rhawn corrected. "And they bring nothing but death."

The puncture on Craig's ankle was already swelling. Lucy could see the poison beginning to take hold and attack his body. Craig's skin was turning a sickly green color. She remembered it from when Rhawn was so sick in the dream and her heartbeat sped up.

God, no wonder the caveman was so twitchy about those icky little vermin. These Ice Age hamsters had almost killed him with their icky little Ice Age hamster fangs. Lucy gave a shudder and bent down to tuck her pant legs into her socks. Animal lover or not, she'd never liked mice. Now she felt totally justified in calling the exterminator on them back home.

Craig's leg was bloating, as the venom raced through his body. It was as if one whole side of him was being inflated, the flesh expanding to a horrific and impossible size. "Do something!" He screamed at no one in particular. His throat began to distend and he wheezed in alarm. "Do something! Do something! *Do something!*"

Taffi did something.

She shot him.

Lucy cried out as Taffi put a bullet right through Craig's skull. "Oh my God!" She gaped down at him for a beat, unable to process what she had just seen. "Oh my *God!* You killed Craig! Jesus! You just *killed* him, Taffi! How could you *do* that?"

"If you'd ever slept with the guy, you wouldn't have to ask." Taffi assured her, not the least bit repentant. "Most boring two minutes of my life. And anyway, what else *could* I do? Nurse him back to frigging health?" She rolled her eyes. "Please. You said yourself we're on a schedule here. He was just going to slow us down with his whining."

Lucy stared at her, unable to comprehend her blasé attitude about murdering their classmate. "*You just killed Craig!*" She repeated at a roar, since the prom queen was still not getting it. "You sat next to him in homeroom for three years!"

"Oh *what*ever." Taffi scoffed in the exact same tone she'd used in high school when she forgot her homework. "Like anyone's going to miss that loser, besides his bookie. He wasn't special. *You're* not special. *I'm* the one who's special. This is *my*. special. fucking. day," she spaced out each word, enunciating them with hard jabs of the gun, "and no one is spoiling it. I'm getting my diamonds and then I'm catching the last boat off of this turd pile."

Lucy very nearly punched her, right in her surgically straightened nose.

"Lucy." Rhawn said quietly, seeing her intentions. "Do not. You will not win through anger. Continue with whatever it is you're doing. Wait until you know it is time for your victory."

"She's not going to win *at all*, Mowgli." Taffi taunted. "Now move." She gave Lucy a shove.

Rhawn shot Taffi a glare. "You are a terrible queen." He informed her seriously and led them through the woods, back towards the river.

They were way, way, *way* too close to Uooloa now. Projectiles the size of old-fashion TV sets were being expelled from the volcano's crater and launched hundreds of feet in the air. Radiant red, they shot out like bombs, crashing to the ground and flattening everything in their path. It still wasn't enough to ease the massive buildup of pressure, though. The sides of the mountain were straining to contain the explosive forces of the volcano and, any moment, they would give way entirely.

"The cave is up ahead." Lucy pointed to the almost invisible opening in the rock behind a vivid blue waterfall. "I saw it earlier."

Rhawn flashed her a baffled look and helped her over the rocks. "Are you sure about this?" He asked, still remarkably composed, given the disasters looming on all fronts, positive that the Savior would do something amazing to rescue him. He wouldn't be nearly so confident if he understood his "Savior" was just Lucy Meadowcroft, from Clovis New York.

Lucy swallowed hard, hoping that she could get them out of this mess. "I'm sure."

"There had better be *a lot* of diamonds in here." Taffi warned them. "Like Marilyn Monroe amounts. Otherwise, you two are going to be really sorry you messed with me."

"Don't worry. There are plenty of stones inside. But they're in the walls, so we'll have to pry them out." Lucy had no idea how diamonds were mined, but she'd seen *Snow White* when she was a kid. Hopefully, "Hi-Ho" was the extent of Taffi's knowledge, too. "We might need pickaxes for the big ones. Does the Clan have pickaxes, Rhawn?

"I am unfamiliar with the word..."

"Are those the *small* diamonds, then?" Taffi interrupted, pointed at the strands looped around Lucy's neck. "Holy crap, I'm going to be *soooo* rich I can just *buy* myself a film career! *And* get a boob job *and* hire Brad Pitt as my sexy butler. *Finally*, I'm going to get what I deserve." She squeezed her way across a narrow path to the cave entrance, dragging Lucy through the frigid water of the torrential falls. "And I'm getting rid of that stupid, smelly dog and finally buying a pony!"

Lucy took one step into the cave and knew her plan

was going to work.

Instead of billions in of shiny carbon, there were bones. The dirt floor was littered with skulls, femurs, ribs, and vertebra, indicating this cave was used as a predator's lair. A big predator. Probably *lots* of big predators. She slowly smiled.

"Lucy, there are no shiny rocks in this cave." Rhawn said in a quiet voice.

"I know."

"Where the hell are the diamonds?" Taffi demanded, heading for the walls to search for the telltale sparkle of gems. "It's supposed to look like Harry Winston's wet dream in here. Why am I not seeing any diamonds? Huh?" She headed deeper into the cavern, not exactly ready to whistle while she worked. "Where did you hide them?!"

Lucy had a brief flash of guilt. Maybe she should try and stop this. "Taffi, don't go back there." She blurted out, before she could reconsider. "Please."

"Shut up and help me look!"

Sanity returned. It was no use trying to save the lunatic planning to kill them. If Taffi had her way, Lucy and Rhawn would join Craig in whatever afterlife this island led to. Besides, that bitch had threatened Rhawn and Lucy was taking that personally.

The prom queen was on her own.

Lucy grabbed hold of Rhawn's arm, preventing him from going any farther into the cave. "Back up." She hissed. "Very slowly." Her shoes were crunching on archeological evidence that would prove her entire thesis true and she didn't even care. "You know how you said I'd know when it was time for victory? Well, it's time."

"You will win the *Ardin*, now?" He guessed hopefully, like a kid all ready for *WrestleMania* to start. "Can we do that by retreating?"

"We can when we're standing in a sabretooth den."

Rhawn glanced around in surprise, as Lucy edged them both towards the door. "I have never seen a long-tooth den. They are very private animals." He sounded interested. "Are you sure?"

"Trust me. I got an A in this." The cavern looked exactly like the diagram in Lucy's final paper. Her conclusion that groups of sabretooth cats lived together in caves. She'd seen the entrance when they fled from the valley and she'd known that this was the pack's home. At the time, she'd regretted that she wouldn't have a chance to investigate it.

Now she just wanted to get the hell out.

A low growl emanated from the dark recesses of the cavern. Then another. Then another. The menacing sounds echoed off the stone walls, making them seem like they were going on and on and on. They came from all directions at once, pitched at the perfect frequency to make all the hairs on the human body stand straight up.

"What the hell was *that?*" Taffi demanded. She glowered over at Lucy. "What have you done now?"

"I went to grad school." Lucy spared a quick look towards the exit, making sure they had a clear path. The sabretooth wouldn't attack them if they were in retreat.

Not when they could attack Taffi instead.

Taffi spun around in a circle, trying to see the threat. "Whoever's there, better back off. I mean it! These are *my* diamonds and I'll fight for them. *All* of them." She waved her gun, heedlessly firing into the darkness. "Stay back or else!"

Instead of scaring them away, the gun instigated the attack. It was the same way Craig had killed the sabretooth in the tar pits. The same noise. The cats *had* been watching from the shadows that day and now they associated the weapon with their dead pride-mate. With murder. With death. With suffering.

With enemies.

Six sabretooth seemed to move as one and the prom queen didn't stand a chance. Lucy cringed, knowing what was about to happen. Taffi's shouting bounced off the wall as she wildly fired at the cats.

It was no use. Even Taffi seemed to realize that. She spun the gun around, aiming it at Lucy. "You can't do this to me!" She shrieked. "*I'm supposed to be the star!*"

Lucy didn't even bother to duck. No bullets were going to hit her. Taffi had just emptied the gun. "Good-bye, Taffi." She said softly. "I'm sorry we were enemies since kindergarten. I'm sorry there wasn't another way."

Fangs as long as rulers flashed, claws rending flesh. The sabretooths silenced Taffi's enraged scream so quickly, it was like the prom queen had never been there, at all. Lucy squeezed her eyes shut, turning her face away so she wouldn't see the carnage.

"The Destroyer is gone." Rhawn breathed. "Just as you said."

"*Go.*" Lucy whispered back. They had to make their escape while the pride was occupied or they would never get out. She couldn't bring herself to look at Taffi's body, but she still felt a twinge of sadness for her.

No one deserved that kind of end. Not even cheerleaders.

Rhawn didn't seem to hear her urging. "You have won the *Ardin* and you used *knowledge* as your only weapon." He met her gaze, looking awed. "You *are* the Savior, Lucy. Even you must see it."

"You really want to start that shit *now?* We have to get out of here!"

"The long-tooths will not harm you. They know who you are." He slowly shook his head. "You did not even have to *strike* Taffi to win, just as you did not have to touch Craig to defeat him. This island and its inhabitants protect you."

"Well, they're doing a piss poor job of it." She shoved him through the waterfall and then stumbled out after him. "We can talk about your goddess kink later, okay? Right now, we have to get back to the beach, before the volcano explodes."

...And that's when the volcano exploded.

The stories of Krakatoa had been right. The sound nearly did rupture Lucy's eardrums. It sent her whole head ringing, like someone had pounded on a gong with a sledgehammer. The reverberations inside her skull had her hands coming up to clutch the sides of her head in agony.

The whole top of Uooloa blew apart, spewing a geyser of lava in explosions of fire. The mountain glowed with the most beautiful and terrifying shades of red she'd ever seen. Electric, searing colors that were almost *alive* lit up the sky.

It was like watching the 4th of July fireworks in hell.

The force of the eruption sent trees blowing backwards all over the island. It also knocked Lucy right off her feet. She toppled into the river, the shocking cold of the water all the more shockingly cold because of the rush of volcanic heat in the air. Lucy's head whacked against a rock below the surface. For a second, she nearly blacked out.

"Lucy!"

She could hear Rhawn's voice bellowing her name and it brought her around. Lucy swam back to the surface, trying to reach him, but the current was too strong. She cursed in frustration. Goddamn it, they didn't have time for this. Lava was pouring down the side of the volcano, melted rock covering the island like a shroud. They *had* to get to the boat.

Except she couldn't fight her way back to shore.

"Lucy!" Rhawn raced along the riverbank and then waded into the torrent after her. "Lucy, give me your hand!"

Lucy reached out to him and missed. She wanted to tell him to go without her and save himself, but she knew he wouldn't, so there was no sense in wasting the oxygen. Air was suddenly a precious commodity. The only way she was going to save Rhawn was to save herself, so she needed to focus on survival. Lucy's feet touched the bottom of the river and she kicked off the rocks, propelling herself towards shore.

Rhawn grabbed her, his fingers sealing around her wrist like a vice. Nothing would've been able to pry her free of his grasp. "Are you, alright?" He demanded, dragging her against his chest. "Are you hurt?"

Lucy shook her head, coughing up water. "This island is *not* trying to save me, Rhawn." She got out. "I think that's pretty fucking clear."

"You're still alive, aren't you? Seems like the work of the gods to me, seeing as how difficult you can be." The river dragged him forward too, sending the both of them hurdling downstream and towards a large lake. "I have never seen one woman land herself into trouble so often."

"I love you, too." She kissed the side of his jaw and his mouth curved. If a guy could smile at you in the middle of drowning and during a volcanic eruption, you knew he was a keeper. "Hey, if we survive this, you want to get married?" She asked, because what the hell better time was there to propose than a natural disaster?

"I am unfamiliar with the word 'married.'"

"It's a ceremony that makes you my mate, for better or worse."

Rhawn shot her an incredulous look. "Why would I want that? I *am* your mate. I do not need a ceremony to give me what I already possess."

"Well, too bad. We're having one. ...If we survive this, anyhow." Lucy held onto his neck, as the current dragged them out to the middle of the lake. The water was deep and cold, but that was the least of her worries. Her eyes stayed on the volcano. The force of the explosion had ripped long, jagged fissures in the ground. It really might tear the whole island apart and sink it beneath their feet. "Rhawn, I *seriously* do not know how we're going to survive this." She whispered.

"You are the Savior. You will save us."

It would be a shame to spend their last moments alive hitting the man she loved, but she was sorely tempted to bop Rhawn on his pretty head. "Would you stop with that crap and just be logical for a moment? You're supposed to be the practical, reasonable, scientific genius in this partnership, so act like it." She looked around, trying to come up with a plan. It seemed like an earthquake had opened up a passage in the lakeshore that connected it to the ocean. Maybe they could get out that way. "Do you think we could swim fast enough to catch up with Warren and the...?" She trailed off, her eyes falling on a strange glow beneath the water.

Something blue and swirling.

And familiar.

Staring at it, Lucy recalled falling off the deck of the

Arden. Below her, had been a whirlpool of blue that glowed with an identical unnatural light. It was exactly the same glowing whirlpool that Rhawn had drawn on his cave wall. Images from his earliest dreams. How many glowing blue whirlpools could there be? It was all the same phenomena and Lucy suddenly knew what it was:

A portal home.

"Rhawn, take us underwater!" She shouted.

"You would prefer drowning to roasting alive, then? I think we should try to reach the beach and..."

Lucy cut off his complaint. "I found your blue whirlpool. Get us down to it. I think it's our ticket to Earth."

Rhawn glanced at the whirlpool, jolting to see it right there in front of them. "I have been to this lake many times. That was never here before."

"Who cares? It's here now. I think it's going to lead us home."

"We do not know that it will take us to Newyork. If it is a magical passageway, it could go anywhere."

"Luckily 'anywhere' is a hell of a lot better than *here*, at the moment." She leaned up to give him a smacking kiss. "Besides, so long as I'm with you, Rhawn, I don't think it matters *where* we end up."

He grinned at that logic and held her tight. "Hold your breath." He instructed and dunked them under the water.

The blue glow sucked them forward, pulling them in. Lucy felt like she was surrounded by something vast and warm. She looked back up at the surface and she could see a brief moment of fiery destruction. Then the water churned around her, obscuring her view. Whatever happened to the island, she would never know.

Lucy held tight to Rhawn, afraid to let him go for fear he'd be pulled away from her. They stayed under for what seemed like forever, caught in the swirling vortex. Then, just as suddenly as it had appeared, the whirlpool vanished again. It spit them out into dark, dark water, and Lucy didn't know which way was up.

Everything was black and it disoriented her.

She couldn't breathe. She couldn't breathe! Lucy would've panicked, but Rhawn was already moving them through the water. They could have been going any direction on the compass, for all she knew, but she trusted him to figure it out. She gripped Rhawn as close as she could, her lungs burning like fire.

Then, they were bursting into the fresh air. Finally. Lucy dragged in greedy gulps of oxygen, pushing the wet hair from her eyes. "Rhawn..." she panted, "you... okay...?"

He nodded, slightly less out of breath, because he was the fittest man on the planet. ...Whichever planet they'd landed on. "Are you alright, goddess?"

"Yeah. Where are we?"

"I don't know. But I do not see a volcano. This is a positive sign."

Considering they were apparently stranded in the middle of an inky black sea at night, Lucy wasn't so optimistic. She looked around trying to get her bearings. It was definitely salt water and there seemed to be some kind of large floating structure a few hundred yards away. It was a ship, except it looked wrong *somehow*. Shit. What if they were stranded on some weird alien future place? What the hell were they...?

She frowned, as a rhythmic, mechanical noise entered her consciousness.

"What is that?" Rhawn demanded, staring up at the sky.

"A helicopter." Lucy breathed, recognizing the sound. The panic faded enough for her to think and she began to get her bearings. "It's a helicopter!" She waved a hand in the air, trying to get the pilot's attention. "Hey, we're down here!"

This wasn't some weird alien future place.

She was back on Earth. Which was weird and alien, but *not* in the future.

This was the same time she'd left. The floating structure off the left was the ship. The *Ardin* was on its side, but still buoyant enough that survivors clung to its sideways decks. The helicopter was searching for anyone still in the water, probably with some kind of night vision equipment.

Lucy began to laugh with relief. "Rhawn, we did it! This is home!"

Rhawn was gaping up at the helicopter, an amazed expression on his face.

"It's alright." Lucy touched his face, bring his eyes around to meet hers. "Sweetie, it's alright. Remember when I told you that picture you drew on your wall was an airplane? Well, that up there," she pointed to the chopper, "is its baby brother. Just a machine someone invented. We're safe."

Rhawn seemed dazed. "We are in Newyork?" He got out.

"No." Lucy grinned as the helicopter's searchlight flicked on and aimed its beam right at them. "But, we're definitely on our way."

A creature moved beneath the water. Something huge and almost... reptilian. For just a second, Lucy processed a long neck and four primeval-looking flippers. Oh crap. Nothing that looked like that had been alive for a couple hundred million years. In fact, she had a real bad feeling about what just swam past them.

"Ummm..." she glanced at Rhawn, "was that a dinosaur?"

"No. It is a *jigon*. It must have traveled through the whirlpool with us."

"Oh." Lucy swallowed, watching the creature slip away. "Okay. Because that *really* looks like a plesiosaurs." Which technically weren't dinosaurs, but still no *way* should it have been alive on planet Ice Age. God, that island was just a paleontological mess. "I think that's gotta be against the law to import *jigon* to Earth. Whatever you do, don't tell anyone we brought it here."

"Just be grateful it is not interested in eating us. I told you, they are monsters." Rhawn seemed unconcerned about letting a Mesozoic creature loose on the modern world. All his attention was focused on the helicopter. "I cannot believe we are really here." He murmured.

She shook her head and decided not to worry about destroying the food web with extinct marine life, for the moment. "When they fish us out, just let me do the talking, okay? And if anybody asks, the loincloth you're wearing is really a designer bathing suit."

"I am unfamiliar with that word." He looked a little overwhelmed. "I am unfamiliar with *many* words, Lucy."

"That's okay. You're a genius. You'll figure it all out."

"Are you sure? I can already tell, this world is very different than mine."

"I'm sure." Lucy gave him a quick kiss. "You'll be fine. Trust me. I know these things. After all, I have it on good authority that I'm the Savior."

Epilogue

"I had a dream last night." Rhawn said in a contemplative tone.

Lucy turned to look at him over the tops of her sunglasses. "It better not have been about some other girl. I might not have magical powers, but I can improvise with the best of 'em."

The two of them were sitting on their beach, watching the sun sink into the vivid blue sea. Island living wasn't nearly so bad, now that they were back in the real world. The lack of volcanoes was a serious plus.

Rhawn's mouth curved. "I dream of no other women, Lucy. You know that."

The caveman was fitting into the twenty-first century like a champ. It would probably take a while before he completely adapted to running water, frozen pizza, and Blu-ray players, but it was still impressive to see how quickly he was learning. He even seemed to be okay with the warm weather, although he did keep the air conditioning cranked up to subzero settings.

"I dreamed of the Clan." Rhawn continued leaning back in his Adirondack chair, his bare feet resting in the gentle surf. Wearing pants might be old hat for him now, but he was never going to like shoes. She could already tell. "It was *more* than a dream. It was a vision. I saw them cross the Infinite Sea. It took them three days and they feared they would be lost forever, but finally they landed on a new island. A place of waterfalls and purple flowers and vast herds of mammoths." He smiled. "They are safe there."

"Thank God." Lucy let out a relieved breath. "I knew they'd be okay, but deep down... I've been worried."

"There is no need to be. I saw Anniah and Warr-en.

They are well."

"Good. He's still a dick, but not a *total* dick. By the end, I feel like he was kinda my friend and I don't have a lot of friends. Plus, he makes Anniah happy. I want her to be happy." She paused. "Do you think we'll ever see them again?"

"I do not know how exactly, but... yes." Rhawn shrugged. "I think we will."

"So do I." Lucy arched a brow. "And if Warren shows up on this planet again, he's going to *love* his statue."

Clovis was erecting a life-size version of Warren on the courthouse lawn. That town really was *desperate* for someone special to come from their zip code. For no reason she could possibly imagine, Lucy had fibbed a little bit about Warren's greatness in her statement to the authorities. In her version, he'd been a cross between Aqua Man and Gandhi, gallantly saving countless lives before he was swept overboard and vanished. The guy who had never been quite good enough was now enshrined in local memory as a hero. They were even talking about renaming the high school in his honor. His parents had never been prouder.

She'd tried to sugarcoat Taffi's demise, too, but it was clear Tony didn't much care. He and Taffi-Two both seemed happy as hell to be free of her. As far as Lucy knew no one had asked about Craig, at all. It made her sad, even though Taffi and Craig's own choices had led to them being unmourned by the world.

Still, Jessica Alba was in talks to play Taffi in the upcoming made-for-TV-movie about the cruise ship disaster. According to the Hollywood idiot who called pitching the idea (and who Lucy had promptly hung up on) it was going to be, "*Titanic* meets *Sharknado*, man! Only – like– if John Hughes directed it."

Needless to say, Lucy was opting out of the project, but Taffi would've loved the idea. In a weird way, she was finally going to be a star.

Amazingly, everyone else had survived the sinking. Lucy doubted any of them would be eager to go to their twentieth high school reunion, but they were alive. Knowing what a miracle that was, she didn't plan to waste even a moment of her second chance.

"Anniah and Warr-en will lead the Clan, after Notan." Rhawn continued. Mammoth, their cute little dog, came trotting over with a tennis ball and Rhawn obligingly tossed it down the beach for him to chase. "Warr-en is learning the language."

"God help those poor people, once he starts talking."

Rhawn chuckled. "I must admit that it is far quieter in this world. I quite enjoy the lack of Warr-en 'ya knowing' at me." He sighed in contentment. "I quite enjoy *everything* here. All my life I dreamed of this world and of you. Now I am living in this magical place, with you by my side, and I have never been happier."

God, Lucy loved this guy. "Me neither." She said sincerely and met his gaze. She no longer had to tilt her head every which way to maintain eye contact with him. His gaze stayed on hers, confident of its welcome. "This is where I was always supposed to be, Rhawn."

"So you finally admit I was right about fate?"

Lucy arched a brow at him. "Well, if this *was* fate, I think I owe it a big 'thank you.'"

"You truly do not miss living in Newyork?"

"No. Well, I miss the bagels, but it's a small price to pay." She looked back out over the water. "I mean, owning our own private island is a lot less stressful than working the checkout counter at a bookstore."

Rhawn was adjusting better than anyone else ever could have. He wasn't even threatening to cook poor Mammoth, anymore. In fact, he seemed to like the scruffy little mutt, once he began to see it as a pet and not a food source. Living in a massive city right away would've been too big of a culture shock, even for Rhawn, though. Lucy didn't want him overwhelmed. It seemed far wiser to start with baby steps. Something familiar for him.

Luckily, there were thousands of tiny islands in the Florida Keys and you could buy one for a couple million bucks.

Which wasn't really a problem, since that necklace Anniah gave her was worth thirty times that amount. Those huge, roughly-cut diamonds meant that Rhawn and Lucy would be financially secure until the next Ice Age rolled around. All they had to do with the rest of their happily ever after was decide between margaritas and daiquiris.

Still...

"I was thinking about the future." Lucy said, reaching for the sunscreen. "About what we're going to do with it, now that we're not being shot at or chased by wolves."

"My plans for the future are watching the sunset, practicing lower kissing with my mate, and eating ice cream."

"Good plans." She grinned over at him. "But, I meant *beyond* the sex and ice cream part." Rhawn loved ice cream almost as much as he loved sex, so she wasn't surprised by his agenda for the evening. That's all a given. The question is: What am I going to do with my life, now? I want to show our daughter that Mom is someone who goes out and accomplishes great things."

He leaned over to kiss her temple. "How could she ever doubt it?"

"I spent fifteen years doubting it." Lucy squirted some sunscreen onto her rounded stomach rubbing the white goo into her skin. All the websites said it was important to wear a high SPF while pregnant. "No more, though. This time I'm going to be who I'm supposed to be, *every single moment.*"

She wasn't worried about what Rhawn would do. He'd just picked up right where he left off. He'd already invented a half-dozen thingamajigs, using the tools and supplies in his new workshop. One of them was some bizarre-shaped umbrella presently shading them and, Lucy had to admit, it worked great. Once he figured out computers, the guy was probably going to be filing patents every other day. She'd already gotten him a phony birth certificate and social security number, because the paperwork for all his inventions was going to be impossible without it.

Also, they'd need it for their wedding license.

Rhawn still thought it was ridiculous that Lucy wanted

a ceremony to declare them mates. To his mind, they were already married. And she knew he was right. They *were* married, in every way that mattered. ...But she still wanted a wedding and she was going to have it. Besides, Rhawn would love the cake. Especially if there was an ice cream layer.

It was all going to work out perfectly. Lucy knew that. Only her job had her floundering. What was she going to do next? For a while, she'd contemplated going back for her Ph.D. A thesis on the Ice Age would practically publish itself, now that she'd experienced it firsthand. Maybe someday she'd give that a try. Or she could track down the *jigon* and become famous for finding the Lock Ness Monster. That would be fun.

But right now she had a better idea.

"I was thinking maybe I should write a book." She told him.

Rhawn liked that idea. Aside from ice cream, books and pillows were his two favorite parts of modernity. "A book about your time on the island?" He asked excitedly. "I could help you with that. I have many stories of men being eaten by large creatures. I think those would be very popular tales with your people." He also loved *Godzilla* movies.

"I'm sure they would, but that's not quite what I had in mind." Lucy murmured. "The book is more about what the island taught me. It'll be for everybody who isn't yet who they always wanted to be. Everyone who needs a do-over. Maybe it can help someone figure things out, like I did." She glanced at him. "I'm going to call it, 'How to Change the World, In Three Easy Steps."

"A very promising title."

"I thought so." She agreed. "Step one is paying attention to how we're *all* special. Because everyone is."

"It sounds like you are becoming not so antisocial, after all." He teased.

"Don't bet on it. Our kid is going to have your stratospherically high IQ and my terrible people skills. I can already guarantee it." She shrugged. "But step *two* is accepting yourself and others for who you are, and not living in the past, so I'm okay with that."

Rhawn reached over to catch hold of her palm. "Our child will be beautiful and kind and brilliant, just like her mother. She could be nothing else." He paused. "I would not mind if she had my eyes, though." Being in a world where eyes came in all colors had helped him to see his weren't a curse, after all. "Or maybe she could have one green and one brown. That would be fair."

"Maybe." Lucy allowed and smiled at him. "Step three is finding someone who inspires you to be your very best self. The person you *really* are, deep inside. And that's what you do for me, Rhawn. I am so, *so* happy. I wake up every day and Choose you all over again."

"You are every dream I ever had." He kissed the back of Lucy's hand, although it probably tasted like sunblock. "I would gladly live in any world at all, so long as you were with me."

"But ice cream world is *way* better than the sabretooth one. Admit it."

Rhawn laughed and moved their joined hands so the rested on her stomach. "*Vando*, Lucy."

She arched a brow. "One of these days you're going to have to tell me why you're always trying to seduce me with the word 'lungs.' It's seriously a weird pickup line."

He smirked. "It seems to have served me well, so far."

"Yeah, let's see how lucky you get *tonight* with that kind of sweet talk."

"It technically means *no* lungs." Rhawn offered, as if that might help make the endearment more palatable.

It didn't.

"No lungs? Lovely. How is suffocation romantic?"

"It's to signify a *feeling*, not the actual lungs in your chest." Rhawn paused as if he was trying to think of an exact translation. "I cannot breathe when I look at you. You make my heart pound and the air still inside of me. You are the very breath in my body." He nodded. "*That* is what I'm trying to say."

Lucy met his gaze, her own eyes filming with tears. "So

it *does* mean 'I love you.'" She said softly.

Rhawn's head tilted. "Yes. I suppose it does."

"I *knew* it." She leaned over to kiss him. "I love you, too, caveman."

Rhawn chuckled at that. "I really do love you beyond words, Lucy Meadowcroft." He agreed with a tender smile. His fingers caressed their growing child and his mouth brushed against hers. "You truly are a goddess."

Author's Note

     Once Upon a Caveman took me about ten years to write. Seriously. I have hundreds of pages of starts and stops, different settings, different characters, different plots... In fact, *Wicked, Ugly, Bad* and *Love in the Time of Zombies* both began their lives as drafts for this book. Crazy right?

     If you've read *Wicked, Ugly, Bad* you might remember that it begins in a psychiatric facility. Well, there was a draft of this book where Lucy was in a mental hospital, due to her caveman dreams and hallucinations. If you read *Love in the Time of Zombies* you might recall that there is a volcano-themed hole on Zeke's miniature golf course. Well, there was a draft of this book where Zeke was the Warren-ish character and that Fiberglas volcano was a gateway to Rhawn's island. I knew within one chapter that both of those ideas were wrong for this story and they went in totally new directions. The trouble was I still couldn't figure out what was right for *Once Upon a Caveman*.

     It can be frustrating to know chunks of a story, but not be able to see the whole picture. That was me and this book for a long time. The first pieces for *Once Upon a Caveman* came so easily. I was stuck in an intro to anthropology class, not paying attention to the professor's boring Power Point. In the glass case on the wall, there was a sabretooth tiger skull sitting on a shelf. The teeth were longer than my pencil. I started thinking about what it must have been like to live in a world where these creatures hunted in the shadows. Instead of taking notes on the brain-size of gibbons, (For real, that was a test question. You see why I was daydreaming?) I started writing down ideas for a time travel story, where a modern girl is catapulted back to the Ice Age. I filled up a whole notebook with my story ideas and then kinda set it aside, unfinished.

     I leave a lot of books unfinished. Far, *far* more than get actual endings. I have to actually *write* something to know if it's going to work. Sometimes it takes me eighty thousand words to realize its crap and I toss it away. Other times, I wait for a while and come back to it with fresh eyes. (I had parts of *Cowboy From the Future* untouched for two years before finally completing it.) For some reason, I always knew I'd finish *Once Upon a Caveman*. I even knew most of the characters names, which are primarily based on fossil sites or other archeological finds. It was the rest that I was still sketchy on, so I decided I needed to do some "research."

It was pretty informal. If I was in LA, I'd take a side-trip to the La Brea tar pits. (Amazing place, by the way.) If I was in New York, I'd visit the American History museum to look at the mammoth displays. If there was a PBS special on the Ice Age, it got DVRed and scrutinized. Heck, my sister and I even practiced Ice Age spear throwing at a mammoth site in Hot Springs, South Dakota. (It's way harder than you'd think.) I knew I was going to write this damn book sooner or later, so I was casually gathering up information.

I set the story in another world so I could play a bit fast-and-loose with the geological landscape of the island. I have always been more interested in history than science and I make no claims about the accuracy of the volcanic activity on the island, aside from the very basics. Any references to historical eruptions like Krakatoa and Vesuvius are true. But could an island sink into the sea? Probably not on Earth. It could get blown apart, though. I leave it up to the reader to decide what happened to Rhawn's island.

I'm by no means an expert on the Ice Age either, but the facts that Lucy relates in the book are true, to the best of my knowledge. There were no dinosaurs in the Ice Age. I just tossed a plesiosaur in because I thought it would be fun. (I also made up *bogas*, but that's about it.) Wooly rhinos existed. So did dire wolves and armadillos the size of cars. Animals were larger then and glaciers covered the northern part of the globe.

With so much water trapped in ice, a land bridge was exposed between Asia and Alaska. This is the most accepted theory as to how people first found their way to North America, although there is also evidence to suggest that some cultures were capable of building boats. These were not stupid people. They had art, music, language, and technology to make their daily lives easier. The more you learn about "cavemen" the more you see, they're not so different from us.

All over the globe, humans lived side-by-side with creatures so bizarre it's hard to even imagine them. Rhawn's plan to hunt the mammoths is one theory of how human groups actually killed them. Humans used their tusks to make huts, their skins to make blankets, their bones to make art and tools... Mammoths were a vital part of their culture. But I can still sympathize with Lucy's horror at the idea of killing something so amazing. There are few things weirder or more awesome than Pleistocene mammals. If you look at some of the cave paintings people left behind in Europe, you can catch a small glimpse into their world and its beautiful and terrifying wildlife.

Anyway, about a decade into my half-hearted, start-and-stop research, my family took a cruise. It was a "boutique" ship, filled with an ever-present staff trained to subdue all resistance with all-you-can-eat sorbet and afternoon shuffleboard. My sister Elizabeth is probably the worst person in the world to stick on a cruise ship full of people who like sorbet and shuffleboard. A battle of wills began. The more the staff urged her to participate in show tune charades (true story), the higher she cranked Johnny Cash on her iPod and ignored them.

Our cruise director was a man named Tony, who might just have been genetically engineered for his job. His perpetual grin and orangey tan were meant for a life on the lido deck. There was no way he'd survive in any other environment. He was also overly, aggressively, patronizingly cheerful and my sister... isn't. Conflict was inevitable. And funny.

"Tony the cruise director hates you." I informed my sister after one of their more entertaining encounters.

"Whatever." She said, not caring about her onboard popularity. And then she added, with the randomness that I love about her, "Hey, that actually sounds like the beginning of a cool book, though."

And that's how *Once Upon a Caveman* was finally born. My sister's snarking, plus a probably-replica skull of a sabretooth cat, plus a decade of do-overs and wrong turns. ...And maybe too many rewatches of *The Breakfast Club*. Honestly, I'm not sure where the idea of the class reunion came from. The book is about becoming the person you always *wanted* to be, so reevaluating your life through a lens of your high school self just seems to fit.

In any case, I hope you enjoyed Lucy and Rhawn's adventure. It took a long time for me to get it right, but I think they're finally both happy with their happily ever after. If you have any questions, comments, or concerns about this book or any other please let me know at starturtlepublishing@gmail.com. We love to hear from you!

Don't miss another exciting novel by Cassandra Gannon:
***Ghost Walk*.**
Available Now!

Grace Rivera just wants to be normal. She's the only member of her spell-casting, fortune-telling family who isn't hunting unicorns or trying to discover the lost recipe for Troll Powder. Trained as a crime scene investigator, she believes in science and cold, hard facts. And right now, the cold, hard facts are telling Grace that she's lost her mind. It started last July, when she "hallucinated" that she traveled back in time to relive a crime before it had even happened. Her resulting breakdown cost Grace her forensics job, so now she's stuck working as a tour guide in her Revolutionary War themed hometown. After a year of rebuilding her life, she's finally convincing herself that she might just have a chance to be normal, again. ...Until a handsome, sarcastic, and really real seeming ghost shows up on her Ghost Walk, anyway.

Captain James Riordan was unjustly hanged for murder on July 4th 1789. Ever since then, he's been haunting the streets of Harrisonburg, Virginia, trying to find some way to clear his name. Unfortunately, it's impossible to prove his innocence as an incorporeal ghost, so mostly he whiles away his un-life watching teen soaps on TV and tagging along on Harrisonburg's nightly Ghost Walk. The tour is supposed to tell visitors spooky stories about the historic town. On this particular night, though, there's a new tour guide leading the group. She's terrible at weaving scary tales. She looks like a Sunday school teacher. She's spreading slanderous lies about him. ...And she's the first person in centuries that can actually see him.

Now Grace and Jamie are working together to solve a two hundred year old crime. From the eighteenth century and back again, the two of them are determined to clear Jamie's name and set history right. Even if it means some time-traveling forensics work. Even if it means Grace has to listen to Jamie lament his lost pirate's treasure (a lot) and Jamie is frustrated because he can't physically touch the one person in the world he's sure is his. Even if it means dealing with Grace's stalking ex-boyfriend, her crazy relatives, and the Rivera's lost recipe for Troll Powder. ...And especially if it means a scoundrel of a ghost and a girl who just wants to be normal somehow fall in love along the way.

Made in the USA
Columbia, SC
08 December 2019